RO]

THE
Escalante
ENIGMA

outskirtspress

DENVER, COLORADO

1

Beads of sweat dripped down my face and bare, brown upper torso as a bright, hot mid-afternoon October sun burned another layer of bronze pigment into the leathery hide of my already deeply tanned shoulders and back. Clad only in faded blue Speedos, I sat unsteadily astride the starboard engine of my PBY Catalina flying boat, as I reached inside the upper cowling and tugged at a stubborn fuel line. I swore profusely as an inconsiderate oaf in an overpowered speedboat inquisitively circled the plane, creating a wash that almost tossed me into the deep, dark blue of Sydney Harbor.

My PBY-5A is a World War Two vintage amphibious aircraft of immense proportions in its day. The -5A model has a wing span of one hundred and four feet. It is sixty-three feet ten inches long and twenty feet two inches high at the top of the tail. It has a giant parasol wing, no flaps, two Pratt and Whitney 1830-92 radial engines rated at one thousand, two hundred horsepower each, a sea level cruising speed of one hundred and sixty nine miles per hour and a stalling speed of seventy-eight miles per hour. It has an incredible range of two thousand five hundred and forty-five miles!

This particular machine was built in 1943 and saw action in the South Pacific in one of the Royal Australian Air

Force sub-hunter squadrons. It is now my very own floating and flying home, and also provides me with a rather precarious living as an itinerant charter pilot. I was doing some routine maintenance on the ancient lady, prior to taxiing her a couple of bays east of our normal home at the old Rose Bay flying boat base. We had been invited to the very exclusive waterfront neighborhood of Elizabeth Bay on the south side of Sydney Harbor not far from downtown, the famous Opera House and Circular Quay.

Several years ago I had inherited the rusting hulk of this old relic, which had been lying abandoned on a far north Queensland beach. With nothing better to do at the time, except to recover from some rather serious recently acquired wounds, I had set about rebuilding her and bringing her back to her former noble status as a vintage flying boat. In the process, I had completely refitted the interior for onboard living.

That had been a hard and dirty year. Too many close encounters, and too many scrapes of steel and lead on my already scarred and battered fiftyish body. As I reflected on that time, I gently traced the most recent of these outrages, a long, thin white scar down the outside of my left thigh, the not so successful outcome of dodging a lunatic bent on carving me up with a ten inch blade in a Darwin backstreet!

Not at all what I had in mind when I came home to the land Down Under after a long spell of flying all kinds of planes in many different countries; anything I could get in the desperately unstable world of a professional aviator for hire.

After several long and arduous years, I had finally fulfilled my dream of finding just such a plane and retiring with her, to spend the rest of my days fishing and beachcombing. I had the plane. I had the lifestyle I had yearned for, living on and reveling in the sights and sounds of magnificent Sydney Harbor. However, the income to support such a life was both tenuous and unexpectedly perilous.

Beyer, my best friend and neighbor, who lives on his own chunky little forty-two feet cruiser at the Rose Bay marina, had managed to salvage both the PBY and me from a state of total dereliction on that far north Queensland beach.

Of the two derelicts, the more difficult task by far was reaching out with patience, friendship and empathy to bring me back to reality and sobriety after the unexpected and devastating death of my then true love. Bringing the seventy year old amphibian back to life turned out to be a catharsis of the soul for both of us. Since then, we had shared many hazardous adventures, all of which Beyer has sworn on the sacred grave of his beloved grandmother, will be his last!

I steadied myself on the cowling and got on with the job. Our good friends Celia and Miles Warner, who live in an elegant, two hundred year old, convict-built sandstone mansion, the manicured grounds of which extend right down to their very own private beach and dock on the bay, had invited Beyer and me to bring the 'Wayward Wind', as we had christened the PBY, around to their place for a beachside cocktail party. We happily obliged. Our lives had been very low-profile lately, literally recovering from an almost fatal encounter with a crazed mob of mid-eastern terrorists menacing a small town in outback Australia.

For some inexplicable reason, they had taken great umbrage to our destroying their training camp, wherein they had been rehearsing a repeat of the New York twin towers assault commonly referred to as '9/11', for a similar attack on Sydney and Melbourne.

The party was in full swing by the time we taxied the craft round to Elizabeth Bay. As soon as we had shut down and anchored, we had two boatloads of revelers, already three sheets in the wind, clambering through the rear gun blisters into the modified observation cabin to excitedly explore my giant floating home.

I was fixing myself a generous Gin Gimlet at the bar in the center section galley when Beyer pushed through the crowd in the cramped dining space forward of the observation deck and shouted in my ear.

"Who is Ronnie McCall?"

"What?"

"I said – who is Ronnie McCall?"

"Ronnie ….." My voice trailed off, my throat went dry, and I suddenly felt warm all over, as fond old memories came flooding back.

"She's on the phone, Mitch! Sounds American."

"As usual, a brilliant and profound observation, but not strictly correct," I replied sardonically. "Gimme the phone!"

I snatched the cell phone out of his hand, pushed forward through the narrow companionway into my tiny portside stateroom just behind the cockpit, and slammed the bulkhead door, cutting the noise by a mere decibel.

"Ronnie? Is this really you? What the ...?"

"G'day mate," she replied, attempting the Aussie vernacular. "It sure is good to hear *your* voice again. Listen, Mitch. I know it's been a long time, and we haven't spoken or written for years, but a lifetime ago, you said if I ever needed help.....well, now's the time. Besides, you're the only person I know in Australia, and the only one I know I can really trust anywhere in the world. I need to talk to you."

"Where are you?"

"At the Hilton near Sydney Airport. I just flew in. I really need to see you. I mean, is there any way......?"

"Stay right where you are! Don't move. I'll be there in fifteen minutes," I said, as I threw the phone on the bed, crawled out through the port side escape hatch, tumbled down into the zodiac secured alongside, and puttered over to the dock. Five minutes later, I was bound for Kingsford Smith Airport, pushing my old electric blue '57 Thunderbird, which I had that afternoon parked at the Warner's, as fast as I dared. It was normally a twenty minute drive. I did it in ten!

Ronnie McCall was waiting in the lobby of the Airport Hilton. She looked as good as I remembered the last time I saw her more than ten years ago. That would put her at about thirty-eight, but she hadn't aged a day; still lithe, slender and in excellent shape. She was elegantly clad in a short, bright yellow sleeveless sundress, which beautifully accentuated her velvety, coffee-colored skin. Her black hair was pulled back in a short ponytail, emphasizing the superb facial contours of her African heritage. We had flown for the same airline in Texas for a while, and she had been my co-pilot many times. She was a great pilot; one of those gifted aviators to whom the passion for flying translates into a totally natural feel for the airplane.

Many times since we had parted, I wished that we could once more share the joy of sitting side by side, bathed in the soft glow of the instruments, the bright moon shining down into the cockpit as we talked and laughed away the airborne hours together. For a professional pilot, there is nothing as pleasurable and intimate as sharing the joy of flying with someone who loves it as much as you do.

I remembered one night in particular. It was a clear, starlit winter evening over north Texas. We were just crossing the Red River at twenty-three thousand feet, bound for Wichita, Kansas, in an EMB-120 Brasilia, then the fastest turboprop in the sky. The cockpit was warm and cozy. The big Pratt 1800 prop-jet engines thrummed with a muted and comforting roar. The autopilot had the plane. She laughed heartily and clapped her hands in response to one of my endless Aussie jokes.

Yet even in the dim cockpit lighting, I could see and feel an abrupt and subtle change in her mood. She suddenly turned away and craned her head back to gaze up at the full moon through her side window. Until that moment, she had been my first officer and my friend; a capable, knowledgeable and skilled pilot – someone I trusted implicitly and looked forward to working with. But in one intense instant, all that had changed.

Fortunately for both of us though, our heightened awareness of each other was interrupted by a loud knock on the cockpit door. We both jumped high enough in our seatbelts to hit our heads on the overhead switch panel. We had barely regained our composure when our flight attendant came bursting uninvited through the door like a storm trooper, with two steaming mugs of coffee.

Our new-found awareness was kept in check for the rest of the flight and in fact never really went any further than that. Oh, we saw each other socially more often. But though we had ample opportunity both at and away from work, by some mutual and unspoken agreement, more on her part than mine I must admit, we would reach a point beyond which she absolutely would not go. At the time, I thought it was because of our differing ethnic backgrounds and ages.

In any case, our unconsummated desire softened into a very firm and long-lasting friendship. Eventually, she accepted an offer to join American Airlines and I returned to Australia, but we stayed in touch. Then gradually, as friendships are apt to do, the letters and calls became fewer and finally faded out altogether.

Now, as she spotted me, it was as if we had never been apart! She rushed up and gave me a bigger hug than at our last parting, when we thought we would probably never see each other again. She lightly brushed my lips with hers, turned to grab her overnight bag, began to pick up her heavy suitcase, which I immediately and gallantly took from her, then she dragged me out into the warm, sublime night.

I pointed out my stately, ancient convertible, which she eyed suspiciously, and then she unceremoniously flung open the right side door and dropped into the red leather bench seat.

Propping my elbows on the door frame, I rested my chin on my cupped hands, grinned broadly and casually asked, "Are you sure you want to drive in Sydney traffic on your first night in town?"

She muttered a barely audible oath as she discovered the steering wheel in front of her and sheepishly slid over to the left side passenger seat. I threw her bags into the back, jumped in, cranked the starter and drove out on to the expressway bound for the eastern suburbs.

"It sure is good to see you again, Ronnie," I said with genuine warmth and affection. "But what brings you half way round the world to see *me*? Was I *that* good?"

She reached over and struck me hard across the left shoulder. "You wish!" she laughed.

"So, how's everything with me old mate?" she inquired, grinning as she reached out to grab my left hand.

"Oh, I'm still in the land of the living, just barely; still appreciating every breath and all the wonders of nature."

"Yeah, I can imagine what wonders of nature *you* appreciate."

"Well, this *is* one of the best places in the world for girl-watching, you know. But to answer your question, I'm sort of retired now, living on my flying boat, just like I always told you I would. I'm my own alter-ego; the airborne white knight, riding out with crooked lance, rusty armor and swayback steed to punish the bad guys and save the fair damsels in distress."

"Oh? Any particular damsel I should know about?" she inquired, pretending to be casual, but giving herself away by the same expression and voice timbre changes I had known so well.

"Not lately, anyway," I replied morosely, recalling with bitter-sweet memories the recent departure of my latest love.

We continued the small talk back and forth for a while, catching up on each other's lives for the last ten or more years. I happened to glance at her as she reached up with a familiar gesture to brush her short, silky black hair back with her left hand. It was then that I noticed a glint of gold on her ring finger.

"When did you get married?" I asked, unable to conceal a touch of bitterness in my voice.

Instead of answering my question, she scrunched down further into her seat. For several long minutes, she remained silent, and then asked "How long until we get there?"

"Oh, another five minutes or so. But I have a boatload of drunks on board I will have to get rid of; unless you're in the mood for partying, that is. Somehow, I gather you're not."

"No! Please, Mitch. I've had a twenty hour flight, and I just want to kick back, rest and talk. We've got a lot of catching up to do."

"We sure do," I replied, wondering why my question had brought about such a sudden mood swing.

A few minutes later, we pulled up in front of the Warner's mansion on Elizabeth Bay.

She stayed put, reluctant to leave the car, until I came around to her side, opened the door and gently but firmly pulled her out of her seat. I reached into the back, retrieved her carry-on and handed it to her as I took her big bag and led her down through the immaculately manicured lawns of the estate and out on to the private pier.

She stood at the end of the dock and gazed in awe for a few moments at the bulky black silhouette of the giant PBY swinging gently at her mooring in the calm waters of the bay.

"You really did it, didn't you? Just like you always said you would."

"Took me a while longer than I had planned, but I got there in the end."

As I stood beside her, admiring the fine lines of both the aircraft and the girl, it occurred to me that the amphibian rested quietly in total darkness; certainly not the noisy, raucous floating house party I had left less than an hour before.

I stepped the couple of feet down into the gray rubber zodiac bumping against the dock, motioned for her to pass down her bags, then reached up for her hand to steady her as she clambered awkwardly into the dingy. The outboard motor started easily with one pull of the lanyard, and thirty seconds later we were coming alongside the left blister in the rear hull of the flying boat.

"Up you go," I said as I helped her on to the short boarding ladder up to the open blister.

In a moment, she was standing by the portside dinette in the rear lounge. I hefted the bags up over the side and followed them into the aft section of the plane.

Ronnie gazed around in stunned amazement at the dimly starlit interior. We needed some lights!

I was just stepping toward the switch on the compartment's forward bulkhead when the hairs on the back of my neck bristled with the primeval sixth sense still inherent in the genes of the hunter and the hunted. I stopped dead in my tracks, all my other senses now alert to danger. My nostrils detected a pungent aroma not normally part of the oily, salty, metallic odor to which I had become accustomed.

I reached back with my left hand, found Ronnie's arm and tugged her gently but insistently to my side.

"Mitch? What is it? What's the mat …?"

She did not finish the sentence. I dragged her down to the deck just as a muzzle flash lit up the bulkhead hatch, immediately followed by the stunning, deafening roar of multiple shots and the angry buzz of large caliber slugs as they reverberated around the cabin.

Ronnie screamed! A sledge hammer blow slammed into the side of my right temple with enough force to stop me cold. I dropped to the deck, stunned. A brilliant display of fireworks exploded behind my eyes. I tried to reach out for the invader as I fell, but I had no control over my limbs.

Through a red haze of pain and shock as I sagged to the deck, I again tried to reach for his ankle as he leapt past me to the open blister. Strictly no go! I could not move my arms, hands or fingers. He was gone as quickly as he had appeared, diving out through the port hatch and overboard into the murky black water. The last thing I remembered before passing out was the urgent, burbling rumble of a high-powered motor as he made his escape into the anonymity of the harbor.

A soft, warm, familiar blanket of peace enveloped me. I felt saddened by the fading thought that I would never again see starry, moonlit nights or bright, golden days from the deck of my beloved flying boat. Then the blanket began to float gently back and forth down the right side of my forehead, dabbing at the wound. I recognized the texture of moist, warm terry-towel cloth.

"Mitch? Mitch! Open your eyes, dammit! Talk to me. Look at me. Wake up. Don't *you* die on me too!"

My eyes fluttered open. My head throbbed with the pounding of a thousand jackhammers trying to drill their way out of my skull. No wound or blow to the head I had previously suffered was any measure of this new assault on my battered body.

Gradually, my vision blurrily returned. I attempted to sit up on one elbow, fell back limply to the deck as a new wave of pain exploded behind my eyes. I clumsily tried to move my arms, hands and legs; found that I seemed to be able to do so.

I looked up at Ronnie, for a moment confused with non-recognition. Then it all came back in a rush. Instantly, with pain forgotten and without conscious effort, I rolled over and up into a crouch, ready to renew the battle with the would-be assassin.

"He's gone. Went over the side into the water," Ronnie reassured me as I relaxed back into a sitting position. I took the towel from her and held it with both hands to my oozing, bullet-furrowed scalp.

"Are you all right Mitch? You look terrible. You have a bloody three inch groove along the right side of your skull. Can you move?"

I opened my mouth to reply, but no words would come. I heard a dry, rasping, squawk which I realized was coming from my own throat.

Finally, after several attempts, I managed to squeak a few words.

"Did ….you get a look at him?"

"No. Did you?"

"All I saw was the flash from the gun. After that everything was a blur."

I reached for her hand. She grasped my own and pulled. I struggled painfully to my feet, stood on badly trembling pins for a few moments as the cabin began to swirl wildly about me.

Putting my arm around her shoulder for support, I limped to the forward bulkhead. I stopped for a moment to flick on the lights, regaining my breath and my balance at the same time, remembered to stoop and duck at the low hatchway, and led her forward through the main living and dining cabin into the cramped quarters of the engineer's pylon area which now served as the galley.

Leaning against the galley bench, I reached for the still hot coffee pot, poured a mug full, took a bottle of Black Label scotch from the shelf above and added a generous shot to the brew.

"Well, what'll it be?" I grinned lopsidedly at her, trying hard to regain my shattered composure.

"Huh?"

"What would you like to drink?"

"Oh. I'm sorry. I can't believe what just happened. I'm not used to being shot at. What kind of maniac would be hiding on your plane trying to kill you? I ….just can't believe it," she said again.

"I have absolutely no idea, but I intend to find out. He must have been one of those already on board for the party; must have stowed away when everyone else left. We'll find out soon enough, when we question the Warners about their guest list. Anyway, what can I get you?"

"How can you think of booze at a time like this?"

"I can't think of a better time to think about it!"

"You're right. I do need a drink! I would like one of those very cold, full strength, Aussie beers you are so fond of bragging about."

"Coming right up, ma'am," I said, reaching with still trembling hand into the small fridge beneath the bench and withdrawing an ice-cold, green can of Victoria Bitter. I popped the top and handed it to her.

As Ronnie took a couple of long swigs of the strong brew, her own fear and shock subsided. She began to gaze around her surroundings with renewed interest.

"Putting aside your reception committee for the moment, I must say that this is pretty …… fantastic! You really own this beautiful tub?"

"Lock, stock and rusty rivets. Complete with new bullet holes, it seems. Rebuilt from the keel up with loving care and attention to intimate detail by my pardner and me. Speaking of whom, he must have decided, with customary consideration and concern for my welfare, to clear the decks so that we would have the boat to ourselves when you arrived….."

Then an ugly thought crossed my mind.

"Wait here for a moment," I said as I sprang forward to begin a search of the boat.

"What is it?" she cried.

"I just thought of something I don't like to think about. Maybe Beyer was still on board when our uninvited guest stowed away. I'll be back in a minute."

I searched the entire boat from stem to stern and found to my immense relief that there was no sign of him or a struggle, or any other blood apart from my own.

"Well, he seems to have fled the scene before our murderous friend hid himself aboard. I'm sure you will meet him very soon. He is probably even now regaling the revelers with tales of his adventures on the high seas, from the North Pole to the South Pacific!"

I took her hand in mine, which was now much steadier after a couple of pulls at the scotch-laced coffee, and led her back through the watertight hatches to the observation deck we had first entered. I turned the lights down low once more, and treated her to her first night-time view of Sydney's magnificent harbor, bathed in the orange glow of a million downtown lights, their amber reflections spilling into the inky waters below.

My badly grazed skull was still throbbing tremendously, but the closeness of her, the sweet musky scent of her, brought long-forgotten feelings and memories of a collage of a dozen special girls in my life rushing back. I hooked my right arm around her elegant brown shoulders and gently pulled her into my side. She resisted for only a moment and then relaxed, as I felt the warm curve of her supple African body gently press against my own.

"It's just beautiful," she whispered.

"Why thank you, ma'am," I replied impishly, my old friskiness returning rapidly. "You feel pretty good too."

She pulled away and turned to face me. "I didn't mean you, you...," her voice trailed off as she saw my grin and remembered my tactless and sometimes inappropriate sense of humor. She affectionately struck me across the shoulder again.

"I didn't mean you," she repeated, "but now that you mention it, it *does* feel good to be close to you again, Mitch."

She squirmed back under my arm and into my side. We stood like that for several wonderful, silent minutes, and then suddenly she shuddered uncontrollably, gently separated herself from me, and led me over to the starboard dinette. She pushed me down into the seat and slid into the booth herself, where she began dabbing at my still oozing scalp again.

"So," I said. "Forgetting our recent excitement, for the moment anyway, let the tale begin. How about answering my first question first, lady? When did you get married," I inquired, frowning at her from under knitted and furrowed brow, and unwisely taking a pull at my coffee as I finished the question.

Without hesitation this time, she looked me straight in the eye and said, "About a month before I met you."

I literally choked on the coffee, coughing and gagging as I tried not to spit it out in a classic double take of shock and surprise.

"*Whaat?*" I exclaimed, as I regained enough composure to speak.

"About a month before I met you," she repeated calmly. "Had I met you first, things might be vastly different now – for both of us."

"Go on," I replied sulkily, my knight-errant ego having just taken almost as terrible a blow as my skull.

She reached over in an attempt to hold my hands. I stubbornly resisted and kept them both below the table – for a full thirty seconds.

As I brought my hands back to the surface of the table, I placed both palms around the almost spilled cup of coffee-scotch. She grabbed my wrists instead, leaned forward and locked her glistening black eyes on mine.

"Look Mitch. I didn't tell you at the time, because …. Well, because I just couldn't, that's all. From the day I met you, I knew you were going to be somebody special in my life, but I couldn't bring myself to admit it for a very long time. And by that time, even before that time, I had become a loyal, devoted and faithful wife."

"So ….why couldn't you tell anyone, especially me?" I croaked, still deeply hurt that after all the time we had spent together, she could have kept something as important as this from me.

"Because nobody else – including my parents at the time – knew that we were married. We met about a year before, in Washington, D.C. I was visiting my older brother Jeff, who is an air force officer stationed in the Pentagon. Or he was! He was taken off flying status when his plane was hit by a missile in the Gulf War and he went down in the drink. A rescue team got to him in time to prevent him from drowning, but he was so badly mangled, they grounded him.

"I guess he knew how to pull some strings, because when they offered him his choice of jobs, he asked for and got a posting to AFOSI – though heaven only knows why he chose an office job like that."

"AFOSI?" I repeated, becoming reluctantly engrossed in her story despite myself.

"Air Force Office of Special Investigations. They're like the anti-terrorist and intelligence investigative branch of the air force. But don't ask me what they really do, because I haven't a clue. Whenever I ask, he just laughs and quotes that old line that if he told me, he'd have to kill me. Sometimes, I get the feeling that he's not joking! Anyway, one day, I was visiting him and he was showing me around the Pentagon. This good-looking officer walks into Jeff's office and he introduces me.

"His name is Major Richard Masters, and he is Jeff's immediate superior. He is about four or five years older than Jeff, and ten years older than me. Anyway, one thing led to another, he asked me out, we began dating, and the rest as they say, is history. He asked me to marry him, I was head-over-heels in love, and readily agreed. I did have some reservations though, because I still wanted my own career as an airline pilot, but he said he would not stand in my way. And to make things more complicated – at least for my parents, who are very old fashioned – he is white! His mother is dead, and he had not seen his father in years, apparently. He said his father had abandoned him long ago.

"Well, to cut a long story short, when I got hired by our old company, I took the job and moved to Texas. Richard obviously could not follow me, as he had his own career – a career I knew nothing about – firmly established in Washington. That was a real problem, of course, because one of us had to commute and it was easier for me, but it got to be a real pain in the butt.

"Then one day he called me in Dallas with some good news. He was being temporarily posted to Texas on a special assignment. He was going to be stationed at the ex-Super Collider facility in Waxahachie, on some sort of super important investigation. He couldn't tell me anything about the project, except that it was above top secret, whatever that means.

"Anyway, by the time I had been flying with you a couple of weeks, and we knew pretty much all there was to know about each other, I wanted so badly to tell you. I almost did, many times, and then, that night – well, you know, something changed between us, or at least we became aware of – other feelings, and I just couldn't bring myself to tell you. I wasn't sure of anything any more, but no matter what I felt for you, in the end, I knew I still deeply loved my husband and had to remain faithful to him."

As she finished the sentence, she slid out of the booth and stood looking down at me. She tossed her head, shaking some loose bangs out of her limpid black eyes, and I was struck again by the stunning beauty of her strong oval face with its deep African heritage. She strode over to stand again at the portside blister, crooked one athletic brown knee and leg on the seat and stared down into the calm, inky water, taking several long gulps of her beer as she did so.

Her slender left hand, unadorned except for the plain gold wedding band, idly played on the coaming, now and then breaking away to salute an occasional mosquito which drifted in on the salty evening breeze. Her bare, bronze legs were muscled and shapely at calf and thigh, probably a combination of her runner ancestry and a good deal of working out as well. The petite yellow sundress only accentuated the flat, hard rear, the shapely hips and the full, firm breasts.

Ronnie gazed in first-time awe out through the open blister at Sydney's magnificent harbor lights. The Opera House and the Harbor Bridge threw incandescent white and yellow reflections into the gently rolling waters of the bay. Rugged battlements of downtown skyscrapers seemed to reach up to touch the soft night air, clear as crystal, where white stars fairly blazed in a cold and frosty sky.

I sat in the starboard booth, playing with my now luke-warm brew as I admired her fine lines and features, and wondered what possible manner of good fortune could have brought her back into my life at this particular time and place.

I shook off my reverie, sloshed coffee on the table as I pushed the cup aside rather more roughly than I intended, slid out of the booth and went back to the fridge in the galley where I withdrew another frosty can of VB. I popped the top, took a long swig, and stepped through to the lounge again, where I once more took up my previous position by her side.

Gently, I squeezed her right shoulder and, following her gaze out into the semi-darkness of the harbor, said "I think you know how I feel about you too, but I also knew, from your reluctance to let our friendship go any further, that it was something like that. I don't blame you a bit.

"Although I'm disappointed of course, from a strictly selfish standpoint. But from the point of view of a tarnished, yet honorable *white* knight – albeit with a deep tan *almost as good as yours* - I admire your loyalty. So, having said that, and knowing that we stand here as very good friends, still alive to share this beautiful evening together, what can I do for you, ma'am?"

She turned to me, placed her slender hands on my shoulders and lowered her head to rest her right cheek against my chest. I put my arms around her waist and hugged her lightly, mentally cursing myself for a fool, and cursing Richard Masters for the lucky sod that he was.

The magic ended all too quickly as she began to sob into my chest. She withdrew, wiped the salty tears from her cheeks, and pushed me down into the portside dinette where she sat close, yet still able to face the water as though it was soothing her troubled spirit.

She heaved a great sigh, brushed her hand through her hair again, and said, "Find my husband and brother for me, Mitch. Please!"

"Whoa! You mean they're *missing?* You didn't mention *that* minor detail."

"It's hard to know just where to start. It's all so....confusing. So damned unreal!"

"Well, let's start where you left off; with Richard at the Super Collider."

"Yeah. O.K. I need to get it all straight in my head anyway. Well, he moved to Waxahachie and found an apartment in town, just a few miles from the facility. It was great for both of us; because I could now live with him and still be close enough to commute to DFW airport.

"Our new relationship was rather strained though, almost from day one, because he wouldn't – or couldn't tell me anything about what he was actually doing. All he would say was that he was acting as liaison between the scientific community and the Air Force, which apparently had some kind of vested interest in some new experiments being conducted there. Anyway, one day when he had been there only a few months, Bob Nolan, the chief of plant security, got sick and took a leave of absence and they asked Richard to double as head of security, which he gladly did. His job in Air Force Intelligence made him the perfect man to take over the position."

"Just a minute," I said, interrupting her monologue. "What did you mean when you said the security boss 'got sick'?"

"Well, it was almost as if it conveniently happened so that Richard *could* take over. The guy was just there one day and gone the next, and they were asking Richard to replace him."

"Hmmm," I stroked my chin thoughtfully. "I haven't got a clue where you're going with all this, but knowing a wee bit about the Super Collider from my friend Beyer, I smell a rat already. Anyway, please continue."

"Well, like I said, everything was going along okay until things started happening that he couldn't explain. When he went to the scientist in charge of the entire project, the guy just brushed him off and told him not to worry about things that didn't concern him. He ….."

"Wait a minute! What kind of things started happening? Can you be a little more specific about that?"

"Well, weird kind of stuff; fires that started apparently without cause. Lights that went on and off throughout the tunnels. Then the main generators began to shut down of their own accord, apparently at random, for longer and longer periods of time, causing massive disruption to the program.

"Computers crashed, and the hard disk memories were sometimes erased. Then, one day about three months after Nolan's disappearance, it ....happened."

She dropped her head onto the table of the dinette and began sobbing uncontrollably. I gently lifted her head off the table, took her cheeks between my palms and wiped away the tears with my thumbs.

"*What* happened, baby?"

The pain and anguish in her tear-filled eyes told me what I had already guessed.

She sniffed, wiped her eyes and nose with one sweep of her hand, and said: "Richard disappeared! The last time anyone saw him alive, he was heading for a section in the main tunnel to meet with one of his security team. The guard had requested his urgent assistance by radio; said he needed Richard down there right away. One of the other M.P.s heard the transmission, and decided to go down in case he needed backup. He found the first one in the main tunnel – dead! But there was not a mark on him, apart from what appeared to be a strange, wriggly shaped tattoo on his left forearm. He said the really odd thing about him, apart from his being dead of course, was the expression on his face. His eyes were still open. Wide open! He looked terrified; as if something had literally scared him to death!"

"How do you know all these details? Who did you speak to afterwards?"

"Right after it happened, Jeff called me from Washington. He already knew about it, and was literally on the next plane to Dallas, by order of their superior at AFOSI, to take over the Air Force investigation in co-operation with the civilian authorities, and to begin an official inquest and search for Richard. But nobody could find any trace of him – dead or alive."

"It probably doesn't have any bearing on the case, but just who *was* their boss at the Pentagon?"

"I never heard of him before. His name is General Nathan Price."

"Doesn't ring a bell. Just thought it might. Go on."

"Well, of course Jeff had moved into our apartment, mainly to take care of me, but also as a matter of convenience, being close to the plant to conduct the ongoing investigation.

"Then, one night about a month after he had been on the job, he came home really excited. I've never seen him so worked up, but something had really scared him that night. He wouldn't discuss with me what he had found out. He just said that it was bigger than he had imagined and that it was way above his pay grade.

"Well, he went to work the next day all fired up and really punchy. He was more nervous than I had ever seen him, but try as I might I couldn't get him to open up. I ... I never saw *him* alive again either!"

Her eyes welled with tears once more, she dropped her head into her hands on the table, and began to sob and shake violently.

I put my arms around her and pulled her close and tight. She didn't resist.

"When did all this happen?" I asked softly.

"About six months ago now," she sniffed.

"Six *months* ago!" I echoed. "I don't understand. If all this happened so long ago, what ....?"

"They lied! They told me he was dead, but they lied! About a week after Jeff disappeared, two strange men came to the apartment. They showed me Air Force I.D. They ....."

"What branch?"

"I can't be sure. I was out of it with grief and worry, Mitch. I don't know. Anyway, they had a local cop with them, so I figured it was O.K. They said they had found Jeff's body in the burnt out wreck of his rental car in the bottom of a ravine about a mile from the facility. His uniform, everything, was burnt off him. They asked me if I was up to going with them to identify the body.

"They took me to the local morgue. Oh God, Mitch, there was nothing of him left to identify. His face was burned completely off! They said they had positive identification from his dental records, but they needed me to confirm his personal stuff. His watch, dog tags, I.D. bracelet he always wore, stuff like that."

"I still don't understand why ...."

"They lied, Mitch," she said again, beginning to regain her composure as anger replaced belated grief. She dug into her dress pocket and pulled out a small, shiny object.

"Whoever faked his death screwed up. They forgot one minor detail. There was one thing missing from his personal effects. They overlooked – or didn't know – that he had not worn this since his hands *had been badly burned* when he bailed out over the Gulf. He always kept it on a special chain he wore around his neck under his uniform. It arrived a couple of weeks ago in the mail in a plain brown padded postal bag. Somebody wanted me to know that his death had been faked! And if they lied about Jeff, they probably lied about Richard, too!"

She tossed an air force class ring on to the dinette table as she finished speaking.

I picked it up, turned it over between my fingers, looked at the distinctive emblem on the face and then peered inside the band and read the inscription engraved there.

Jeff McCall, class of `88.

"How do you know it's really his? Could be a fake."

"Notice the tiny nick at the top of the *J*. The engraver started to spell Jeff with a G; the English way – see how the script curves a little too much around to the left - then realized his mistake. You can hardly see it, and even though he works in intelligence, only someone who knows him intimately would know to how to duplicate that error."

Suddenly the hairs on the back of my neck stood on end.

Blaine, ever the white knight sniffing out a dragon to slay, smelled the fiery breath of a very large brute out there, requiring immediate attention and dispatch. As if in answer to my unspoken thoughts, a loud hail from the dock brought me back to the present.

2

"Blaine! Mitch, are you awake?" the deep bass of Beyer's voice rumbled through the darkness.

I gently eased out from under Ronnie's soft and sensuous curves, let her head rest once again on the table, and slid out of the dinette to reply to the bulky black shape silhouetted on the dock.

"Well, if I wasn't, I certainly would be now, after that booming whisper of yours," I sarcastically shouted back.

"Is it …er …convenient for me to come aboard, or should I have the Warners drive me back to my boat?"

"No! Hang on a minute," I replied sharply, as I leapt out through the blister and down the couple of feet into the zodiac. "I need you right here!"

"Uh-oh, I don't like the sound of that," he loudly responded, apprehension rising in his voice.

I again started the little Honda outboard, cast off and seconds later pulled up to the dock. Beyer carefully lowered his huge, hairy bulk into the tiny, unstable craft.

"What did you mean by that?" he asked cautiously.

"What?"

"Don't fence with me, Blaine! I know you well enough by now. I very thoughtfully asked you if I should be driven home, considering your, ah, possible delicate circumstances, and you said, and I quote, 'No. I need you right here.'

"Blaine, I know from long experience that you never, ever, need me right here unless the lady in question has a problem which requires the talents of a thinking man who utilizes brain instead of brawn. And that, my friend, generally leads yours truly into harm's way; into dire peril; into mortal danger; into ….."

"Beyer?"

"Yes?"

"Shut the hell up!"

"Oh, I *see!* So it *is* one of those, is it? Speaking of which, I could have sworn I heard shots a while back. Did you hear anything?" he ended mockingly.

Now it was his turn for sarcasm. He probably could not see the condition of my scalp in the darkness. I ignored him. Neither of us spoke again until we had secured the zodiac, and climbed back aboard the PBY.

Beyer had to literally turn sideways and duck his head at the same time to get his enormous bulk through the frame of the blister.

As he straightened up, he turned, stared agape at the condition of my scalp with its oozing flap of loose hair and skin, and said, "So! I did hear shots! And quite obviously at least one of them hit its mark."

"I don't think I was the mark," I said casually.

Ronnie lifted her head off her hands and glanced with tear-stained eyes at me then Beyer, and back again.

"What …. What do you mean?" she asked, her black eyes widening at the implication of my remark.

"Simply that whoever sent you that ring knows that you know your brother is still alive.

"But we will let Beyer here figure that out. He's the genius. Beyer, this is Ronnie McCall. Ronnie, meet my good friend and neighbor, and occasional lifesaver, Doctor Beyer."

The mountain in question came striding forth, hands outstretched as if he was greeting a long-lost daughter. He halted before her and bowed deeply.

"Just Beyer, please! Ah, my child. Yes indeed! I spoke to you on that infernal and most wretched of inventions, the cellular telephone, only an hour or two ago. What a distinct pleasure it is to meet you. And how *is* Dallas these days? It has been many years since I had the pleasure of ....."

Although she was obviously still very distressed, she suddenly grinned, then snorted and guffawed out loud, covering her mouth as she did so, trying to hide her rude outburst.

Still chortling uncontrollably despite her anguish, she responded automatically, as so many others have, to Beyer's instant and inimitable charm, raised her hands across the table to his, and returned his warm and comforting father-ly grip.

He immediately squeezed his abundant girth into the tight-fitting dinette and, still holding her hands, turned to face her and gently said, "My child, you are even more striking than this clumsy oaf had intimated. He did not mention the minor detail that you are *African*-American, and no doubt, from your extraordinarily exotic features, have ancestry in the Yoruba tribe from the Ogun province of Nigeria ...."

"How could you possibly *know* that?" she asked incredulously.

"Don't even ask him," I interjected. "He'll spend all night telling you. He will tell you he knows your family history right down to your DNA just by estimating the height of your cheekbones, but the truth is he guesses most of it by letting you do all the talking, and then he fills in the blanks. He's very good at it."

He ignored me and continued; "Now my child, how can we be of service to you? What is it that brings such a charming lady halfway around the world to visit this maladroit and boorish friend of mine?"

Her smile faded as she remembered her reason for being here. Beyer took her hand and placed it against his ample and hairy chest.

"There, there, my dear. No worries, as people of Mitch's inadequate breeding are apt to remark. We will get to the bottom of what is troubling you, even if we three have to travel half way round the planet to solve it. Right, Mitchell my boy?"

"May not be quite that simple, Beyer old buddy. But first of all, we need to bring you up to date. I have a few technical questions for you when we're done."

Having said that, I proceeded to fill him in on all that Ronnie had told me up to now about the disappearances of her husband and her brother. Ronnie sat and listened, occasionally interjecting with a correction to my version of her story.

Beyer did not interrupt once during my monologue, but I could see from his changing expressions and the increasing furrows on his brow, that he probably knew, with typical Beyer knowledge of all such complex matters, a lot more about Super Conducting Super Colliders than I ever would.

When I had finished, I went to the fridge to get us all some refreshments. I had a feeling this was going to take some time. My head was beginning to throb again, and I knew Beyer's forthcoming response was not going to make it any better. I was right! He immediately launched forth into his own lavish dissertation on the Collider, more I think, for his own mental revision than as a courtesy to his ignorant listeners.

"Hmmm. The SSC. What an absolutely fantastic masterpiece of infernal engineering and science that could have been, if only the idiotic, moronic, politicians in Washington had not, in their usual meddling and avaricious ways, cancelled the project at the alleged behest of the lobbyists who have them totally in their filthy pockets! They sold their souls and their technical knowledge overseas, and now, apart from a smaller version of the collider at the Fermilab facility west of Chicago, the only one in the world effectively doing any research is the one under the French-Swiss border near the little French village of Crozet – the Large Hadron Collider.

"Since the nineteen thirties, scientists have been using accelerators to smash atoms together and analyze the debris, and with some impressive results. They discovered that matter in all its complex forms seems to be made up of just a few simple particles operating under a handful of basic forces. But this so-called standard model is a puzzle that is not quite complete, and finding the last pieces would take something like the SSC.

"When atomic nuclei smash together with unprecedented energy in the Large Hadron Collider, they hope to create exotic particles and states of matter suspected to be abundant only during the first instants of the universe.

"The ten thousand superconducting magnets in the collider's planned fifty-four miles of underground oval tunnel were going to accelerate protons to nearly the speed of light, then crash them together with unspeakable power! Nobody really knows just what the outcome of such incredible power would be. It could theoretically have the effect of causing a tremendous explosion of such magnitude and devastation as to literally wipe surrounding cities off the face of the planet! On the other hand, it could open up an entirely new field of controlled – and controllable energy of such immensity as to completely change the course of human history. Such a source of appalling supremacy would be coveted by the world's military leaders as a means of total world domination, of course.

"I suspect that Erich Laudaman and his associates were very disappointed when the project at Waxahachie was cancelled in 1993. I believe …"

"But that was twenty *years* ago! And who is Erich Laudaman?" I inquired, not wanting to flaunt my ignorance, but curious enough to risk Beyer's condescending reply.

"My dear fellow," he said, raising his eyebrows in feigned horror at my inexcusable lack of knowledge of current affairs, "Erich Laudaman is only *the* pre-eminent Nobel

Prize-winning fusion-physics scientist in the world today; possibly the only man alive who was capable of bringing this fantastic experiment through to a successful conclusion.

"His frustration and disappointment at the shutdown of the Collider project was of course, unbearable. He pleaded for the SSC before Congress, arguing that this was the ultimate quest in human exploration and development. Before we can even begin to think about traveling the vast distances of interstellar space, we have to develop a totally different method of propulsion – even of travel itself! We need to completely change our narrow and limited scientific perspective on time and space, and focus on a new kind of travel ...."

"You mean, like time or dimension travel?" I interjected again.

"Precisely, my boy," he replied, warming to his subject and pleased that I had grasped at least some idea of what he was talking about.

"And Laudaman had many allies, from all over the world. They spoke of regaining America's leadership in science and technology, and of the jobs that projects like the SSC would generate, and of the practical spin-offs, including improvements in superconducting materials and computer software; which will all be desperately needed now that we have re-commenced the moon landing program.

"Nevertheless, the project's super price tag – originally estimated at five billion dollars, but up to eleven billion by the time it was shut down – was a perpetual and powerful counter-argument, particularly by scientists from other countries. Specialists in other fields of science resented such largesse being heaped on a relatively small number of researchers at a time of national belt tightening. At least, that was their argument for closing the project down.

"Now just about all the American taxpayers have for their two billion dollars already spent is a complex of empty buildings and fourteen point seven miles of tunnel under the Texas prairie!"

"And an ever-deepening mystery," I added thoughtfully, scratching my stubbly chin and gazing at Ronnie, who had been silent throughout Beyer's discourse.

"Yes," Beyer went on as if I had not spoken, "there is no single country that can afford such a big project. In the future, scientists will have to rely more on international partnerships. The Large Hadron Collider is financed by a consortium of eighteen countries. It is only forty percent as powerful as the SSC would have been, but it has a good chance of doing comparable work. Of course, that will not be much consolation to all the people who converged on Waxahachie, Texas, expecting to take part in the grandest experiment of our era."

"Including Ronnie and Richard Masters, and Jeff McCall," I said, growing impatient with his apparent lack of concern for Ronnie's plight.

"Yes, yes, I am terribly sorry, my dear. I do get carried away with these things. This has been something close to my own heart for some time. I was personally extremely distressed when they cancelled the project. I do not know whether Mitchell has told you, but I am a semi-retired astro-physicist. Naturally, I have a great interest in such incredible projects. So much so in fact, that I believe, from what I have heard, that we should prepare ourselves for immediate launch and dispatch to what were once known as the Great Plains of Texas!"

"In the *'Wayward Wind'*?" I asked incredulously.

"Precisely, my boy."

"Whoa. Hold your horses, or whatever retired physicists hold, Beyer. You may be a great scientist, but you have absolutely no idea of what is involved in planning for a flight across eight thousand miles of Pacific Ocean in a seventy year old World War Two flying boat."

"Nonsense, my boy! What do you think this magnificent machine was designed for? Exactly that! Crossing vast oceans. Why, I remember when Sir Gordon Taylor, the famous Australian pioneer aviator, did just that in a PBY much like this one. He even wrote a book about it entitled 'The Sky Beyond' …."

"O.K., O.K., I get your point. When do we leave?" I grinned.

Ronnie's jaw had been dropping continuously during this entire exchange, so that it was now almost resting on the table. At the same time, her eyes were growing wider and wider, in total disbelief at what we were so casually discussing.

"You're both raving mad," she uttered. "You can't be serious! You … you don't actually intend to fly this ….this …"

"Aeroplane. Flying boat, actually," Beyer interjected helpfully. "As I said, that is precisely the reason it was designed and built; a long-range patrol, reconnaissance and rescue bomber. And that is precisely what we shall do with it – again. Reconnoiter, rescue and possibly bomb! What?" he said, winking at me with growing excitement.

"Good grief!" I replied in frustrated but decidedly happy agreement. "Don't I remember you whining not thirty minutes ago about 'mortal peril', so forth?"

"Rubbish! The lady needs assistance. Now go do whatever it is you tarnished knights of the air do to prepare for the fray, while I take care of Maid Marion here."

Reluctantly, I left my place on the other side of 'Maid Marion' and went forward to begin a long night's preparation of flight and fuel planning, food, beverage and water requirements, and all the hundred and one things that needed to be taken care of prior to a long over water flight, and a long stay away from home.

As I was stepping through the hatch into the forward compartment, Ronnie called after me, "Mitch, what did you mean by that remark before about me being the target?"

I replied as calmly as I could.

"Simply that as I can't think of anyone who wants to kill *me* right at this particular moment, and given the fact that there may be several people, including possibly some in the United States government who for whatever dark reason want to kill your relatives, those same people may not want you alive either, to tell anybody else what you may know."

"Oh." She said meekly.

I shouted back to Beyer and said, "Just when did you plan on us getting under way, 'old boy'?"

"Oh, I expect that first thing in the morning will be soon enough."

"First thing in the ....!" I choked off my reply. I did not want to appear to Ronnie to be reluctant to get going. I was usually the one to make rash decisions like this. I knew he was just beating me at my own game for the benefit of the lady in distress, so I took my own advice and shut the hell up.

Ronnie spoke again, realizing, I think for the first time, that we were actually serious, and that we were in fact literally going to 'fly' to her rescue.

"Well, I'll be damned!" she said, her face now beaming.

"Most of us are," I replied matter-of-factly as I ducked forward.

3

A few minutes later Beyer slid out of the dinette, squeezed through the narrow water-tight hatches, clambered through the main dining saloon, sidestepped past me in the galley and into the cockpit forward of my own tiny stateroom. With practiced ease he forced his bulky frame through the cramped space under the instrument panel and into the front gun-turret and anchor compartment.

"What are you doing?" I called after him.

"Preparing to weigh anchor, of course. We have to taxi back to Rose Bay, so I can return to the 'Pauline O'Neal' and assemble the things I need for the journey. Some of us *do* require the simple accoutrements of life on an extended voyage, like a change of clothing or two, not to mention my octant and star charts."

"Octant and *star charts?*" I repeated in stunned disbelief.

"Of course! How else are we going to navigate our way across eight thousand miles of Pacific Ocean, and half the continent of North America?"

"Well, I was thinking of something a little more modern and accurate – like our GPS, for instance."

"Global Positioning System? Don't be obscene! I can assure you that I can fix our position on the surface of the planet just as accurately with star and sun shots as you can with that electronic satellite tracker. Besides, what if the thing fails in the middle of the South Pacific? Electronic gadgets *do* fail, you know. What if the U.S. Air Force decides to turn off the damned satellites just when we happen to need `em?"

"All right, all right, I should have known you would use this as a perfect opportunity to hone your astral navigation skills. But we're keeping the GPS up and running, just on the off-chance that some time during our five day flight, it might get cloudy."

"Oh, very well. But I do not see why ....did you say five *days*," his voice climbing an octave or two on the last word.

"Of course," I mimicked him. "How long did you think it was going to take the old girl to get us across at only about a hundred and ten knots in long-range cruise? Surely a man of your superb mathematical skills can figure out that eight thousand miles divided by a hundred and ten equals almost seventy-three hours of flight time, not allowing for tail winds, plus about another forty-eight or so in required refueling and rest stops. Five days."

"Oh. Well, let's get on with it then. All the more reason to proceed with all possible dispatch," he shouted from his hole up front.

"Yes sir!" I replied, turning to the cockpit myself to crank up the engines for the twenty minute taxi back around to our regular mooring at Rose Bay.

Ronnie had followed me up front. She paused to peek into my mini-stateroom on the left side of the companionway, just behind the cockpit. She then turned forward and stared in astonishment at the ancient instrument panel. After all, this plane had been flying thirty years before she was even born! I motioned her with a nod and a grin into the right seat. She happily obliged, and slipped into the cracked green leather of the old bucket. It felt good to have her there beside me again.

I checked the main bus switches on the bar between the control yokes, set the fuel valves, pushed the props into high r.p.m., checked the mixture controls were in 'Idle Cut-Off' and cracked the throttles.

I gave the engines a quick prime with the electric boost pumps which had long since replaced the old hand wobble pumps, turned the ignition switches to 'Both ON', called out to Beyer up in the nose to clear the right prop for me, to make sure some clown in a boat was not under the wing, then hit the right starter switch. The engine turned with a familiar whine. She fired almost instantly, belching blue oily smoke out the stubby exhaust. I shoved the mixture into 'auto-rich', then performed the same ritual with the left engine.

Beyer let go of the mooring line which he had removed from the bow cleat, and we were under way. Soon we were slicing through the moonlit, sparkling waters of the harbor which was still alive, even at this late hour with ferries, yachts, and tour and pleasure boats of all kinds. I had all my navigation, taxi and landing lights on so I could be seen clearly. Boat traffic had no idea how big this thing was, or how long the wingspan and it was extremely hazardous to taxi at night.

The old Pratt and Whitney radial engines idled along with their familiar clatter as they turned the giant props through nine hundred revolutions per minute.

Beyer's head and upper torso still protruded through the bow hatch, his thick black hair streaming back in the breeze and the spray of our passage. He turned and waved at Ronnie, his huge white grin flashing in the moonlight.

She grinned back, returned his wave, and turned to me. In the reflection of the harbor lights, I saw in her dark eyes a glow of warmth and peace and awe. Yes indeed! It was good to have this girl back at my side as my friend and my co-pilot, despite the fact that she was married, and that our mission, if successful, would guarantee my losing her again – forever.

She must have read my thoughts, for her expression quickly faded; she turned away and looked straight ahead through the windshield. A single, silver tear trickled down her left cheek and dropped unchecked into her lap. And in that moment, I knew that no matter what I wanted, or how I felt about this girl, my first and only thought must be to get her husband and brother back, and to hell with my own romantic notions!

Ronnie McCall - now Masters - was my friend. If nothing more could be, I valued that friendship as dearly as I did Beyer's, and it was good to have her back!

Ten minutes later, we shut the engines down and slowly drifted up to our own familiar mooring buoy in Rose Bay, right in front of the ramp and the giant concrete slab which once served as the floor of Ansett Airlines' Sandringham flying boat maintenance hangar, now, like so many similar ones around the world, long gone.

Beyer picked up the line with his pike, turned it a couple of time around the bow cleat, and secured it firmly.

Ronnie turned to me and spoke for the first time since we had left Elizabeth bay. "You really live like this? It's still hard to believe. What a fabulous life! What a beautiful place. Oh Mitch, I'm so happy for you. This is a pilot's dream. Anyone's dream. I wish …."

I looked at her with one cocked eyebrow, hoping she would say what I wanted to hear, but she did not finish the sentence.

Instead, she twisted out of her seat, rested her right hand on my shoulder and slid out of the cockpit. As she did so, she squeezed my shoulder, looked down at me and said with a forced grin, "C'mon mate. We've got work to do. If you two are serious – and I know you are –you have what's left of this beautiful evening to teach me the fundamentals of flying and navigating this bird over eight thousand miles of Pacific Ocean, as you so recently pointed out to Beyer. So let's make a fresh pot of coffee and get to work!"

"I could not have put it any more succinctly myself," that worthy chimed in as he struggled awkwardly back into the cockpit. "You two do what you must. I, for one, am going home to my stately little craft to pack, make some phone calls and other arrangements, and last but not least, try to accrue a few brief hours of precious rest. From past experience, I suspect that the only real sleep I may ever get from now on is the longest sleep of all, once this adventure has begun!"

He stepped over the sills of my stateroom and chartroom, through the galley and the main saloon, and climbed out through the port blister. With one leg inside the aircraft and one outside on the boarding ladder, he turned to us and added, "Mitch, I am going to call a few friends in high places, to give us an extra edge or two. This is a powerful group of people we may be dealing with; possibly even agencies of the United States Government itself. I think we should go very well prepared to ....ah, defend ourselves."

With that, he disappeared into the darkness.

Seconds later, the outboard sputtered to life and receded in the direction of the marina.

"What did he mean by that?" Ronnie inquired, turning to me with a worried frown.

"Oh, he's just being overly dramatic, as usual. Just wants us to be extra careful with our planning, because it's such a long trip, and because we'll be foreigners in U.S. airspace," I lied.

"Oh. Where does he live, anyway?"

I took her hand and led her once again to the huge open Plexiglas blisters in the observation lounge. The flying boat was swinging gently on her mooring, nudged by a light breeze from the south shore. About fifty yards away, in the misty amber glow of marina dock lights, we could just make out Beyer's distant silhouette climbing aboard his chunky little round-ended cruiser. The 'Pauline O'Neil' was his own retreat from a world which in his opinion was rapidly reverting to barbarism and anarchy.

"He lives aboard?"

"When he's not off in some obscure location on the planet, giving or listening to a seminar on some even more obscure subject of interest only to advanced analytical minds such as his."

"He's that clever?"

"Trust me, mate. That man has one of the most brilliant scientific minds in the world. As a result, he also moves in a small but influential group of very powerful men. He's a great asset, as well as a great friend. Why he chose me to side with, I'll never know. I'm glad he did, though. Without him I'd be a dead man; many times over."

Ronnie stared out at the silent, boat-filled marina for a few moments longer, heaved a long sigh, and then turned back to me.

"Let's get to work then," she said again.

"O.K.," I replied with some reluctance, falling to the task at hand.

"I'm sure glad I have an aviator of your experience and knowledge to help me with this. We have one hell of a job ahead of us, preparing for a trans-Pacific flight in just a few hours. I'll dig out the charts; you can start on the endurance and range problems. Work out the fuel burn per leg, taking into account the winds aloft, which I will get for you shortly, while I figure the navigation bit, so forth.

"We are going to be very close to maximum range on a couple of these legs, and I don't want to join the ranks of other famous flyers like Kingsford Smith and Amelia Earhart by disappearing 'somewhere in the South Pacific.'"

So saying, I went forward to the former radioman's station on the starboard side, just behind the cockpit and opposite my cubby-cabin. I reached into several different steel pigeonholes and brought out the dozen or so charts, tables and books of graphs we would need to plan the long flight. I took them all back and dropped them on the starboard dinette in front of Ronnie.

"The very first thing we're going to need is a long-range weather forecast. As I reminded Beyer, this little crossing is going to take us about five days, compared to the fifteen or so hours it took you to get here on that seven-forty-seven. We are going to need to arrange for fuel and servicing at the islands we decide to land on.

"We'll also have to arrange the more mundane things like diplomatic privileges – temporary visas, permission to land, so forth. I am assuming that Beyer, despite his claim that he is going to sleep, will be on the phone most of the night arranging that end of the program. That is his special forte`; talking people in high places who are full of their own importance into allowing us safe passage through in-hospitable and interminable paperwork."

"What about entry into the U.S.?" Ronnie asked with a frown. "Surely that will take more than a phone call from Beyer. We're talking about a foreign-registered aircraft and crew, except me of course, entering the States for possibly quite a long time. Can he do that?"

"He can do that," I said, confident from previous experience that Beyer's ambassadorial talent could arrange such a formality with little difficulty.

She stared in horror at the mountain of charts before her, and asked, "Do we really need all this stuff? Why can't we just use Flight Plan.com?"

I laughed heartily and replied, "Are you kidding? They don't have any data for this old tub. I have one of the last copies of the Pilot's Flight Manual and accompanying performance charts in existence."

She looked at me quizzically, shrugged and began to sort through the debris I had placed before her on the table. She selected a large sectional chart of both the South and North Pacific, then searched for and found the PBY's range and endurance tables. She took up a pencil and my old E6B navigation computer, placed the pencil between her gleaming white teeth, tossed her head to flick the bangs out of her eyes, and got straight to work, opening and spreading the charts all over the table.

I watched in admiration for a few moments, seeing her old flight instructor experience returning with aplomb as she quickly set to the daunting task I had given her; that of planning an eighty-some hour flight across eight thousand miles of almost empty ocean in an ancient aircraft that until about an hour ago she had never even heard of, much less had any kind of experience with.

She looked up and grinned around the pencil, flashing those perfect teeth at me. When I didn't move, she removed the writing instrument from her mouth and said, "What? I thought you were going to get the weather. Are you going to make me do *all* the work, as usual?"

I laughed hard enough to make my head start throbbing again.

"You're right! I did do that," I replied. "Although I do recall doing the aircraft walk-around for you in some very unpleasant weather, just so you wouldn't have to go out in the freezing wind and snow."

"Yeah, well, I'll be real interested to see how you walk round *this* airplane!"

I laughed again. "I know I'm good, but I'm afraid walking on water is above my pay grade," I replied as I reached into a drawer built into the underside of the dinette and pulled out a laptop computer. I cranked it up and moments later I was hooked up to the wireless internet and getting an instant weather brief.

Ronnie looked stunned, and then threw the pencil at me. "You bum! You mean to tell me you want *me* to do all this stuff by hand, the old-fashioned way, when you can plan it all on the *internet?*"

"That's the problem. I can't do it all on the internet. This bird is so old, there is no on-line data available for it. Oh, I could manually load the stuff in, but by the time I did that, I just know you can have it all done anyway."

She snatched the pencil back and, feigning disgust, got back to work.

I began to look around the cabin and after some invective-filled minutes of searching, found what I was looking for.

"Trouble with these damned cellular phones is that they won't stay in one place like the old land line. You always have to remember where you dropped the bloody thing last time you used it, which in this case was when you called me. Needless to say, I dropped it in a big hurry to fly to your side," I said, puffing my chest out in a vain attempt to garner the lady's affection.

It was her turn to laugh. She guffawed in spite of herself at my comical pose.

"What's so damn funny about that?" I pouted. "Can't you picture me as a Flying Sir Galahad?"

With that, she dropped her instruments, slid out of the dinette, stood up, took my wrists and lifted my hands to rest them on her shoulders. She moved in close to me and leaned forward, put her arms around me, and kissed me lightly on the lips. Her closeness and her natural scent, combined with a hint of patchouli, sent a fiery rush of excitement through my body, but before I could respond, she placed her lips against my left ear and whispered huskily.

"You will always and forever be my friend and my *white* knight. If things were different, you would be more, much more than that."

She pulled away from me, locked her beautiful black eyes on mine, and added, "Mitch, I can't tell you how much you mean to me – now and back when. So please, let's get to work before I forget why I came here."

She didn't know – or maybe she did – that with one very powerful gesture and those few intimate words, she had forever made it impossible for me to forget why she had come. And if we were successful, I would probably lose her again. Story of my life!

"You're right, of course," I said despondently, looking away from her with an unfamiliar stinging in my own blue/gray eyes. "Where is that *damned* phone, anyway?"

"In your left hand," she whispered, smiling as she directed her gaze to it with a sidelong glance.

"Thank you very much," was all I could manage to think of. "Now, as you suggested, I shall sit down, gather my widely scattered wits, and proceed to obtain the weather. Either that bullet knocked more sense out of me than I guessed, or you have a knack of taking a man's mind off the task at hand, madam."

"Why, thank you sir. Totally intentional, of course, I assure you. Now, about these eight thousand miles of ocean. Perhaps we should begin, or it *will* take us all night!"

"What will?"

"Sit down and make that call," she replied, pushing me gently back into the dinette. She cleared some room for me to write and manipulate the laptop, and then got back to her charts.

I made the call.

After a couple of rings, the phone at the Kingsford Smith Airport Meteorological Bureau was answered, and a familiar voice spoke to me. "Sydney Met Office. Dawson here."

"G'day Tony. This is Mitch Blaine. Got time for a brief?"

"Hey Mitch! Good to hear your voice, you old bugger. When you and Beyer gonna take me for a ride in that rust-bucket of yours?"

"Never, if you insult Beyer's magnificent engineering and mechanical genius like that," I retorted, only half joking.

"Aw, c'mon, you know I'm just kidding. You know that waterfowl of yours is the envy of every boat and aviation buff on Sydney Harbor. What kind of brief do you want? Let me guess. You're gonna fly some hapless sheila up the coast to Lake Macquarie for a dirty weekend and you want a nice, romantic rainy day to keep the lady in question on board and below decks. Right?"

"Not quite. I want a long-range forecast for the entire Pacific Ocean from Sydney to Los Angeles, via Fiji, Kiribati and Hawaii for the next week. I'm looking at the weather charts on the magic box, but it doesn't extend out far enough, and anyway, there is nothing like the human touch, fallible as it may be."

"You want *what*? You can't be serious! You're not really thinking of taking that thing across the bloody pond, are you?"

"Dead serious. Besides, somebody flew her down here from the States in the first place."

"Yeah, but ….but that was seventy *years* ago," he stammered, still not quite sure that I was serious.

"Well, never mind that. We really do need that forecast ASAP, Tony. We're planning on taking off at first light, or just as soon thereafter as possible."

"First …. You mean, *in the morning?*"

"Yeah. You were partly right. There is a sheila involved. We kind of have an urgent mission to the U.S. to save a fair damsel in distress from an ugly ol' dragon."

"Another one? Oh well, it's your neck, mate! Let me get on this and I'll call you back as soon as I have something, all right?"

"Roger that. Talk to you in a little bit."

So saying, I hit the 'End' button, dropped the phone, and turned back to Ronnie.

She was patiently waiting for me to finish the call, so she could ask me some pertinent questions about the performance of the aircraft for her computations.

"So?" she inquired.

"He's going to call me back. You'd think he's never had a request for a Pacific briefing before. He must give 'em a dozen times a day to the QANTAS boys and all the other U.S. bound flights."

"But never to a crazy loon who wants to take five days to do what those other guys do in thirteen some hours, I suppose."

"No excuse for his damned temerity! He's a public servant," I scoffed. "Used to be standard procedure for these Met types forty or fifty years ago, when airlines with real pilots flew real aeroplanes like the Super Connies, DC-7s, so forth, across the pond."

She rolled her eyes and took up her pencil again.

"Now you're *definitely* showing your age," I barely heard her mutter under her breath. "Anyway, as I have never flown a *real aeroplane* with *real* engines," she mimicked, "you're going to have to give me a little help with some of the terminology here."

"Fire away."

"Let me see if I have this right. These engines are Pratt and Whitney R dash 1830 dash 92 radials, with 1200 take-off horsepower. Normal cruise horse power at seven thousand feet is 1,050. Her empty weight is twenty-thousand, nine hundred and ten pounds, and gross is thirty-three thousand, nine hundred and seventy five?"

"Absolutely correct, but we'll use her gross overload weight of thirty-five thousand four hundred and twenty. We'll need every pound of it in fuel on a couple of the legs, and we will have to use the JATO rockets on those."

"JATO rockets? What the hell are they?" she inquired, perplexed at the unfamiliar term.

"Ah lassie, as Beyer would say. Now you are showing *your* age – or lack of it. You have not been in the world long enough to remember such things. JATO is an acronym for Jet Assisted Take Off. They were one of the first offshoots of the infant American rocket industry.

"Back in the late thirties, early forties, when the weight and complexity of aircraft was rapidly outstripping the power available to get them aloft, some bright fellow discovered a practical use for the first primitive rockets. They found that, particularly with overloaded flying boats, they could not get the aircraft out of the water because of the tremendous drag of the water itself in getting the bird up on to the planing 'step'.

"This severely restricted fuel and payloads, and consequently range and endurance until they came up with the brilliant idea of strapping a few of these new-fangled baby rockets to the sides of aircraft for extra initial thrust during the take-off. After the usual mishaps, they found that it actually worked – most of the time.

"In the case of the PBY, it was found by trial and error, as was the case in most aircraft design, that four rockets, two on each side just forward of the blisters, fired sequentially in opposite pairs, the first pair as the bow came out of the water and the second just as the bird was getting over the hump and on to the step, worked the best. You could now take an extra-heavy PBY and still get her out of the water with over twenty-four hours of fuel on board."

Ronnie's mouth fell open and she gasped in amazement.

"Twenty-four *hours?* That's more than the range of any airplane today, isn't it?"

"Any civilian airplane, anyway," I replied. "So we'll plan on using the rockets on the longer legs, unless we happen to be taking off from a very long runway, instead of doing a water take-off."

"O.K., but I can't plan non-stop on the really long legs; which appear, from calculating on this chart, to be from Fiji to Hawaii at three thousand, seven hundred and seventy-six miles, and from Hawaii to L.A. at two thousand, two hundred and twenty-eight. Looks like from here to Fiji is a cake-walk at only one thousand, seven hundred and thirty-eight miles!"

"Yeah, right! And her maximum range is only a little over twenty five hundred miles, so we will have to break that leg from Fiji to Hawaii at Kiribati. Wait until you have had your beautiful black booty strapped to that pilot's seat for eighteen hours nonstop, and we'll see how much of a cake-walk you think it is. But you're right about the distances. Now if only Dawson would call me back with the weather, we can figure the fuel burns and estimate the times aloft."

As if in answer to my musing, the cell phone tinkled and I began anew my search for the damn thing, muttering about its heritage under my breath.

To my chagrin, Ronnie calmly reached under the debris on the table, pulled out the offending instrument, and handed it to me.

I glowered at her, swiped it out of her hand, and pressed the 'Receive' button.

"Hello?"

"G'day again, Mitch. This is Tony. I think I have every-thing you need for your epic emulation of Kingsford-Smith. You got a pencil?"

"Ha, ha. Very funny!" Weathermen are not widely known for their great sense of humor. Just the facts, man."

"Oh, all right," he said sulkily, sounding rather hurt that I did not seem to appreciate his wit. "It looks like you've got plain sailing, so to speak, till you get to about a hundred miles north of the Samoan Islands. Clear skies, light winds, mostly out of the southwest at ten to fifteen knots. Some occasional stratocumulus at ten to fifteen thousand. After Samoa and right up till you get almost to Hawaii, there is a tropical depression building, starting at about Kiribati. Could turn into a real nasty bugger. When do you expect you will be getting there?"

"Hawaii? Oh, if all goes well, probably four days from now. Assuming the bird behaves herself and we don't have any unex-pected problems with local bureaucrats, so forth, along the way."

"Well, you'd better be careful. This thing looks like it is building fast. I'll e-mail you a printout if you like, along with everything else you need."

"Thanks Tony. I appreciate it. I'll get another update just before we leave, and then at the stations en-route, of course. We will try to get around it if we have enough gas."

"O.K. Good luck. Don't forget you owe me a ride, so don't go and sink her before I get my chance."

"Another feeble attempt at met man humor. See you later, chum."

I clicked off and dropped the phone back on the table. Ronnie had, with pencil end gripped firmly between her teeth, been working with the computer on our fuel problems while listening to my half of the conversation. She now looked up with a frown, removed the pencil, and asked, "Bad news?"

"Not really. Pretty good weather most of the way, actually. Just a little tropical depression building between Samoa and Hawaii, but we should be able to skirt it with the gas we'll have on board. How are you doing?"

"No worries. This is fun. It's been years since I actually had to do some manual flight planning. Everything on the new planes is done for you by computer. I've never in my life planned a flight like this, so you had better check my calculations."

"Don't worry. As Captain James T. Kirk of the Starship Enterprise once said to Mister Spock, 'I'd trust your best guess over anyone else's facts', but …."

I was interrupted by the tinkling of the phone once again. "Hello?"

"Mitch. I've changed my mind. I'm coming back on board tonight. You can get my bunk in the tail cone ready. I have made some phone calls, and we need to talk about a few things before we take off. Is she ready to fly?"

"As ready as she was when you left. Why? What's up?"

"Never mind. I'll tell you both when I get there. Put the coffee on."

I hung up and said, "I don't like it."

"What?"

"Beyer's coming back on board to stay the night. That's not like him at all. In the first place, he really does like his sleep, and secondly, he never, ever wants to stay on board when I have a lady on deck, no matter how platonic it is. I don't like it," I said again.

"But that's ridiculous," Ronnie said. "Surely he knows from what we already talked about that….."

"He gets embarrassed very easily, as you do. He values our friendship – and our respective privacy – highly, and draws a distinct line between those two aspects of our lives. That's probably why we have remained so close for so long."

"Where is he going to sleep?"

"Well, we actually have a convertible bunk in the amidships sofa, but he prefers to sleep back there," I said, nodding in the direction of the aft end.

I took her hand and gently tugged her out of the dinette. I opened the watertight hatch in the rear bulkhead of the cabin, to reveal a much smaller compartment with a tiny rectangular porthole on the right side in the tail section of the aircraft.

"Wow! What's this?"

"Used to be where the tunnel gun was mounted, for firing below and behind the aircraft. The tunnel hatch is still there, and has served as a secret escape route for us on more than one occasion, but as you can see – or rather, can't see – it's now concealed by a removable platform which supports that air mattress, which serves as Beyer's bunk when he sleeps aboard. He always gripes about having to squeeze his generous bulk through this hatch, though."

"I can imagine! What a neat hidey hole. This whole ship is just a boy's dream of adventure come true for you, isn't it?"

"Yep. And why not? Not too many people, rich or poor, can claim they are living their childhood dreams. But life is much too short to do otherwise; especially in the white knight business."

Ronnie looked at me quizzically, as another thought came to her.

"While we're on the delicate subject of sleeping arrangements, before this, I noticed only one other bed on board. Yours, up forward. And very comfortable it looks too, I might add."

"Ah yes, milady," I replied, bowing low as I spoke. "My cabin is now your cabin. You may take up residence forthwith. As forthwith as when you finish your work with the charts, that is."

With that, I released my grip on her hands, and turned her in the direction of the dinette again.

For my part, I kept my promise and disappeared forward through the aircraft's compartments to my cabin. I tidied it up for her and returned to the main saloon just forward of the observation deck. This was once the crew's bunk compartment and I had considered converting it to my own bunkroom, but in the end decided that it was too high a traffic area to be practical as a private stateroom.

However, it did make a wonderful day cabin. The main sofa here, thanks to Beyer's ingenuity, easily converted into a comfortable sleeper. I went back into the galley and put on a fresh pot of coffee. As I stepped aft once more, I heard the putt-putting of the outboard, followed by a slight bump, as Beyer drew alongside.

4

Standing by the ladder, I waited to help him aboard. Moments later, he again lowered his huge frame through the blister. Without his usual gregarious salutation, he dropped his duffel bag untidily on to the deck and sidled over to slide himself into the dinette as close as he could get to Ronnie.

"Blaine old chap, I think you have picked a beauty this time."

"Well, actually, I didn't pick her. She picked me, remember?"

Ronnie threw a foreign object at me. Beyer simply scowled until his bushy brows became joined in the middle.

"Don't be so predictable! And go get us all some coffee. I am going to require your undivided attention."

"Yessir! You're the boss," I replied as I snapped him a mock salute, turned and marched forward to the galley again.

Ronnie turned sideways to look him in the eyes and asked rather brusquely, "What's going on, Beyer?"

"Let us wait until Mitch gets back, my dear. I believe I have news of the greatest importance to our plans."

Hearing that, I poured three mugs of hot, black coffee, grabbed a bottle of scotch and was back at the dinette with them in two minutes. As I slid one of the steaming mugs before him, Beyer poured a generous dash of the scotch into it, then very theatrically picked it up and took several long sips before speaking. When he did, he dropped a bombshell!

"You remember I said a while ago that the reason the SSC project was discontinued was because of an overwhelming vote by the House and the Senate? Well, I have just been talking to a very good friend of mine, who shall remain nameless, and who is employed in one of the uppermost echelons of the United States government.

"After the usual pleasantries, I managed to innocently swing the conversation around to how deeply disappointed I was that the SSC had been shut down several years ago, and wondered if those morons in Washington had any idea whatever of the incredible wealth of knowledge they had managed to suppress by handing the project over to the European consortium.

"There was a long pause on the other end of the phone, and I thought he had been cut off. Then he spoke very guardedly, as if he really didn't want to tell me anything, but had to trust somebody. He said that voting members of the House had been 'persuaded' by high officials of the Defense Department to vote to kill the project – for the usual reason – in the interests of national security. They were apparently convinced that this was a 'world project' and far too important to leave to a few maverick scientists spending billions of tax-payers' dollars in a big hole in Texas."

I was dumbfounded. "Are you actually telling me that it was a government and military conspiracy to shut the thing down? Why would the government of the United States take such a risk of being exposed to their own people – not to mention the rest of the world – as just as corrupt as every other two-bit dictatorship?"

"Because they are, of course," he replied simply. "And what's worse, they don't give a damn! They are arrogantly aware of being the richest and most powerful government on the planet, and believe they are above even the will of their own people. And unfortunately for us, we will have to deal with that corruption on every level, not knowing where or whom, in order to attempt to ascertain where Ronnie's brother and husband are located – assuming they are still …."

Ronnie looked defiantly at him and her eyes flashed angrily as she said, "They *are* still alive. I *know* they are!"

"Of course they are, my child. Please accept my apologies for being so tactless. That is usually the domain of my clumsy friend here. But in answer to your question, Mitchell, I believe that the answer lies somewhere in the magnificent red desert of the Four Corners area of the U.S. – more specifically, the Navajo Nation."

"The Navajo Nation …?" I repeated, thunderstruck by this latest incredible revelation.

I was accustomed to his sometimes outrageous disclosures, but Ronnie was now twisting sideways in her seat, staring at him as if she believed he had taken complete leave of his senses.

Suddenly she snorted, then snickered, and then doubled over until she was banging her head on the table, laughing uncontrollably. I caught the bug and soon the two

of us were literally in convulsions, unable to stop guffaw-
ing despite Beyer's loud assertions for us do to so. Finally, I
managed to pull myself together.

I wiped the tears from my eyes and repeated carefully,
"The Navajo Nation? I know I am going to regret asking
this, but what exactly is that, and what does it have to do
with the disappearance of Ronnie's brother and husband?"

Beyer now rolled his eyes at me as if I was a total imbe-
cile and began another lengthy dissertation.

"The Navajo Nation - Diné Bikéyah - in the Navajo
language, is a semi-autonomous Native American home-
land covering about 26,000 square miles - 17 million acres,
occupying all of northeastern Arizona, the southeast portion of Utah, and northwestern New Mexico. It is the
largest land area assigned primarily to a Native American
jurisdiction within the United States.

"The Nation encompasses the land, kinship, language,
religion, and the right of its people to govern themselves.
They have their own police force, called the Navajo Tribal
Police, and their own form of self-government which is as old
as The People itself. Members of the Nation are often known
as *Navajo*, but traditionally call themselves *Diné* - sometimes
spelled in English as *Dineh* - which means *the people*."

Beyer looked from me to Ronnie and back again.

"It is painfully obvious to me that it is going to take far
too long to try to explain the connection, so what I suggest
is this. What is the time? Nearly eleven. How long before
we will actually be ready to depart?"

"Apart from finishing up and submitting the flight plan
for the first leg, which we can do on-line, we're ready. We

can launch at daybreak. If we leave at six, and if we have the forecast tailwinds, that will put us into Fiji at about three a.m. their time, but that's O.K. We can land at Nadi Airport and sleep until mid-morning if need be. There are several good hotels right by the airport."

"Perfect! Very well. As I said, the connection between the SSC and the Four Corners desert is not all that is involved in this affair. I believe it is more complicated than even I can imagine, so I shall brief you both en-route. Fifteen hours or so should be enough time to bring you more or less up to speed on the history of the world."

Ronnie and I grinned at each other, but managed to wipe the smirks off our faces. I suppressed the urge to laugh out loud again by speaking solemnly in my most authoritative aircraft commander's voice.

"All right Beyer, you stow your gear in your hole in back, then get on the horn again to whomever of your highly placed acquaintances can arrange our temporary entry visas, so forth."

"Already done, old boy."

"Naturally! I should have known. Ronnie, you finish up the plan on that first leg. Just what we need to get started for Fiji. We can adjust our heading and power en-route using, dare I say it, Beyer's calculations," then I whispered, loud enough for him to hear me, "backed up by the GPS of course.

"I'll call the airport and let the fuel guys know we will be over bright and early in the morning; make sure they have enough Avgas on hand to fill the plane. They will be overjoyed. On the rare occasions that I say the magic words

'Fill `er up!' they just can't help but smile. Fifteen hundred gallons is a lot of gas – and a lot of bucks. Speaking of which, Beyer ...," I raised my eyebrows inquiringly at him.

"Of course. *My* credit is *always* good, thank God."

"O.K. Let's do it."

"Oh. One more thing," Beyer added. "I checked with the Warners. As far as they know, there were no party-crashers. They knew everyone who showed up at the party, and they personally escorted everyone who wanted to come aboard down to the dock; which means, old rope, that either the would-be assassin was known to the Warners, or he sneaked on after I escorted the revelers off the boat prior to your return."

"Either way," I replied, tenderly touching my weeping scalp wound, "we can expect another attempt at any time en-route."

Thirty minutes later, Beyer was settled comfortably in his cubbyhole, Ronnie had completed her preliminary calculations to ensure that we wouldn't run out of gas somewhere in the South Pacific, and I had just returned from giving the entire aircraft a thorough check, inside and out, for her epic journey.

"That should do it," Ronnie said wearily, looking up as I stepped back into the blister compartment. "Say, it's been almost thirty-six hours since I left home. I just realized how tired and grimy I feel. Any chance a girl can get a shower on this tub before I go to bed?"

"Of course! I'm sorry, mate," I said. "I should have offered it sooner. Follow me, and I'll show you the peculiarities of our bathing facilities."

So saying, I led her forward, stopped just short of my cabin, opened the door to the tiny head, ushered her into the cramped space, and then squeezed in behind her.

"Nothing to it, really. Just like any old trailer or houseboat. Gravity feed tank gives you your water. Turn this switch on to run the pump that keeps the header tank full. It's hotwired to the ship's batteries. The water heater also runs off the batteries. It won't be as hot as you're probably used to, but it's not too bad. The toilet also works like one on a boat…"

"Hey, I'm not a total wimp, ya know. I'm sure it will be just fine."

"O.K. There are fresh towels in that locker behind you. One more thing," I said, opening the inside door to my cabin. "This is the only head on the plane. As you can see, it has two doors. Don't be alarmed if, in the middle of the night, you hear strange rumblings from in here when you are in my bed. Holler if you need anything else."

I turned to step out of the cramped space. She grasped my arm and pulled me back into the shower stall. She put her arms around me, pulled me close to her and looked up into my eyes again.

"Thanks Mitch."

"For what?"

"For understanding; for what you and Beyer are doing; for being there."

"Shucks, ma'am," I said, feigning humility in the Texas style, "this is what I do, you know. Besides, you're worth much more than a ten thousand mile trip in a seventy year old airplane. I wish I could tell you how much, but ……" my voice trailed off.

I didn't know what else to say that hadn't already been said, so I reluctantly backed myself out of her embrace and out of the stall, climbed up into the cockpit, and slumped into my pilot's seat. This was where I really felt at home, and was most at ease in times of stress; and this was definitely a time of stress. It always was, when I found someone I really cared for, and knew the love could never be returned.

I sat in my seat for a long time, checking and re-checking every dial, knob and switch, mostly to take my mind off Ronnie, but also because I knew our lives were going to depend on this ancient flying machine for many days and weeks to come.

Had I any clue as to just how much our lives would depend on the reliability of this machine, I may very well have changed my mind about this whole white knight business!

5

When I had checked everything in my 'office' that it was possible to check, I sat for a long time staring out at the ceaseless activity on the harbor. It was a calm, beautiful night, and I never grew tired of the feel of the boat under me, rocking gently in the slight swells.

For a time, girl activity in my cabin behind me also kept me mentally entertained. She ran the shower for about twenty minutes. No problem there. Filtered shower water was pumped in directly from the harbor, and re-filtered before it was voided overboard again. When the water stopped running, little girly noises and fragrances wafted through the bulkhead at my back. She had to know that I was sitting up here, and I wished that she would open my cabin door, poke her head out, and invite me in. No such luck!

A few minutes after midnight, I squeezed out of my seat and silently padded back through the aircraft to my own lonely half-acre of bed in the main saloon. I lay awake for a long time, wondering what Beyer's comments about the Utah-Arizona desert had to do with two men missing or dead in Texas, fifteen hundred miles or so to the east. Finally the gentle nudging of wavelets against the hull, and the creaking of lines in a stiffening breeze lulled me into a restless sleep.

Sometime in the early hours, I was partially awakened as Beyer crept past me to use the head. After that, I heard nothing until five a.m., when I became vaguely aware of a presence moving around me. A few minutes later, the unmistakable aroma of freshly brewed coffee brought me totally awake.

I sat up and poked my head around the bulkhead hatch into the blister compartment. Ronnie grinned at me from the starboard dinette, removed the ever-present pencil from her teeth, and shoved a steaming mug in my direction.

"Wake up Australia!" she cheerily quipped, showing no signs of the melancholy mood that had gripped her last night. "I've been up for hours, re-working my calculations. Why don't you get some actual clothes on and come in here and check 'em for me, huh?"

"In that order?" I inquired, ducking back as another foreign object hurtled through the hatch and past my head. "And a very good morning to you, too," I responded as I immodestly dragged on my old khaki shorts and stepped cautiously over the coaming into the dinette beside her.

I yawned, rubbed my eyes, leaned over and kissed her soft, caramel cheek, then awaited her response.

She looked up and frowned at me, but her wide black eyes softened and I thought I caught a momentary glimpse of the old attraction. Then she seemed to come to some inward decision. She slid sideways toward me, pecked me on my left ear, and passed the coffee she had poured me. "Drink! Beyer is already up and preparing breakfast. The least you can do is look at my fig..."

I had opened my mouth to make another painfully predictable Blaine wisecrack.

"...numbers – and I'll just have to watch *everything* I say, won't I?"

"Yes, ma'am. O.K., let's see what you've got here."

I took a look at her copious notes and numbers, then shuffled through the litter on the table and found the PBY-5A Pilot Operating Instructions. The manual was open at the page titled 'Cruising Control Chart'.

I picked up the pencil which Ronnie had discarded, and began to work through the chart.

"Let's see here. What did we say? Nineteen hundred and sixty miles, roughly, to Nadi airport? At our best long-range cruise of fifty-five percent power looks like around thirty-one inches manifold pressure and eighteen hundred r.p.m., with a fuel flow of approximately seventy-four gallons per hour."

"Down to our gross weight of thirty-three thousand pounds for this leg, then up to our density altitude line again, gives us a true airspeed of about one hundred and eight knots. Nineteen sixty divided by one oh eight is eighteen hours at seventy-four g.p.h., equals about thirteen hundred and thirty two gallons."

I glanced across at her figures. Identical! When I looked up in amazement at Ronnie, her lips were pulled back from her clenched teeth in a huge grin of satisfaction.

I briefly glanced at the Range and Endurance Prediction Chart, confirmed that her numbers once again matched my own quick calculations, and that we would indeed have enough gas to last us the eighteen hours aloft. I was just about to repeat my good morning gesture to her when Beyer came blundering through the hatch, balancing a tray full of breakfast goodies in one hand and clinging to the side of the hatch with the other.

"Oho!" he boomed, full of good cheer. "Now that we are *all* up and about, I presume we can get on with the business of hoisting this beastie aloft and into the unfriendly skies beyond."

"No worries mate" I replied, as I moved over to let him slide his giant bulk into the dinette. He had other ideas though, and managed to squeeze himself in on the other side of Ronnie, crushing her between the two of us so that she barely had room to raise her hands to her plate.

Breakfast, in typical Beyer over boost of grilled bacon, tomatoes, potatoes, scrambled eggs and toast, with more coffee and orange juice, was downed amidst a flurry of excited conversation about our forthcoming adventure.

"So how's the damaged noggin this morning, old chap?" Beyer asked, frowning at my still slightly oozing and reddening scalp.

"None the better for your asking. I thought that by now you would have come up with some wild theory as to the identity and purpose of the would-be assassin," I replied smugly.

"Oh I have, old fruit. I most certainly have. But that can wait until we are all buttoned up and well and truly on our way."

"One can only imagine," I mumbled around a last mouthful of dry toast, "Very well. Let us indeed get this show on the road. We still have to slip over to the big airport to gas up."

So saying, I pried myself out of the dinette, led the way up forward to the cockpit, and slipped into the familiar green cracked leather of my seat to begin the pre-start drill for the countless time.

Beyer followed, aware of his duty as first mate in the bow to cast us off once we had the engines running. Ronnie stopped long enough in the rear to gather up and return the breakfast things to the galley amidships, so they didn't fly all over the place when we started our take-off run.

Just as I was about to begin the Before Start Check, she slid into the right-hand seat, picked up the old cardboard checklist, and waited for me to call for it after I had done the flows and set the knobs and switches for the starting sequence. It was like old times!

By the time I had both engines clattering at idle power, Beyer's bulk was protruding from the bow-hatch, pike in hand, awaiting my order to cast off.

"Let `er go, Beyer," I shouted to him through the side window as I gave him the thumbs up.

He slipped the line, I advance the throttles just a hair, and we were free, running out into the swells of Rose Bay. The wind was out of the northwest, and we would have to taxi around in circles while waiting for the oil temps to come up and checking for boat traffic at the same time.

While I was waiting, I picked up the hand microphone and called Sydney Approach to get permission to take off and join the landing pattern at Kingsford-Smith.

"Sydney Approach good morning. This is Catalina Papa Bravo Yankee requesting clearance to depart Rose Bay inbound for Kingsford-Smith."

"Papa Bravo Yankee, Sydney Approach; g'day Mitch. You are cleared to depart Rose Bay, climb over north end of the bridge and join left base for runway one six left. No other traffic."

"Join base for one six left, roger. Call you again in a few minutes."

Ronnie joined in the fun. "How about I read the checklists to you like we had to do in the airline? It'll give me a chance to get familiar with the controls and procedures."

"O.K., Shoot!"

"Roger that. Elevator, rudder and aileron tabs."

"Checked."

"Rudder lock."

"Off."

"Auto-pilot."

"Off."

"Landing Gear."

"Up and locked."

"Wing floats."

"Down and locked."

She went on with the seemingly endless litany of checklist items required to be completed prior to commencing our take-off, finishing with the familiar 'Before take-off checklist complete, *sir!*"

I grinned at her. "Thanks mate. Oil temps and pressures are in the green. You ready for this?"

"Can't wait!"

"O.K." I mashed the intercom button on my control yoke and spoke to Beyer through his headphones, which he now had firmly placed over his huge bear head. "Beyer, get your head down and close that hatch. We're ready!"

His great, black thatch disappeared and the bow-hatch slammed down. "I'm ready. Let's go," he shouted back.

I tugged the overhead throttles back into idle and let her swing into the wind. I checked once more for boat traffic in my path, glanced at Ronnie again, made sure her seatbelt and shoulder harness were secure. She tossed her head and grinned back at me.

I again grasped both throttles firmly in my right hand, nudged them slowly forward, at the same time pulling the control yoke all the way back into my stomach with my left hand. The great Pratt and Whitney radial engines bellowed. I glanced down at the manifold pressure gauges and stopped advancing the throttles at forty-eight inches.

A plume of white spray rose up around the bow of the huge flying boat. Her nose came up and she squatted on the rear of her 'step'. I held the yoke hard back. The white plume came up around the cockpit. I slowly eased the yoke forward and she settled into her planing position, slightly nose-high.

We were up and running!

"Floats up," I yelled at Ronnie over the roar of the engines.

She hit the float switch on the instrument bar connecting the two yokes, and craned her head out her side window. Hydraulic pumps whined as the wing floats came up and snugged into their wingtip positions.

The 'Wayward Wind' sliced through chop churned up by the northwesterly breeze. Wavelets drummed against the hull, making a terrible din as she fought to break free. We were light, with little gas on board, and as the airspeed quivered on seventy knots, I eased the yoke back a fraction. She lifted out of the waves, shaking the spray off her like an old dog, and sniffing the air ahead with her bulbous snout.

I lowered the nose slightly to build up speed. Ronnie clapped her hands with glee as we zoomed low over the masts of the boats in the harbor. I put the Cat into a gentle climbing turn over the north end of the spectacular Sydney Harbor Bridge and reduced the power to twenty-two fifty r.p.m.

The view below was fantastic! I never got tired of looking at it. The sun, a sphere of molten copper, was just slipping out of the ocean beyond Sydney Heads beneath our starboard wing, tinting red roofs with gold and the harbor with silver; an exquisite sight on any morning, but particularly this one, the dawning of a new adventure with two old friends in our magnificent flying machine.

We swept over the north-side towers of the bridge, waved to the giant clown mouth yawning at the entrance to the old Luna Park, and lined up to join left base to a southeasterly landing at Kingsford-Smith Airport. Middle Harbor and Cockatoo Island Naval Dockyards swung beneath us, and then we were in a gentle left bank to join final.

"Papa Bravo Yankee, Sydney Approach. You are radar contact. Continue approach for one six left. You should see a QANTAS 747 at your three o'clock for one six right. Call the tower on one two four decimal seven abeam downtown. Talk to you on the way out, Mitch."

"Thanks Cliff. Talk to you soon."

Ronnie had spoken not a word in the seven or eight minutes since we took off. She was far too captivated with the excitement of the short flight and the incredible view of Sydney spread out before us.

"You still with us, mate?" I inquired.

"Are you kidding? This is the most fun I've had since I first learned to fly. Better, in fact! Who needs a jet when you have this? You gonna teach me to fly this baby?"

"You can already fly it. I just need to teach you how to get her on and off the water. There's nothing to it, for an aviator of your talent."

I glanced at the airspeed indicator as I eased the throttles back for the approach, and shoved the prop levers forward to maximum r.p.m. At ninety knots I wanted the wheels. I had already briefed Ronnie on the landing gear operation.

"Gear down, Ronnie."

"You got it," she replied with alacrity, reaching for the selector valve handle on the forward panel. She flipped it to the down position, confirmed that the safety catch had clicked into place, and checked the "W" down and locked indicator light.

Moments later, I eased us into a flare over the threshold of those eight thousand feet of concrete, the gear rolled on, and we rumbled off the runway at the first high-speed taxiway.

Ronnie was still grinning at me as we taxied to the general aviation ramp to begin our lengthy fueling operation. Beyer stayed with the ship to supervise – and pay for – the loading of almost fourteen hundred gallons of aviation gasoline. Ronnie and I hitched a ride with an airport security vehicle over to the Met. Office, where we received updated print-outs of the Pacific weather forecast promised us by Tony Dawson the previous evening.

Dan Thompson, his shift relief, outlined the trend of the pressure system we would be following, and reiterated Tony's warning about possible bad weather as we approached the Hawaiian Islands. Thirty minutes later, we were back at the Cat. Ronnie, with print-out in hand, began studying the winds and temperatures aloft, mentally comparing her calculations of last evening with this morning's predictions.

Beyer's massive bulk was precariously perched on top of that giant slab of wing, ensuring that the fuel and oil caps were secure.

"How's she going, Beyer? All buttoned up?"

"Ready as we'll ever be, old horse. You owe my American Express card five thousand, six hundred and fifty-eight dollars!"

"No worries mate. It's on account; on account of I can't pay, that is," I chuckled.

"Very amusing. I dare say it will be 'on account' forever, as usual."

I ignored his griping, glanced at my watch and decided it was definitely time we were not here. I followed Ronnie into the ship. Beyer awkwardly clambered down between the two Pratts on to the top of the fuselage and made his way back to the blisters. Ronnie was already in the co-pilot's seat, flight plan and paperwork on her lap, teeth gripping the ever-present pencil, fingers twirling the E6B in a flurry of last-minute computations.

I leaned into the cockpit, admiring her work, her enthusiasm and her attractive African features once more.

"You don't have to do that, you know. We do have the GPS to take care of our navigation for us."

"I know, but I'm kind of with Beyer. If he's going to do sun and star shots, the least I can do is practice my dead-reckoning nav."

"Suit yourself."

I ducked through the hatch and slid into my seat, then turned to peer back into the dimness of the main companionway.

"You with us, Beyer?"

"Absolutely, old rope. I'm traveling in style this time."

He waved from the main saloon, my erstwhile bedroom three compartments back, where he had buckled himself into one of the big, comfortable day chairs by the portholes.

"Well alrighty then! Let's get rolling. Checklist please, number one," I said, inviting Ronnie to participate in the routine again.

She ran through the engine start checks with me, and minutes later we were cleared by the ground controller in the tower to taxi out on to the same runway we had recently landed on. We completed the before take-off checks and then we were ready to go.

"O.K. mate, because we're so heavy with gas, if we lose an engine, you confirm it and feather the prop pronto or she won't fly. We'll run the checklist, call the tower and come back in and land. If we can't make the runway, we'll land in Botany Bay. Any questions?"

"No questions boss. Let's do it!"

I scanned the instruments and gauges with practiced eye, tightened my belt, reached for the overhead throttles, and eased them forward. I held the brakes momentarily as I again checked the engine instruments. Twenty-four hundred lusty horses bellowed and snorted blue smoke. As the huge flying boat shook and vibrated from stem to stern, I released the brakes and the old girl began to lumber down that almost two mile stretch of concrete.

The airspeed quivered, then began to register. Forty knots, then fifty, sixty, seventy. At eighty knots she wanted to fly. I gently eased the yoke back. She responded sluggishly. This was the first time I could remember taking off at such a high gross weight; and unknown to Ronnie, the massive fuel load did not *quite* account for that entire incredible payload!

As the airspeed went through eighty-five, I tugged the yoke more firmly. The nose wheel lifted off followed seconds later by the mains. I waited until I had a positive rate of climb on the vertical speed indicator.

"Positive rate," Ronnie called, barely audible over the engines.

"Gear up!" I shouted back.

She already had her hand on the lever, waiting for my command. She loosened the safety catch then raised the lever to the 'UP' position. The starboard engine hydraulic pump whined and sucked up the mains into the sides of the fuselage, and the nose wheel into its compartment.

I reduced manifold pressure and r.p.m. to climb power and we were away, done with the ground for about eighteen hours. We banked left over Botany Bay in a wide sweeping turn to set heading on a north-easterly course for Nadi in the Fiji Islands.

The tower controller came back on as we climbed through five hundred feet. "Papa Bravo Yankee, call departure on one two nine decimal seven. Good luck, Mitch."

"One two nine point seven. Thanks mate. We'll need it!"

The sun was already high in the windshield, the Pacific sky that brilliant, clear cerulean blue which can only be seen in this virtually smogless country of ours; a great day to begin our flight into mystery and intrigue.

Ronnie dragged her face away from the magnificent sight receding beneath her side window, turned and flashed that flawless and irresistible grin.

"Wow!" the lady yelled over the din of the howling Pratts. "What a ride. What a sight. What a *plane!*"

"She's all yours," I said, turning the controls over to her. She took the plane with aplomb, and was still smiling broadly when Beyer's hairy visage appeared in the cockpit hatchway.

He released the jump seat – woefully inadequate for his proportions – from its stowage, locked it into position, and dropped heavily into it, shoving his massive shoulders into the narrow space between and behind us. He took the spare headset down from its peg, stretched it almost to breaking point, and fit it over his bear-like head.

I gave Ronnie an initial heading, allowing for the forecast quartering tailwind from the southwest, fine-tuned the climb power settings, sat back, folded my arms, and awaited Beyer's verbal assault.

Forgoing his customary repartee, he immediately launched into his long-awaited monologue.

"Now then, as I said last evening, it is going to take quite some time to brief you two, but eighteen hours should be plenty of time for you to absorb the facts.

"First of all, I need to bring you both up to date on a conversation I had last night which somewhat expands on what Ronnie has already stated. Ronnie, you mentioned one of the personnel in the tunnel had died rather inexplicably. What you did not mention, no doubt because you did not know, was that he was a Native American – more specifically, a Navajo; not terribly significant in itself, but when you put a few other facts together, it does become very important.

"Many cultures – the Navajo and Hopi tribes included - believe that there are certain places on the surface of the earth which are spiritual locations where the energy is right to facilitate prayer, mediation and healing. These are called vortexes, and are believed to have energy flow that exists on multiple dimensions.

"These places, for obvious reasons, are very sacred sites to native Americans and other indigenous cultures. The Navajo Creation legend itself tells of First man and First woman who were created and brought to the surface through a series of underworlds. The Navajo story of their origin is rather long and complicated, with many versions. "However, in a nutshell, it says that The Creator fashioned the Natural World. He and his first creations, the Holy People, made humans, birds, animals, and all of the Natural World was put in Hozjo or balance. All of the

Natural Worlds depend on each other. The Navajo say they are glued together with respect, and together they work in harmony. To the Navajo, this present world is the fourth. The place of emergence into this level was 'Xajiinai', a hole in the world we know. The Navajo believe that these places of emergence are accessible through their kivas."

Fascinated as I was with Beyer's monologue, I could remain silent no longer.

"Beyer?"

"Yes?"

"This is a very nice story, but just exactly where are we going with all this? What has it got to do with Ronnie's husband and brother, much less the supercollider in Texas?"

"Very simply that I believe the supercollider location is one of the aforementioned vortexes, better known as a portal. I suspect that the location was chosen in the first place for that very reason. The strange things that were happening there are, I hypothesize, a direct result of interaction by forces as yet undetermined. Furthermore…"

I turned around in my seat and looked over my sunglasses at him from a distance of about two feet, to make sure he was not pulling my leg. Even Ronnie, who had been listening intently to his lengthy discourse, squirmed around to face Beyer.

"But I thought you said that it was shut down by politicians for financial reasons."

"That, I have now discovered, much to my chagrin, was nothing but a clever ploy, to distract any would-be investigations into the shutdown. The politicians were themselves duped by a *very* sinister plot to cover up the whole affair, under the pretext of the usual reason – national security!"

"Good grief!" I expostulated. "Don't you think that's just a *little* bit far-fetched?"

"Not at all, old horse," he countered, slightly miffed that I doubted his incredible disclosure. "As a matter of fact, I happen to have it on very good authority that that is precisely what happened; so if you will allow me to continue?"

"Please do."

"Thank you! My source, who shall remain nameless for the time being, assures me that he knows this to be so, because of personal knowledge of the People."

"What people?"

"Don't be absurd! The Navajo refer to themselves as The People. The man who died in the supercollider was a 'guardian', who….."

"We already established he was a guard," I interjected again.

"Not a guard; a 'guardian'. There is a difference; a *big* difference! You see…"

"That's all very well and good, Beyer," I interrupted again rather impatiently, "but I say again, what has all this got to do with ….?"

"The problem is," he went on as if I had not spoken, "the man in the supercollider tunnel died, I suspect, protecting access to the portal."

That really shook me.

I glanced over at Ronnie. She was not amused either. She simply looked at me, shrugged her shoulders, and continued her silent vigil at the controls. Neither of us wanted to even think that what he was saying might in any way, shape or form be true.

"Oh boy! Come on, Beyer," I scoffed, without any humor at all, "you've *got* to be kidding! Are you actually suggesting that there are portals into other dimensions, that the supercollider just *happened* to be located right on top of one and that the Navajo nation has been arbitrarily appointed the 'chosen' race to secure these entrances?"

"Yes and no. I suspect that the answer to your first question is yes. If so, however, I also suspect that the location of the supercollider was selected precisely *because* those who were putting the project together *theorized* that if they could smash atoms at exactly the right speed and frequency, they may discover the secret to opening the portal.

"What the fools obviously did not realize, of course, is that these dimensional windows, if indeed they exist, are open *all the time* under the right circumstances, which of course we do not know.

"If the Navajo Creation legends are in any way believable, entering one of these portals may lead to one or more of their 'other worlds' which could in turn invite disaster on the world as we know it."

"Good grief, man! Do you know what you're saying?"

"So," he went on, ignoring me, "if we were to find evidence – even at this late stage of our development – of a previous, or alternate civilization, not on another planet, which we were all assuming and hoping for, but right here in our own back yard, what a blow to the ego that would be! We just couldn't accept that it could be possible. Our universe has been getting smaller and smaller as our quest for knowledge and intelligence has become more acute."

I could stand it no longer!

"Beyer, this has been a fascinating discourse, but *please* don't tell me that *any* of this has anything at all to do with the disappearance of Richard Masters and Jeff McCall."

"On the contrary, old rope. I believe it has *everything* to do with it. But I have to introduce you to the association, or you will have no earthly clue as to why Texas is only the starting point of our quest."

6

"Only the starting point?" I echoed shrilly, noticing that Ronnie, although remaining silent, had clenched her teeth so tightly that the jaw muscles were knotting discernibly. She stared fixedly out through her forward windshield, but there was no sign of tears in her eyes.

"Precisely, my boy."

"Well, before you continue, please give us a moment to check our position and make sure we are going to *get* to Texas."

So saying, I checked the GPS, which has to know where it is before it leaves the ground, so that it can constantly update its position with its big brother satellites orbiting overhead. It showed we were about ten miles south-east of our desired track, and that we needed to turn seven degrees left to intercept the new direct course to Fiji.

Ronnie and I checked and reset our gyro compass cards, and she made the appropriate course correction. I tinkered unnecessarily with the controls and made minute adjustments to the power settings to ensure our best range, causing the incessant and barely muted roar of the engines to change pitch slightly.

Ronnie, who had remained silent during Beyer's entire monologue, now broke her own reverie with a tinge of acid in her voice.

"Mitch, how do I engage the auto-pilot on this ship? I want to make sure I don't miss anything. I'm more than just a little bit curious myself as to how Beyer is going to relate my husband's and brother's disappearance to an apparent anomaly in a time-space continuum in Texas."

"Well said," I responded. "It's not exactly an auto-pilot in the modern sense you're used to," I added, pointing to the old Sperry gyro- pilot control in the center of the main instrument panel. "Really just a wing-leveler with a primitive altitude hold."

I reached back and turned the main 'ON-OFF' control handle on the door frame above Beyer's head, then flipped the switch on the panel and adjusted the wing-leveler with the rotary knob.

"See? Nothing to it."

"Got it," she replied.

The altimeter was just approaching our initial target altitude. "Leveling off at four thousand," Ronnie added.

"Roger. Make our cruise power settings as calculated, and we'll adjust 'em as necessary when we check our fuel burn in an hour or so."

She did as I asked, and then we both settled back to await Beyer's Revelation, Part Two.

"Are you both quite ready?"

"Go ahead!"

"*Thank* you! Now Ronnie, I realize that all this sounds very far-fetched, and impossible to relate to your own grief and concern at this time, but trust me, it will come together. However, having told you what I have, and in order for it all to make some kind of sense, I need to digress yet again."

I rolled my eyes, crossed my arms and sighed.

"Go back to what I said about a conspiracy. Let's just suppose, for argument's sake, that one of the scientists on the project, who also happens to be one of the world's leading experts on advanced propulsion research, was experimenting with a new but extremely dangerous and highly unstable source of infinite energy, suspected to exist at the very core of matter as we know it. Let's also say that this person has discovered that, when harnessed properly, it could finally take us off the Earth and into the farthest reaches of the galaxy."

"Enter Dr. Erich Laudaman, most notably of SSC fame," I exclaimed in a rare burst of perspicacity.

"Precisely! Let us also suppose that, unbeknown to Dr. Laudaman or his colleagues or superiors, there was a conspiracy afoot to quash his experimental atom-smasher, for reasons which shall shortly become obvious."

"Beyer?"

"Yes?"

"Are you making this up as you go along?"

"I shall give that comment the contempt it deserves and pretend to ignore it. Blaine, I am not sitting on this ridiculous perch, cramped into this tiny space in this noisy machine four thousand feet above the South Pacific Ocean for my own health. Please remember that. I have gone to great pains and considerable personal risk to obtain this information."

"I apologize."

"Accepted. If I may continue ....?"

"Please do!"

"It would seem, according to my friend of whom I spoke, that the parties involved in the project were instructed that the Super Collider – or perhaps more specifically, Dr. Laudaman himself – had to be shut down, to be prevented from revealing his secrets of energy and propulsion.

"At first, it was assumed that delays, confusion, and budget overruns would be sufficient to postpone the progress of the project. When these methods did not prevail, pressure was brought to bear on members of the House to suspend funding. Finally, as you know, the entire project was voted down by Congress.

"Twenty years later, as we now know, Richard Masters and Jeff McCall, both of the United States Air Force Office of Special Investigations, were dispatched to the site. Overtly, they were to investigate acts of sabotage against some new and secret project."

"But what have acts of sabotage against a civilian project got to do with the air force?" I persisted, more bewildered than ever. "And why would Washington want to suppress information about a new energy source? You'd think they would be delighted to announce such a discovery."

"Simply this, old trout. Certain powerful members of the House, the Senate and the Armed Services Committee were informed – perhaps threatened would be a better word – by the intelligence communities that it was in their best interests and those of their country to shut down the Super Collider before its incredible secrets were revealed. I suspect that what they – the intelligence people, that is - really wanted was to kill the project in the public eye so they could covertly have it all to themselves."

Neither Ronnie nor I were prepared for what he said next.

"I also suspect that the project has been ongoing under an incredibly tight veil of security, and that in spite of, or perhaps even because of – McCall's and Masters' investigation - they were either accidentally or deliberately taken through the aforementioned portal."

"*Whaat?*" Ronnie and I shouted in unison. The hairs on the back of my neck stood on end, and a chill went all the way down my spine. I shuddered involuntarily and squinted out the cockpit windshield through the glare at the empty, copper sea and the deep indigo sky.

It was a good thing that the old gyro pilot had some measure of control over the ship. Had either of us been hand flying at the moment of Beyer's astonishing statement, I'm sure we would have lost control of the aircraft.

"My God!" was all that I could muster.

Ronnie's bottom jaw dropped a good two inches, then slammed shut. The pencil she was gripping snapped in half.

"Now do you see why they couldn't let Dr. Laudaman finish his research?"

"I think so," I replied. "His experiments at the Collider were in dimensional travel. If he had succeeded, they would have such an advantage over the rest of the world, they just could not be allowed to let that happen. They may very well have discovered a way to get to anywhere in the galaxy, for that matter, in literally no time.

"They, that is the military and the government, could not let us *common* peasants in on a secret like that. Like you said before, Beyer, to their warped way of thinking, it would totally and forever change our own perception of ourselves and where we came from."

"Precisely! Well said, my boy."

"Doesn't exactly bode well for Dr. Laudaman's health, does it now?"

"I shouldn't think we will find *his* body either, if that's what you mean."

I sat for a long moment, trying to absorb some of what my friend Beyer had just revealed. It was all too incredible to be true, and yet, acutely aware of his knowledge of all such matters, I knew it must be so, beyond my comprehension as it may be.

"Beyer?"

"Mmm?"

"Exactly who knows we're coming?"

"Oh, only my friend in Washington who gave me all this information, as far as I know. I had to tell him, of course, in order to arrange our visas and give us unhindered passage into and around the States in this lumbering, very visible beast of ours. Why do you ask?"

"The fewer people who know we are coming, the better chance we have of staying alive," I said, aware of yet another very itchy feeling at the nape of my neck. "Who is this mystery person, anyway?"

"Normally I would not divulge his identity. However, as there is no way that it can go any further than the three of us, I think it is safe to tell you. We met many years ago at a post-graduate seminar in advanced nuclear and laser technology, specifically aligned to the promulgation of the Strategic Defense Initiative."

"You mean Star Wars?"

"Exactly. His name you are probably not familiar with. He is the head of the Special Committee on Funding Procurement for S.D.I. His name is Nathan Price."

I almost fell out of my pilot's seat! It was at that precise moment that I knew we were, as Beyer so succinctly put it, 'in mortal peril'.

It was my turn to astonish Beyer, for a change.

"*General* Nathan Price?" I inquired smugly.

"How did you …."

But before he could complete the sentence, Ronnie, recovering from his stunning multiple revelations, chipped in. "He is my husband's and brother's commanding officer. It was he who gave me all the details of their disappearance. He also happens to be the Commanding Officer of the United States Air Force Office of Special Investigations," she added scornfully.

This time it was Beyer's turn to register extreme shock, surprise and anger.

"But … but, that means I have given all our details to the very man who may be at the center of the mystery surrounding their …" his voice trailed off, as the significance of the situation dawned on him.

"So you think we are up against the United States Government?" Ronnie asked despondently.

"More specifically, at the very least, the air force I'm afraid, my dear," Beyer responded as he pried himself out of his jump seat, stowed it back against the bulkhead, and retreated aft.

"Where are you going?" I inquired, regaining some of my own composure.

"I have had my sensitive buttocks strapped to that uncomfortable perch far too long. I am going to prepare some liquid refreshments, and then I am going to take a sun shot, just to ensure that we are indeed on course, despite the random calculations of that ridiculous black box of yours!

"By the way, speaking of the vagaries of the United States Air Force, you *do* realize of course, that the Defense Department has the capability at any time they please, of turning off their GPS satellites to prevent civilian or foreign government use in case of national emergency?

"Where would we be then? I'll tell you, old trout! We wouldn't have a clue. We would be as hopelessly lost as Amelia Earhart."

Before I could open my mouth to frame a suitably acerbic reply, he turned his winning charm on Ronnie once more.

"What would you like to drink, Ronnie my dear? Coffee? Tea?"

"No thanks Beyer. After all that you have told us, I feel like a very strong alcoholic beverage, but I'll have to settle for one of those big bottles of water, please."

"Very well. Mitchell?"

As I could think of not one suitably unbecoming reply to his insults to both my intelligence and the limitations of my GPS unit, I sulkily replied, "Coke, thanks."

"I shall be back shortly. I intend to leave my watch on Sydney time so that I know what meal my stomach is attempting to tell me to prepare. Running towards the sun as we are doing, at the incredible warp speed of one hundred and ten nautical miles per hour, it will be dark before it is lunchtime!"

"Can't have that, can we? You might very well fade away to a mountain," I admonished, finally getting in a sarcastic jibe. "Speaking of which, if my own watch is correct, you have been orating nonstop now for over four hours. It *is* time for lunch! How 'bout a sandwich or three?"

"Blaine, you are incorrigible! However, you are also correct. I shall bring your libation forward, then go and prepare a repast reminiscent of the grand old QANTAS days of the Order of the Double Sunrise," he said, disappearing aft.

Ronnie turned to me and, her infectious grin returning, asked "What the hell is he talking about now?"

I chuckled and said, "The correct title is the *Secret Order of the Double Sunrise*, and he is referring to a much-coveted certificate that the old QANTAS Empire Airways once gave to passengers who survived two sunrises of continuous flight in this very type of machine during World War Two – except it was the straight flying boat, not the amphibian version – to save weight for fuel. Between the Germans and the Japs, they had all the oceans and most of the airways of the world bottled up, but the airspace over the Indian Ocean was pretty well wide open.

"Australia, the U.S. and Britain had to have a means of getting VIP civilian and military personnel to England, so QANTAS was asked by the Australian Air Force to pioneer a flight from Perth to Colombo in what used to be Ceylon – now Sri Lanka. It took over twenty-four hours nonstop. In fact, I believe the record on one trip was thirty one hours. A very exclusive club, I can tell you; something akin to those who flew on the Concord a generation later."

Before she could reply, Beyer had reappeared in the cockpit doorway with our beverages. "Sandwiches coming up," he said ebulliently.

Shortly thereafter, as promised, he brought us a sumptuous tray of canapés, sandwiches and small pastries. He had obviously been busy loading more than just gasoline while Ronnie and I were at the weather briefing office in Sydney. Knowing his healthy appetite for the good life, the catering truck must have also taken a goodly chunk of his seemingly endless supply of credit.

We droned on through the bright glare of noon. The sun climbed high and gradually passed overhead. A silent lethargy overcame us. We sat transfixed by the muffled roar of the Pratts, the brilliance of the searing light and the fullness of our bellies.

Time lost all meaning.

As Beyer had observed, we had no really accurate way of measuring exactly what time it was anyway without any known landfall to go by. The only thing that would really affect us would be crossing the International Dateline as we flew abeam of the Samoan Islands about seven hundred miles northeast of Fiji, but that would not be until sometime tomorrow, after we had rested in Nadi.

Hours went by and the white glare gradually changed to a softer glow. The sky beyond began to darken to a deep indigo; fluffy balls of cumulus became tinted with pink-orange rays from a dying sun behind us. Our first day in the air was almost done. We had been aloft now for over ten hours. Another seven or so would see us safely in the bar under a palm tree and a thatched roof at the Mogambo Airport Hotel in Nadi.

Ronnie and I settled into a routine of taking over the controls about every two hours or so, while the other got out of the cockpit and walked around to stretch cramped muscles. Beyer intermittently doubled as navigator, world historian, executive chef and Australian Ambassador when it came to the tricky art of radio communications and international diplomacy with the bureaucrats of every island monarchy and banana republic in the South Pacific into whose airspace we strayed.

The sun finally dipped into an empty, silent ocean behind the tail of the aircraft. As twilight gently wrapped around us, Beyer showed even more enthusiasm for practicing his astral navigation skills. With boyish delight, he came up to the cockpit much more than I either needed or cared for, to show us precisely which square inch of the chart we were currently flying over, "just in case that ridiculous little GPS suffered from a satellite-induced anomaly".

However, according to that same little black box, we were averaging a twenty knot tailwind, which would put us into Nadi almost an hour earlier than we had anticipated. At one-ten a.m., with fifty-five miles left to run, the lights of Suva on the island of Viti Levu began to show up as a pale glow on the horizon.

"You want to take her in?" I inquired of Ronnie, knowing by now that the question was superfluous. The girl loved to fly! That's all there was to it. She never showed any sign of fatigue, and even when I insisted she take her break from the controls and go rest in my bunk, she was back up begging to fly again practically before I could get comfortable in my seat.

"You bet!" she grinned, taking the controls off the gyropilot and putting the Cat into a slow, gentle descent.

I inched the manifold pressure back with the throttles and put the mixtures to 'Auto Rich'. I closed the cowl flaps, checked that the carburetor air controls were set, then picked up the microphone and spoke to Nadi Approach Control.

"Nadi Approach, good evening. This is Catalina Papa Bravo Yankee, fifty miles southwest inbound, descending through three thousand for landing with ATIS information Delta."

A thick, Fijian accent came back immediately. "Bula, Papa Bravo Yankee. We are expecting you. Please cross the coast at one thousand, five hundred and enter left base for runway two. Call tower on one one eight decimal one, and welcome to Fiji!"

"Thanks Approach. Request clearance to overfly Suva, and then track around the south and west coast to line up with the runway."

"No problem, man! You the only traffic we got this time o' night. Just call tower on right base. Bula, Bula."

"Bula to you too," I echoed, returning the traditional Fijian greeting which doubled for hello, goodbye and just about everything in between.

I pointed through the windshield at the approaching lights of Suva. "Aim for downtown, then hang a left and fly down the coast. Once you're over the coastline, keep those lights over there on your right. That's Nadi, and the only thing there is the airport."

Beyer, who had magically rejoined us on his jump seat, began a not unexpected commentary for Ronnie's benefit on the general history of Fiji and its capital city, Suva.

We zoomed over the city, and then doubled back to the southwest coast of the island, descending to pattern altitude as we did so. We could easily make out the white surf pounding the length of deserted, palm-fringed beaches as we swung around the west coast and lined up for the ten and a half thousand feet long runway at Nadi International.

"Nadi Tower, this is Papa Bravo Yankee joining right base for runway two."

"Bula, Bravo Yankee. Clear to land. Where do you wish to park?"

"General Aviation would be fine. I'm sure Customs is expecting us. Could you do us a big favor and call the Mogambo? Have them send a van for us in about twenty minutes."

"Sure, man. No problem. Taxi to your parking area on this frequency. The agent will be waiting for you at the G.A. Terminal. You can clear customs there. Welcome to Fiji!"

"Bula. Many thanks."

"Gear down, props max r.p.m., landing check all the way," Ronnie commanded as we turned final.

I hit the gear selector valve handle, made sure it locked in place, checked the 'down and locked' light, and then pushed the prop levers up to maximum r.p.m.

"Hold your speed at about eighty knots for the approach," I cautioned her. "Start easing your power back at about fifty feet, and hold a constant pitch with the nose just above the horizon. Should give you a nice, smooth approach and touchdown."

She did as I suggested, and even though she had never landed this type of ship before, seconds later she touched down as if she had been flying a Catalina all her life. The huge main wheels squeaked onto the runway, she held the nose up to bleed off airspeed, and then gently lowered the nose wheel to the ground.

"Nice one! Couldn't have done better myself," I complimented her. She turned, tossed her head, and gave me that clenched-teeth white grin which I was beginning to fall in love with all over again.

"Thanks mate. I *love* this airplane!"

"Yeah, me too."

I took the controls and taxied us to the ramp. We shut her down and climbed stiffly out of our seats. Before we could get to the back of the plane, Beyer was already opening the portside blister and greeting the resident customs agent as a long lost brother.

I don't know whether he actually knew the giant black Fijian, or simply regarded him as one of his own because of his immense size. Anyway, by the time Ronnie and I had jumped down with our passports, paperwork and overnight bags in hand, the man was already leading Beyer in the direction of the waiting van, slapping him on the back, conversing with him in Fijian, and looking over his shoulder at me, laughing heartily at some obviously derogatory comment Beyer had made about my manhood or aviating abilities.

He opened the rear side door of the van, ushered Beyer in with a flourish, turned and walked back to the G.A. terminal with an occasional rearward glance in my direction, chortling and shaking his huge curly head as he did so.

I handed Ronnie up into the rear seat of the van, then clambered in beside her and slid the door closed.

"What was all that about?" I inquired curtly.

"Diplomatic relations, old horse. Just taking his mind off getting too picky about inspecting us or our machine."

"At my expense, by the sound of it."

"Not at all, dear boy. Don't be so sensitive! Just told him the truth; that we had come all the way from Sydney, that we had been flying for seventeen hours or so and that we just wanted to get to bed."

"And….?"

"And, uh, that you are a terrible pilot and a worse lover, and that even though your African woman had been flying all day, she would still be better able to stay awake for playtime than you would."

He ducked too late. We both struck him simultaneously from behind, but the blows were as feathers to his incredible bulk.

"Well, that's gratitude! Never can *satisfy* you, Blaine. I more than likely just saved us from exposing the Cat's venomous claws, thus avoiding a possible international incident and possible indefinite internment. Ronnie, I *do* apologize for dragging your good name through the mire, but the men here are typical of the uninhibited cultures in the South Seas – for that matter, probably anywhere – and take great pride in openly and innocently discussing their sexual prowess, and that of their women."

"Whether you like it or not, the very first question he asked me was who you belonged to, and what you were like, er …. Well, you know. Naturally, I knew if I amused him with a little anecdote, it would take his innocent mind off his job. Please forgive me."

"Well, I don't know. That's a pretty big affront where I come from, Beyer," she said, scrubbing at her graceful brown chin. "But I guess it was in a good cause, although I can't possibly imagine what that might be. And we *are* heading to the hotel less than five minutes after leaving the plane. I guess I can forgive you if you buy the beer."

"I *like* the girl," I echoed.

"Done!" said Beyer. "The local brew is quite superb, and very strong. I should think one or two will hit the spot and put us into a sound and restful sleep almost immediately."

"Speak for yourself," I chipped in again. "And please let me know next time you intend to take my name in vain with the authorities."

"Blaine, this one was easy. Be grateful for a little banter with a burly Fijian with a sense of humor. From now on, dealing with the authorities is going to get tougher – literally to the point of life-threatening. To use you own vulgar vernacular, don't knock it!"

Five minutes later, we rolled into the hotel lobby driveway, with its typical island wood and stone entrance, thatched palm fronds on the roof and bamboo pole lanterns flickering in the light breeze.

We checked in, took three rooms adjacent to each other and close to the lobby and the open-air restaurant, and stepped into the deserted bar. The sleepy receptionist, who apparently doubled as bartender, left his post at the desk and came over to slide behind the bar.

Beyer ordered three tall, frosty glasses of the ubiquitous local lager, Fiji Bitters, which as he predicted turned out to be quite superb. When we had quaffed our first frothy, long-awaited draft, I wiped the foam from my lips with the back of my hand and spoke our common thought.

"Well, I think after one or three more of these, I will be ready for about twelve hours' solid kip."

"Here, here old trout! The next leg of our journey is going to be by far the longest; nearly twenty-four hundred miles. Have you done your arithmetic? Are you absolutely positive the Cat has that kind of range?"

"Ask my executive officer here."

"Well, it's going to be tight - real tight," Ronnie chipped in. "At one hundred and twenty knots ground speed, it's going to take the best part of twenty-three hours. That puts us at the absolute limit of our endurance, and that's assuming the charted minimum specific fuel consumption of sixty-nine gallons per hour at about forty-five percent power and a hundred and five knots true airspeed.

"We'll be hanging off the props. If that tailwind doesn't hold, or if we have to deviate around any of the weather forecast to hit Hawaii about the time we get there, we're not going to make it. We will probably have to ditch a couple of hundred miles short."

"Thank you very much," said Beyer. "Precisely why I am so glad you are with us, my dear. Had I left such planning to Blaine here, he would have assured me that we had 'no worries' of arriving at our destination, and we would no doubt be floundering around in the Pacific, off all known sea lanes."

"Oh come *on*, Beyer. Don't be so damned melodramatic! I know my own airplane well enough to be able to figure out our maximum endurance. Sure it'll be tight, but we'll make it."

"See what I am talking about my dear? His hopeless optimism has more than once been the cause of our near demise in the past. I would appreciate your *carefully* working your calculations once more and coming up with a viable alternative. Perhaps we should land at Pago Pago and re-fuel there before we continue. Would that not shorten our leg length to Honolulu by about five hundred miles?"

Ronnie frowned thoughtfully, then cocked her left eyebrow at me. "You know, mate, he might be right. We *will* be pushing the edge of the endurance envelope. Pago Pago is only about seven hundred miles northeast, and only a couple of hundred miles off our direct track to Hawaii. If we filled up there, we would be well within safe range and endurance for the rest of the trip. Give us some extra gas to maneuver around that weather if we need to."

"O.K.," I replied rather reluctantly, deferring to her better judgment. "But what about diplomatic relations, Beyer? Can we even land and get gas there if we want to?"

"Already taken care of, old fruit."

"Already ....?"

"I can read a map too, you know. I have personally established contact with my diplomatic friends in every island nation between here and Honolulu, just in case we do encounter some such unexpected difficulty along the trade routes. Not that I don't trust your judgment, Mitchell. Just being very, very careful. We have a long and perilous journey ahead of us."

"Great! It's nice to know I have such a trusting, confident and well-connected friend."

By the end of our third beer, we were all so drowsy we could barely hold our heads up. With silent and mutual agreement, we left the lonely, empty bar and staggered the short distance to our respective rooms.

I did not remember hitting the bed. My next conscious awareness was of golden, dust filled rays of sunlight streaming through the slits in the bamboo blinds. I squinted blearily at the bedside table clock.

The red digital display winked at me as it flipped over to 10:12 a.m. I leapt out of the big king bed and stumbled groggily to the bathroom, splashed cold water in my face, fumbled for my electric razor, ran it quickly over my two day stubble, brushed my hairy teeth, then stepped into a cold and reviving shower.

I dressed quickly in a fresh, short sleeve khaki shirt and jungle green shorts, slipped on my comfortable old brown boat shoes, and brushed my short, wiry, sea and salt blonde hair. The door slammed behind me as I left the room and, feeling refreshed and ready to face another long day in the air and whatever else lay ahead of us, strode to the dining room to be greeted by my two friends who were already halfway through their tropical fruit breakfast.

Beyer bellowed his customary greeting. "Oho! His lordship arises to seize the day and grace us with his wonderful company, I see."

"And the same to you too, Beyer," I replied determined not to let him goad me, my eyes only for Ronnie as I approached the table.

She flashed me her ineffable grin, enough to warm the cockles of any man's heart. In response, I went around behind her chair, stroked her still-wet, shiny black hair, and leaned down to kiss her lightly on her right ear. Then I dropped into the vacant chair, rubbed my hands together eagerly, and looked around the now almost full room for someone resembling a waitress with a coffee pot in her hand.

"Now then, now then, my friends, let us break the fast and proceed with all haste on our mission to locate and liquidate the bad guys," I declared enthusiastically.

"Absolutely, old boy! A beautiful day to launch ourselves into the blue on the next leg of our journey into the unknown."

"I take it, Beyer, that with your usual and customary efficiency, not to mention the magic of your seemingly unlimited supply of credit, you have managed to arrange for the Cat's tanks to be filled to the brim?"

"Naturally. And what's more, Blaine, I am keeping close tabs on the many thousands of dollars you owe for the privilege of my escorting you on this little mission of mercy. The price of aviation petrol in these climes is outrageous! I expect full recompense at the conclusion of this expedition, or I swear the Cat will not fly again until such has been received."

"Yeah, yeah, no problem. Testy this morning, aren't we? Did we not get enough beauty sleep last night, *old boy*?" I mimicked.

"Very amusing. I suggest you follow your own advice and order a large and filling breakfast. It may be the last decent meal we partake of until we reach the epicurean delights of the Sandwich Islands."

"The Sandwich Islands?" Ronnie repeated, swallowing a mouthful of fresh pineapple and raising a questioning eyebrow. "I didn't see any Sandwich Islands on the maps."

"Of course not, my child. They have not been charted as such for over two hundred years. Nevertheless, on charts of ancient mariners, you will still find the Hawaiian Islands depicted as the Sandwich Isles. The famous English explorer, Captain James Cook, of Her Majesty's Bark 'Endeavour', credited by British historians of the era as having discovered almost the entire then-known universe in both the northern and southern hemispheres, named the islands in honor of the Earl of Sandwich, Lord of the British Admiralty at that time; the same gentleman, incidentally, after whom the humble sandwich was in fact named. He...."

"Beyer?"

"Yes?"

"Shut up!"

"*Now* who is being testy?" he replied, thoroughly insulted.

"Amazing," Ronnie laughed, again awed by the apparently unplumbed depths of Beyer's general knowledge.

"He carries a book of geographical trivia with him at all times for the specific purpose of astounding young ladies with his incredible erudition," I mumbled around a purloined piece of bacon.

"Rubbish!" he replied. "Simply a matter of such basic knowledge that any fool – present *female* company excluded, Ronnie – who claims to possess an elementary education, should know."

I pretended to ignore him, looked up at the huge Fijian lassie patiently hovering by my left shoulder with pencil poised, and gave her my order.

"Lots of coffee, please, followed by your special omelet, crispy bacon, potatoes, grilled tomato and onion, more toast and a large, fresh pineapple juice."

"Anything else, sir?" she inquired politely with her lilting island accent, though her raised eyebrows and huge brown eyes indicated a silent comment on my ravenous appetite.

"That'll do for now, thanks. Coffee as soon as you can, though."

"Right away, sir."

True to her promise, my cup was brimming in ten seconds. I took several long, appreciative gulps, then got on with the task at hand.

"All right. It's ten forty-five. We should be away by noon. Means we'll be in Pago Pago by about seven tonight.

Say about an hour to gas up and flight plan the next leg; we should be able to head straight on for Hawaii. We'll take turns to fly and sleep on the long haul. Should make landfall about twenty hours later. Let's see, about eight p.m. Honolulu time. Sound about right, Beyer?"

"Give or take an hour or two. Don't forget we will be crossing the International Date Line about a hundred miles this side of Pago Pago. We will have to adjust our chronometers back a day and recheck the local time when we arrive."

I nodded my head as I began to wolf down the huge plate of food which had magically appeared before me in record time. In equally record time, I finished the excellent breakfast, gulped down the last of my coffee and juice, and pushed back my chair to stand, rubbing my stomach with grim satisfaction as I did so.

Ronnie looked aghast.

"My Goodness!" she exclaimed. "Do you always eat like that?"

"Like what?"

Beyer snorted. "Only when he is either hungry or in a hurry, one of which applies at all times."

"Very amusing. I hope your sense of humor extends to paying for rooms and breakfast for the three of us. Let's get going."

I stood, grabbed my own and Ronnie's overnight bags placed beside the table, and led the way to the front desk a few feet away.

"My friend here," I said, indicating Beyer coming up behind, "will be settling our account. Do you have a van and driver available to take us to the airport?"

"Yes sir. Right away."

"Bula!"

Beyer paid the bill with one of his ever-present credit cards, grumbling all the time about 'bludging pilots who can't afford the price of a glass of water'.

The van pulled up just as we stepped out into bright, tropical sunlight. The temperature hovered right around ninety-five degrees, but as not even the guest rooms were air-conditioned, we were already accustomed to the stinging, humid heat. Five minutes later, we were pulling into the general aviation parking lot.

I had been slightly apprehensive that an armed guard might be present at the aircraft, preventing our boarding or departing. Beyer's diplomatic magic seemed to be holding, however, and after a brief look over what limited weather forecast was available, we submitted our flight plan and strolled out to the big Cat unhindered.

"Ronnie, why don't you walk around her while I climb inside, power up, and get us a clearance. It's going to be hot as hell in there. I'll open her up and see if I can't cool her down a bit before you come aboard."

"Sounds good to me. I'm ready to get airborne."

So saying, she began the external portion of the daily pre-flight inspection check.

In the meantime, Beyer wandered over to the tower to give the local controllers the personal touch with his famous charm, expediting our departure and arrival formalities for the next leg to Pago Pago.

7

Twenty-five minutes later, we were once again climbing our way northeast over endless stretches of empty, sparkling blue Pacific. We soon returned to our routine duties, and the hours seemed to pass more quickly. The reliable old Pratt and Whitney engines pulled us along with their comforting, deafening clamor, turning the giant props at a little more than thirteen hundred r.p.m.

Isolated, lonely specks of palm-fringed islands occasionally marked our slow but steady progress across the infinite expanse of ocean to our next stop at Pago Pago.

Beyer marked our passage over them with his customary effervescence.

Niaufo'ou. Tafahi. Niuatoputapu. Then, six and a half hours later, Tutuila and Pago Pago.

I never ceased to be amazed by Ronnie's enthusiasm and delight at every little detail of what to most pilots would be a tiring, uneventful, incredibly boring flight.

She clapped her hands with delight every time we spied so much as a lone seagull practically keeping pace with our stolid progress. Each island's stark and lonely beauty seemed to remind her of her own heritage, as she felt the pull of long dead ancestors beckoning her home to her native land.

Soon we were descending again, down through the burnished blue and into our first U.S. Territory at Pago Pago

International Airport. The island customs officials here were a little more obtrusive than our friends at Nadi, but thanks to Beyer's incredible charm and charisma, he had the inevitable paperwork completed and our tanks topped off with fourteen hundred gallons of high octane aviation gasoline in little more than an hour.

It was now just past eight p.m. local time, the day *before* we had departed Sydney, as we had now crossed the International Dateline. The sun was setting and the fierce equatorial temperature was abating, but the air was stagnant and heavy with moisture. We were at absolute sea level, but I worried that a computed density altitude of almost two thousand feet was going to make our overloaded PBY perform like the proverbial flying pig during our take-off roll.

I was very glad that we were taking off from a ten thousand feet long, jumbo jet capable runway. An ocean take-off – even with the added thrust of the JATO rockets – would be terrifying at the very least, and catastrophic at worst, if one of the engines decided to so much as hiccup while trying to get her on the step, or during the water run.

One hour and eighteen minutes after we had touched down at Pago Pago, we were rolling on to the runway for the longest leg of our journey, although the leg from Honolulu to Los Angeles was in fact only forty- three miles shorter.

The tower controller cleared us for take-off. I took the controls, stood hard on the brakes, and eased the power up to forty-eight inches of manifold pressure. The twin Pratts bellowed in response, R.P.M. gauges rose to 2700, cylinder head temperatures soared to the maximum of 260 degrees

C. I eased my toes off the brakes. The old girl shuddered, and then slowly began to trundle down the almost two miles of concrete before us.

At about sixty knots, I put in some right rudder to counter the torque of the mighty radials trying to take her into the trees to the left of the strip. At seventy-five, I gently tugged at the yoke. She was heavy all right! Didn't want to fly at all. With all the gas on board, we weighed just over thirty-five thousand pounds, and the density altitude was robbing her of lift and power.

I let the speed build to eighty-five, then ninety. At ninety-five, twenty knots beyond normal take-off speed, I again eased back on the yoke. The five thousand feet runway marker passed us as the nose wheel came off the ground. Sluggishly, reluctantly, the giant main wheels left the safety of solid concrete and the Cat was free. Sensing that she was done with the earth once more, she seemed to shake off her torpor and struggled into her natural element with new-found zeal, and we were clean and climbing away free.

We roared over the end of the runway, zoomed up into a right turn over the island of Tutuila, and set course for Hawaii. The vertical climb indicator hovered around four hundred feet per minute at ninety five knots.

The tower handed us off to departure control; we gave our obligatory check-on, and began our slow, ponderous ascent to seven thousand five hundred feet. Twenty minutes later, we leveled off, pulled back the power to our calculated maximum endurance setting, and settled back for the long haul.

A golden-orange glow enveloped the aircraft as the setting sun sank into the vast Pacific behind us on our starboard quarter.

"You want the first shift?" I asked Ronnie, knowing it was a futile question.

"Of course!" she grinned, tossing her dark bangs in the now-familiar mannerism. "Go back and make yourself at home. I'll see you in Hawaii."

"Yeah, right. If you can stay awake at the controls for the next twenty or so hours, you're a better man than I."

"Naturally!"

"You're getting as bad as Beyer, too. Where is he, anyway? He's usually on the jump seat for take-off."

"He said something about getting his octant and charts ready for some 'real' navigation. I think he's back in the blister compartment, stargazing already."

"Figures. Okay mate, you need anything before I go? Coffee, sandwich, sticky bun?"

"Let me have one of those bottles of water, would you?"

"Sure thing." I unbuckled my harness, squirmed out of my seat, and ducked through the narrow cockpit hatchway. Far back in the blister, I glimpsed Beyer at the portside dinette, octant to his eye, peering out through the Perspex blister at the velvet cloak of a star-spangled sky above.

I took a cold bottle of water up to Ronnie, retreated back to the galley and put on a fresh pot of coffee. When it finished brewing, I poured a cup each for Beyer and myself, took them aft and handed one of the steaming enamel mugs to my bulky friend. As he had littered the portside table with his charts and instruments, I slid into the starboard blister booth opposite him.

"Well, are we lost yet?" I inquired mildly.

"Don't be obscene!" he retorted hotly. "I have not yet begun to plot our position accurately, and as we are little more than an hour out of Pago Pago, it is hardly even a challenge to my superb astral navigation abilities to take a star shot just yet.

"However, when sweeping the sky north of our position just now, I did observe a rather strange phenomenon."

"Oh? Such as?"

"I'm not quite sure. I am checking my charts right now but it appears that there is a new, or at least an uncharted star cluster forty degrees southwest of the Crux, and …."

"The Crux?"

"Our very own Southern Cross is the layman's term. On astronomical and even astrological charts, the constellation is known simply as the Crux. Anyway, as I was saying, there appears to be an unknown – to me at least – grouping of stars about forty degrees – relative to our position of course…"

"Of course."

"…. Southwest of the Crux. The really perplexing thing though, is that they appear to be moving towards us – and at an impossible rate!"

"How can that be?"

"I have no idea, old chap. Here. Take a look for yourself," he said, holding the instrument out to me. I slipped out of my booth, took the proffered device, placed it to my right eye, aimed up through the portside blister, and tried to focus on what he was pointing at.

"I don't see anything. As a matter of fact, I *literally* don't see anything. All I see is some kind of shimmering blackness overhead. No stars, no nothing."

"Don't be ridiculous!" he retorted, snatching the thing from my grasp and returning it to his own trained eye. "The sky is so clear and untainted out here, there is a veritable *host* of …."

His voice trailed off suddenly, then, still with the instrument fixed to his right eye, he suddenly exclaimed, "Oh my God! Oh my …"

"Beyer! What the hell do you see?"

"I … I don't know. I think …"

"What? What is it, man?"

He lowered the octant, turned to me with eyes bugging out, and swallowed hard several times.

"I think something of immense proportions is hovering directly over our aircraft, virtually blotting out the stars."

"*Whaat?* Like what?"

The hairs on the nape of my neck bristled with a familiar tingle of alarm.

"Beyer, you're not going to tell me we are having some kind of close encounter, are you? That's absurd!" I added, refusing to believe what he was saying. I had never in all my years of flying ever seen a UFO, although I knew of many pilots who claimed they had, and I sure as hell didn't want to start now.

"Take another look," he said, his voice now icy calm, as he handed the device to me again.

I did so, but this time could see nothing but a brilliant, star-studded heaven directly above.

I gave the instrument back to him. "Beyer, I'm sorry. I don't see anything at all directly above us. I do see something off in the distance though. I think we were just skirting under the base of an overhanging cloud layer, making it appear that there were no stars over us."

He again aimed his view skyward, and then in a calm, studied tone said, "Yes, I believe you are right, old man. Sorry. I don't know what came over me. I could have sworn …… Never mind!"

He slumped down heavily into the dinette and with visibly trembling hands, took a long and noisy sip at his coffee. "I ….could have sworn ……" he repeated, again not finishing the sentence.

"Get it off your chest, mate," I said, sliding into the dinette beside him. "What did you really think you saw?"

Instead of answering my question, he glanced at his watch and asked one himself.

"What time do you have?"

"What time do I …?" I glanced down at my own wrist. "Just after ten-fifteen Pago Pago time. Why?"

"We took off at eight, didn't we?"

"Near as dammit." Again I asked, "Why?"

"So we have been airborne only a little over two hours then?"

"What's gotten into you Beyer? Ten-fifteen minus eight makes two hours and fifteen minutes of flight time. It took us almost twenty-five minutes to climb to cruise altitude because of our weight. When we leveled off, we set cruise power, I sat with Ronnie and we chatted for an hour or so. Then I came back to the galley, made some coffee, and I have been here with you for about another fifteen minutes. Like I said, what's gotten into you?"

"Never mind," he said again, rather sharply this time.

Then, deciding to expound on his thoughts after all, he said, "Blaine, it has just occurred to me that in all our many lengthy discourses together over the years, up until a few minute ago, we have never broached the subject of UFOs. Why is that, do you think?"

"I have absolutely no idea old horse," I replied, using his own vernacular. "I guess it just never came up. I have never personally seen a UFO, and although I have an open mind, and have read a good deal about the subject, I just don't know of anyone in my own circle of friends – including you, unless you have been keeping more from me than I suspect over the years – who has had any kind of personal experience with them.

"*Have* you had any experience with them?" I scowled at him, suspecting now that he knew more about this phenomenon than he had previously disclosed.

Instead of answering, he again countered with a question. "Have you ever heard the term 'missing time'?"

"Missing time? You mean, apart from the time that seems to disappear during your monologues? No. What the hell is that?"

"Very amusing, Blaine. Were it not for my monologues, you would still be a mental Neanderthal. Let me give you another."

He proceeded so to do!

"Since 1947, when the first 'official' UFO event took place at Roswell, New Mexico, there have been literally thousands of alleged sightings involving this phenomenon. Most of those classified as the 'third kind' – that is, personal contact, involve 'missing time'. That is to say that the person or persons reporting the incident also claim to have 'lost' what can amount to minutes, hours or even days of their lives. There is no apparent explanation for these extraordinary claims, and those to whom they are reported simply write them off as either hallucination or confusion about what has actually happened to the 'victim'.

"Add to this that also since 1947, the U.S. government has constructed an immense facility in and around a huge complex known only as 'Area 51' comprising several dry lake beds and what they have been busy building underneath them, which is anyone's guess. But the best guess is that they conceal flying discs of purportedly extra-terrestrial origin, which they have been reverse-engineering for over half a century. It is also alleged that they have another facility near Dulce, New Mexico, where they are actually working *with* aliens, trying to....well, never mind. That's another story – way too fantastic and too frightening to even contemplate.

"Also, the U.S. Navy, not to be outdone, has been suspected for many years of conducting similar experiments in the Atlantic Ocean in what has become known as the infamous 'Bermuda Triangle'. The result is that just about every modern convenience we use today, including your magic GPS, is alleged to have been obtained from this incredible technology."

"Yes, but what has any of this got to do with our seeing anything here, and indeed, our mission itself, if anything?" I interrupted.

"I believe that our mission, if successful, will uncover something that has been hidden for millennia – and we will therefore become *VERY* expendable in the rush to cover up what we might discover – or rediscover."

"Rediscover?" I echoed.

"I believe that what we may stumble upon had been known by the very earliest generations of Native Americans – and other civilizations on earth – thousands of years before the Asians or Europeans ever invaded and conquered all the continents on the planet."

"Good grief Beyer; isn't all this just a little bit far-fetched – even for you?"

"Anyway," he continued, "that is a brief explanation of *some* of what I know of the UFO phenomenon."

"Brief? Did you say brief?" I exclaimed, again glancing at my watch and realizing that almost an hour of *real* time had gone by since Beyer had begun his lecture.

"I want to hear more, but I had better go check on Ronnie, and make sure she's O.K. up front. She'll be thinking we have jumped ship – or been abducted!"

"Not at all amusing, Blaine. Go ahead. I have just thought of something that may be of particular relevance to our own current investigation. I shall explain when you get back."

"Can't wait!" I lied, leaving the booth to duck forward through the hatches to the cockpit.

When I reached the front office, I leaned into the cockpit with my fingers gripping the top of the hatch frame.

Ronnie was still wide awake, guzzling at the inevitable bottle of water and craning her head to stare up and out of the forward windshield at a clear, black, star-spangled night sky. I watched her for a moment, silhouetted as a pale shadow in the soft yellow glow of the instruments. She half-turned in her seat as she felt my presence.

"Hey. What's up?" she grinned, shouting over the din of the old Pratts. "Thought for a while there that you had left us. Sure is beautiful up here. I can't get over how clear the sky is. I've never seen so many stars."

"Ronnie, this is probably a dumb question, but has the sky been clear up here the whole time you have been alone?"

"Excuse me?"

"I mean, did you by any chance happen to notice if we passed under a big cloud base about thirty minutes ago? A big, black, cloud base?"

"Can't say that I did. And I have been star-gazing most of the time you were gone. Why? Is it important?"

"Maybe. Did any of the stars seem to be moving quickly or erratically?"

Her grin faded, and was replaced by a quizzical expression. "No. You're starting to spook me, Mitch – pardon the pun. Is everything all right?"

"What about the time? What time do you have?"

She glanced at her oversized wristwatch. "I have eleven-ten, aircraft time. O.K. Mitch, I'm a big girl. Let's have it! What's going on?"

"Oh, nothing really. Beyer is letting his over-active imagination run away with him. He thinks we had some visitors a while back."

"Visitors? Up here?"

"I think all the events of the last few days are making him edgy, that's all. Let's drop it. I'm with you. I don't see anything out there but stars, our instruments and radios are functioning normally, and as far as I can tell we are still flying sublimely through the South Pacific night."

Ronnie shuddered involuntarily, and with renewed vigor began her surveillance of the heavens. I squirmed with practiced ease into the narrow confines of the cockpit and dropped into my seat beside her.

"Go take a break and get yourself a cup of jar," I ordered. "I'll stand watch for a while. You've been up here for over three hours now."

"I'm just fine. Honestly."

"I know you are. But we have a long way to go, and I'm going to need you wide awake and alert in a few more hours. The airline traffic in and out of Hawaii will require our undivided attention as we get closer to the islands."

"Guess you're right. I could use a trip to the head, anyway. I'll go talk to Beyer about flying saucers for a while. Ha, ha," she quipped.

"Do us all a favor. Please don't! I don't want him to get all worked up about *that* again! I thought he was going to have a seizure a while back, when he thought he saw a UFO. We can't afford to lose him!"

"Don't worry. I was just kidding. I do not want to invoke the wrath of the gods way out here, if there *are* any snooping around watching us."

8

Alone in the cockpit with the familiar but incessant barrage of clattering noise and drumming vibration, I succumbed to the trance-like state caused by long exposure to such mind-numbing fatigue.

My thoughts wandered to the lonely islands passing below in the darkness, and I imagined the soft trade winds again caressing my body, as they had done countless times before. High overhead, the stars still shimmered brightly and I thought I could see luminescence sparkling on the boundless ocean beneath the aircraft.

On solitary watch, I felt the giant flying boat swaying gently in swells of invisible air waves. I watched endless processions of familiar constellations float across the inky blackness around me; the same stars which had guided ancient pilots in their great double-hulled canoes toward Hawaii thousands of years before. My mind slipped easily back to a Pacific world unimaginably different from our own, when fast canoes sailed these vast expanses of ocean.

Some years ago, while still a pilot in the Australian Air Force, I flew over the Bismarck Sea for the first time. I remembered the stark, isolated beauty of the strings of small islands that appeared through puffy white clouds beneath us, separated one from the other by deep blue ocean. This maze of islands and channels had been the proving ground, as it were, for some of the greatest navigators and boat-builders of Earth's history.

These great voyages of Polynesian discovery were over long before any Asian or European explorer even knew of the existence of the Pacific Ocean. Captain Cook, the infamous British explorer and navigator, had been ordered to explore the 'unknown' waters of the southwestern Pacific during 1769-70. More than a century earlier however, in 1642, the Dutch explorer Abel Tasman had sailed from Batavia (now Java) across the Indian Ocean to Mauritius, then south and east to Tasmania, named after himself, of course! He then sailed on eastward until he sighted a 'large land, uplifted high', where he made contact with very warlike people in large canoes.

This land he named New Zealand, but after twenty-three days, Tasman sailed off without even landing. When Cook reached New Zealand in 1769, he soon realized that he had found Tasman's discovery. The country was inhabited by a fierce, savage, but sophisticated people who opposed his landings in many places. He observed fortifications built on strategic promontories and soon found that Maori spears were such formidable weapons that only British muskets were effective against them!

In a brilliant and patient display of seamanship, akin to that of his contemporary Lieutenant William Bligh, when cast adrift by the mutineers of His Majesty's Ship 'BOUNTY', Cook charted New Zealand in 1769-70, finding not a continent but two large islands. As for the people; 'I suppose they live entirely upon fish, dogs, and enemies', wrote Doctor Joseph Banks, Cook's botanical scientist.

The Maori reputation for warlike behavior, and even cannibalism, deterred European visitors, despite the North Island's abundant Kauri wood, ideal for ships' spars. Even into the early 1800s only the boldest whaling skippers visited the Bay of Islands in the north, sometimes recruiting Maori seamen for their expeditions.

From New Zealand, Cook sailed across the stormy Tasman Sea and made landfall on a flat and sandy coastline. His ship 'ENDEAVOUR' dropped anchor and her scientists, led by Banks collected specimens of numerous unknown plants, prompting the name Botany Bay. 'ENDEAVOUR's crew also made their first contact with Australian Aborigines. Cook himself commented that they might have a seemingly wretched existence, but they 'live in a Tranquility which is not disturbed by the Inequality of Condition'.

Leaving Botany Bay, Cook sailed northward past a deep bay he named Port Jackson (now Sydney Harbor), then up through the Whitsunday Passage, which he also named, and the labyrinthine Great Barrier Reef, where 'ENDEAVOUR's hull was punctured by a reef, necessitating an extended stay for repairs at what is now Cooktown. He eventually returned to England, completing one of the epic voyages of modern exploration.

However, on the far side of the world, Cook's new continent remained unexplored until the British government passed the Transportation Act of 1784, which authorized the removal of convicted felons from overcrowded, unsanitary, decommissioned warships anchored on the Thames, to 'Places or Parts beyond the seas'.

In 1786 the government decided to found a penal colony at Botany Bay, and the following year eleven ships and almost fifteen hundred people under the command of Captain Arthur Phillip set out from England on an eight month voyage to Australia. The fleet anchored in Botany Bay but soon moved to Port Jackson's sheltered roadstead, named Sydney Cove after Home and Colonial Secretary Lord Sydney.

The new settlement was a brutal place, marked by regular floggings and hangings, but it grew by way of offering hundred acre land grants and convict slaves to corps officers who served in the outpost. Each year, until popular sentiment stopped the practice in 1840, as many as five thousand new convicts arrived in New South Wales. Had they not, Australia would probably not have been colonized – on the east coast anyway – for at least another half century.

As it was, many of the former convicts themselves, when released or pardoned, were also granted large tracts of land and in time became wealthy property owners in their own right, responsible for much of the later exploration and development of the country.

James Cook never returned to Australia, but he made two further voyages throughout the Pacific. In the course of his second voyage, he touched briefly on one of the outer islands of what is now Fiji. It was left to his sometime lieutenant, William Bligh, to be the first European voyager to sail throughout the archipelago. Bligh accomplished this feat in the open long-boat in which the mutineers of '*BOUNTY*' had set him adrift! He was subsequently appointed governor of New South Wales, in part for his remarkable achievement.

Cook's third voyage from 1776-80 took him from New Zealand to the Cook and Tonga Islands, then to Tahiti and up into the North Pacific to Hawaii, where he met his death at the point of a Hawaiian spear......

A sudden flickering of the cockpit instrument lighting interrupted my reverie. Then, without warning, all the lights failed completely. Total darkness was followed by a heart stopping, explosive backfire from the port engine. My head jerked to the left in an involuntary reflex action, striking the side window at the same time as I observed a huge jet of yellow flame shoot out the stubby exhaust stack. The PBY yawed violently to the left. I instantly knocked off the gyro-pilot and grappled for control of the stricken aircraft.

The engine backfired several more times, and I knew we were in serious trouble. I reached up for the left throttle, yanked it all the way back, did the same with the prop lever, then hit the propeller 'feather' button, in a vain attempt to get the blades edge-on into the airflow to reduce drag. Nothing happened! I tried again, but the prop would not feather. I could not maintain altitude on one engine with an unfeathered prop with the amount of fuel we still had on board. We had over seven hours run to Hawaii, with nothing below us but wild, rolling ocean. We were not even on a regular sea-lane, where we had a chance of being picked up by a ship when we ditched.

Ronnie was beside me again within seconds, slipping silently into her seat and strapping herself in automatically, followed closely by Beyer, who stuck his giant head into the cockpit and was naturally the first to speak.

"Sounds serious, old trout. What can I do?"

"Left engine just quit on us. Looks like we have a major electrical malfunction too. I can't get the left prop to feather, and we can't stay up for very long on one engine. Ronnie, get on the radio. H.F. first, then V.H.F. Give continuous all-stations Mayday calls. You know the drill!

"Beyer, go back and get ready to start jettisoning equipment. We have a lot of extra weight back there that we don't really need for survival – at least, not out here in the ocean. You can start with the gun and the other stuff stowed in the tail. At this point, anything heavy will help."

"Righto, old boy. I'll be on the intercom. Keep me posted," he replied as he pulled a headset off a peg on the bulkhead behind me and headed back down the companionway.

Ronnie was giving me a most peculiar look, but took up her microphone and began a steady stream of Mayday calls in her calm, professional voice. If she suspected that we had minutes left before we died by either impact, drowning or exposure to the sharks and the elements, she gave no indication of it in her voice, but after a few attempts, she stopped and looked at me again. "I don't think I'm getting out. I think the radios are dead too."

I stared at her in blank disbelief, and snatched up my own mike as I continued to wrestle with the controls, struggling desperately to hold the crippled ship on an even keel and in a steady descent. Despite my efforts, she was sinking inexorably towards the ocean swells at over five hundred feet a minute, and I could do nothing to reduce the descent. At this rate, we would be in the drink in less than eight minutes!

"Mayday, Mayday, Mayday, this is Catalina Papa Bravo Yankee," but my voice trailed off as I realized from the hollow echo and lack of carrier tone in my headset that Ronnie was right. The radios were indeed dead.

Then, just as I was thinking that things could not get much worse, the right engine quit!

We were now a big, powerless, glider. The only sound was the wind howling around the wing struts and fuselage, and the pounding of our own hearts in our ears.

Our rate of sink almost doubled, even at her best glide speed of eighty-five knots. We were going into the ocean! Four thousand feet, three thousand, two thousand, one thousand feet above the black, rolling swells of the South Pacific.

At five hundred feet, I knew we were going to die. It was pitch black outside and I could not even see the surface of the ocean I was about to attempt to ditch on; nor did I have the local altimeter setting, which meant I did not know precisely how high we were above the waves. It was impossible! Strictly no go! We had less than thirty seconds to live.

Then Ronnie was shouting in my ear over the shrieking of the wind, and pointing to the control yoke.

"The rockets!"

"What?"

"The JATO rockets. Can we use them?"

The light of her perspicacity struck me like a physical blow. Why had I not thought of them myself?"

"Of *course* we can use the bloody things!"

My right hand leapt to the rocket arming switches on the yoke. I toggled all four of them to 'Arm', and mashed the red buttons of the two forward rockets, at the same time hauling the yoke back into my stomach with all the strength I could muster. "Get on it with me," I yelled at Ronnie.

She didn't need to be asked twice, and I felt the increased back pressure immediately.

The aircraft responded instantly, yawing violently as the left rocket fired a split second before the right one.

The needles on our altimeters both registered zero as she leveled out, and ever so slowly began climbing away at almost three hundred feet per minute. I had no idea how close we had come to impact with the ocean swells before we began to climb, and I didn't want to know! Seconds later, however, I felt the acceleration begin to slow as the rockets burned off their precious fuel. I hit the 'fire' buttons of the remaining two rockets and again felt the very temporary but blessed surge of acceleration push me back in my seat as they lit off.

I knew that we had only a moments' reprieve before we again began to plunge towards the inky, unforgiving depths below. I got busy on the engine controls. I shoved the dead propeller levers all the way forward, selected auto-rich on the fuel levers, and set the throttles at about one third power.

"You've got her," I shouted to Ronnie. She held back pressure on the yoke while I hit both starter buttons together. One engine starting was not going to do us any good at all. I needed both of them, and I needed them *right now, dammit!* This was the last shot I was going to get. Trying to start both engines at once was going to drain what was left of the ship's batteries in about thirty seconds.

The left prop was still unfeathered and wind-milling pretty good already. The right one came out of 'feather' quickly when I reset the button. As our airspeed dropped off and the wind noise died in the climb, I heard the starters whining and the engines clattering. Suddenly the clattering was interspersed with coughing and backfiring. Then both Pratts caught and began to roar almost simultaneously.

I shoved the throttles all the way forward, giving her emergency power at full manifold pressure. She fairly leapt away from the dark sea below. I got back on the yoke with Ronnie. Our acceleration and rate of climb slowed as the second pair of rockets burned out, but we were climbing. We were climbing!

The cockpit lighting flickered, and then came dimly back to life.

"Thank God," Ronnie sighed, wiping her forehead with trembling hand and tossing her hair out of her eyes. "What the hell happened?"

"I have ….absolutely no idea," I replied, aware of the tremor in my own voice, and wondering if I sounded as relieved as I felt. My eyes automatically scanned all the instruments, searching for the least sign of anomaly. Everything appeared to be 'in the green', however.

Beyer's head magically re-appeared between us in the cockpit hatch. "What the hell happened?"

"Is there an echo in here?" I inquired, my sense of humor returning rapidly as the gravity of our situation abated. "I say again, I have absolutely no idea. One minute everything was running fine, and the next we had completely lost our electrical system including, I suspect, the engine magnetos which are supposed to be self-sustaining and independently powered. It just doesn't make any sense at all!"

Then a thought struck me. "Beyer, did you start to toss anything overboard?"

"No. Almost threw myself overboard though, thanks to you. I had the blister open with an armload of – non-essential equipment – about to jettison, when we pulled up and began to accelerate like a space shuttle off the launching pad. You could have let me know you intended to fire those damned rockets," he added sulkily.

"No time. Two seconds later and we would have been in the drink. You owe your life to Ronnie's brilliance and quick thinking!"

"I am not at all surprised," he fawned, bowing his head to the lady in question. "I am deeply indebted, madam, and will be forever your faithful servant."

The subject of his benevolence grinned and replied, "Why, thank you sir. But it was nothing, really. I'm sure Commander Blaine would have been imbued with the same stroke of genius just in the nick of time."

"Ha!" Beyer responded.

"Ronnie, much as I hate to admit it, Beyer's succinct response is correct this time. We were literally seconds from a very ugly and untimely death, and the rockets had not even occurred to me. You deserve all the credit for that one, and I'll be the first to admit it."

"Well then, admit something else to me. *What*, and I quote, 'gun and other stuff stowed in the tail' unquote?"

"Er, yes. Well, remember when I showed you Beyer's quarters in the tail of the plane, and said there was originally a tunnel gun there for shooting the bad guys coming up behind? Well, there still is; hidden very cunningly under Beyer's mattress in a cleverly constructed fairing. Only we have a slightly more modern gun than the original thirty caliber machine gun; a three thousand round per minute Gatling Gun, to be precise!"

Her big brown eyes grew wide in shock and apprehension.

"Why, for goodness sake? And how did you get hold of such an arsenal? That kind of stuff is not exactly readily available at Sporty's Pilot Shop, is it?"

"Let's just say that although I am officially retired from the Australian Air Force, there have been times when Beyer and I have been asked to perform some rather unofficial clandestine missions, using our special talents and the unusual capabilities of this particular aircraft; tasks that would be diplomatically embarrassing for the Australian government and physically impossible for the current equipment in the Australian Air Force inventory."

"I see. So in plain English, you're spies!"

"Not at *all*, my child," Beyer cried, outraged that he could be even remotely suspected of being such a low form of life. "As our tarnished knight here stated, we are merely occasionally – very occasionally, I might add – approached by one of Blaine's former superiors to, shall we say, do some civilian reconnaissance work for them, which sometimes entails penetration into territory spuriously claimed by our various Asian neighbors to the north. Blaine, having the compulsive-aggressive disorder he has, naturally insists on a little protection in case we are ever accidentally or wrongfully placed in harm's way."

"I see. So in plain English, you're spies," Ronnie repeated, this time, grinning hugely at Beyer to indicate she understood perfectly what he was trying to say.

Beyer heaved a deep sigh and backed out of the cockpit. "I shall be in the galley preparing some fresh coffee and a midnight repast. I think we are deserving of some refreshments to celebrate our renewed – and totally undeserved – lease on life. I'm not sure how much more of this kind of excitement I can stand."

Turning back to my instruments, I scanned them suspiciously for several minutes, half expecting a repeat performance of our recent near demise. Ronnie said nothing for a long time. She slumped down in her seat, resting her right foot upon the corner of the instrument panel.

Finally, she gave me a sidelong glance and said, "That firepower back there has just reminded me of something I have been meaning to ask you since before we left Sydney, but forgot about in all the excitement of the last few days. What did you mean when you told Beyer you didn't think you were the target of that lunatic with the gun on the first day?"

Squirming uncomfortably in my own seat, I echoed Beyer's giant sigh, delicately dabbed at the latest unwarranted attack on my person, and regrouped my recently scattered wits.

"Quite simply because there was no reason – at that particular moment in time – for anyone to be trying to kill either Beyer or me. I have been giving it a lot of thought. The Warners invited us to a party, asking us to bring the Cat around. The guest list was entirely theirs. Not long after some of those guests were on board, many of whom I did not know before that night, I get a phone call from you. I pick you up, drive you home, being followed all the way, I might add – a minor detail I neglected to mention before – and when we arrive, the ship is empty, we think!"

"Followed?" she repeated with raised eyebrow.

"Yes. I didn't think anything of it at the time, but I should have been more situationally aware of my tail. Now we know that Beyer himself evicted all the revelers but one, and there is absolutely no possibility that he could have known anyone remained on board. Question: is it merely coincidence that we were invited to entertain our friends' guests the same night that you arrived? Or, assuming the Warners can be trusted, did someone else in their large, elite social circle ask them to ask us if we would entertain that night?

"Supposition: I think someone wanted very badly to make sure you didn't get to talk to Beyer or me for very long, and they didn't care about how recklessly or noisily the deed was done, as long as you were quickly silenced. Or to put it as unpleasantly as possible, Ronnie, I think they knew you were coming!"

She was staring at me with mouth agape. Her bottom jaw had been dropping steadily as the implication of what I was saying sunk in. Now it snapped shut so tightly, I thought she would chip some of those beautiful white teeth.

"*What?*" was all the lady could muster.

"My sentiments exactly. Our big problem is, if whoever '*they*' are knew you were coming, and obviously know their first attempt to eliminate you failed, then they also know that we have joined the fray. At least, we must assume that they know. Which means, of course, that they will be expecting us, and that we will be operating in enemy territory from the gitgo, completely exposed, and in a ship that already stands out like the proverbial you-know-whats. And of course, it also means that they will undoubtedly try again," I added prophetically.

"All of which makes me wonder if our recent almost fatal plunge towards the briny was an accident at all. When I think about it, the chances of our losing *both* engines *and* our electrical system at the same time must be at least a million to one. I'm sure Beyer can give us a more exact estimate."

"Precisely one point seven eight million to one, old horse. And *that* is precisely what I have been meaning to discuss with you since our recent exercise in astral navigation," Beyer finished as he shoved his mighty head and shoulders through the hatch, pushing a tray of sandwiches and coffee ahead of him.

Ronnie took the tray as his lordship settled uncomfortably on to the totally inadequate jump seat once again. "Do you mean to tell me that somebody in the *United States government* is actually trying to *kill* me?" she inquired incredulously.

"That would be my best supposition at this point. At least, I believe that we have to continue under that assumption. I can think of no individual or organization with a price on Blaine's head right now, although lord knows, there could be thousands of them!"

I resisted the temptation to strike him.

"But *why?* What could anyone in the government possibly have to gain by killing me? I'm just a pilot who happens to be the wife and sister of a couple of missing air force officers."

"Precisely, my child."

I half-turned in my seat, settling deeper into it as I did so, and helped myself to a sandwich and a mug of steaming coffee as Ronnie continued to unconsciously hold the tray. I was almost back to my cool, collected self, and I could tell that we were in for another verbal barrage from Beyer. We still had a long way to go to Hawaii. It would help to pass the time!

"Let's back up a little from Blaine's scenario. Let us suppose that someone very high up in the U.S. Air Force, or even higher than that, in the government itself, has a very good reason for not wanting us to discover that either or both of our missing airmen are alive – assuming, of course, that they are. Let us also surmise that your husband – or brother – discovered something of such magnitude that their own lives were in jeopardy if they spoke of it. It would certainly not be the first time that the CIA or any other branch of the intelligence community has been ordered to eliminate an individual 'in the interest of national security', which can be loosely translated as 'to save somebody's acute embarrassment or worse, their *own* precious behind."

"But....that's preposterous," Ronnie replied, not yet quite prepared to accept everything Beyer said as gospel. If we lived long enough, she would eventually learn to take all he said at face value. "How could they get away with it, and even if they could – again, why me?"

"It's a good thing we're still a long way from Hawaii," I commented dryly.

He ignored me!

9

"Let's assume a hypothetical situation. Let us say it just *happens* that a certain pre-eminent scientist, and at least two others we are aware of, have mysteriously disappeared off the face of the Earth, so to speak, apparently to prevent them from enlightening the rest of us – in his case, of a fantastic discovery – and in the others' case, the conspiracy to prevent such enlightenment."

I could stand it no longer. I harrumphed loudly to interrupt his monologue.

"What *is* it Blaine? I take it you disagree with some of my assumptions?"

"Talking about enlightenment, would you please enlighten me as to why, if somebody was carrying out such a large-scale conspiracy, they would assign a controversial and high-profile figure to a project they were presumably trying to conceal, and then send two of their most senior and experienced inside intelligence operatives to investigate the very thing they were trying to cover up in the first place?"

"I'm coming to that. Patience is definitely not one of your strong points, Blaine!"

"Please continue."

He glowered at me.

"Let us suppose – again hypothetically of course – that there exists within the thin facade of the U.S. government, a 'secret' government much more powerful and much more Machiavellian than the so-called *real* leaders of the country could ever hope to be."

I stared at Beyer for several long seconds, thinking he had at last gone quite mad! I said that was the most ridiculous thing I had ever heard of, not wanting to believe what I was hearing about the modern world's seat of democracy.

"Even if such a ludicrous theory is true, what pray tell has *any* of that got to do with the Supercollider? Even assuming there is such a group, and they *have* that kind of power, why would they let someone go run a new research program at the Collider if they intended kidnapping or killing him, and then follow up with an investigation, where the investigators themselves are done away with? That makes no sense at all."

"They *had* to post Laudaman to the Collider site," he responded thoughtfully. "They *had* to get rid of him, and a new project at the collider facility was the perfect place to hide him. Sending him there, however, was just an act of gross deception, because *somebody* already *knew* about it!"

"I know I'm going to regret asking this, but knew about what?"

"Why, the dimensional portal, of course!"

"What the *hell* is a dimensional portal?"

Ignoring my question, he continued, "Unfortunately, he got too close to the truth, and became another unsuspecting and expendable pawn in their master plan. They were feeding him information a little at a time, to make him believe that he was solely responsible for the 'discovery'. But I feel certain that he must have suspected something. He is — was — a methodical man. I will guarantee he has left some kind of record or log of his day to day activities. If we find it, I think it will answer all our other questions. As for Masters and McCall, I can only guess at that part of the scenario."

"*You* have to guess, Beyer?" I inquired acidly.

He continued to ignore me.

"Disinformation, old horse, is their specialty. Everything relates to covering their own tracks. Nothing is more important."

I found myself staring at my old friend with a deep suspicion dawning behind my eyes.

"Beyer?"

"Mmmm?"

"How do you *know* all this stuff?"

"Simply because, old trout, I was once invited to join their exclusive little club, and was given the third, fourth and fifth degrees, and told as much as they dared tell me, without actually giving away all their rotten little secrets."

"*Whaaat?*" Ronnie and I echoed together.

True to Beyer's form, the story unfolded. Many years ago, long before he had rescued me from dereliction on that north Queensland beach, he had been on a sabbatical, working voluntarily on a special astronomy project for the Smithsonian Institute, when he had been approached by a colleague at the American Institute of Astronomy, who had invited him to a very exclusive luncheon.

He agreed with alacrity at first, believing that this was simply more recognition for the work he had been doing in the U.S., but he became most uneasy at the increasingly demanding security levels he had to pass through for a mere luncheon engagement, which he eventually discovered was to be held in one of the hundreds of honeycomb cells in the underground facilities beneath the Pentagon. He was, after all, a mere scientist, and a very reclusive one at that.

Of course, the luncheon turned out to be a very cautious and tentative exploration of his knowledge and his loyalties.

They were already familiar with Beyer's complete background and history from birth, including his astounding educational accomplishments. They were also aware of the fact that he had become a United States citizen in a special one-on-one ceremony at the White House, performed by President Reagan himself, in recognition of his contributions to the American Astronomical Society and the president's own Strategic Defense Initiative.

My own bottom jaw had been sagging uncontrollably since the beginning of this latest Beyer revelation. I finally summoned up enough cerebral sagacity to speak, after swallowing several times.

"Good grief, Beyer," was all my astonished brain could manage to articulate. Ronnie was in considerably worse vocal condition. She was quite speechless!

"Anyway, the long and short of it is that I turned them down," Beyer continued. "I could see where they were trying to lead me, and I did not want any part of it. Besides, I would have had to leave my country and my home and permanently reside in Washington, D.C., with all the other lunatics there. And I did not want to be tied down to the kind of exposure, where everything I did, everywhere I went in the world, would be monitored by some spy, satellite or drone somewhere, for fear of my spilling some above top secret information, either accidentally or on purpose. So I turned them down. As it is, I am quite sure they keep tabs on me anyway, even though I know nothing of their actual secrets. Paranoia is rampant in such a group."

"I don't believe it," I muttered, my mind still unable to fully comprehend the implications of what he had just told us. He had not revealed any of this to me in all the years I had known him!

"We're already dead! They know we're coming. They know all about us. No *wonder* they were trying to knock Ronnie off! They were trying to stop us before we even got started. The only thing that surprises me is that they haven't tried again by now. Or maybe they have," I added, recalling our most recent dive toward imminent death. "I'm amazed any of us are still alive!"

"Don't be so melodramatic, Blaine. As I have repeatedly tried to convince Ronnie here, I am a scholar, not a spy, and they know that I know their tactics of ridicule, lies and disinformation would ruin my life and years of work if I dared to bring any of this into public light."

"All the more reason why you haven't had a fatal accident long ago, my friend," I said, recovering some of my shattered composure.

Our discussion was interrupted by a noisy crackle in our headsets as the High Frequency radio began to squeal. The tinny voice of a trans-Pacific air traffic controller somewhere on one of the isolated islands below came in to us, requesting a position report. We were far outside the

range of normal radar, and were therefore required to report our position every sixty minutes until we were back in
communication on normal V.H.F. channels.

Several more hours dragged by, boring and uneventful
compared to our almost fatal plunge into the deep, dark
depths of the vast Pacific, and then we were back in radar
range and in communication with the area controllers of
Hawaiian airspace, who of course knew we were coming,
by virtue of our flight plan and position reports passed
along by the lonely Pacific radio men.

Soon after, we were commencing a normal descent
into Honolulu International Airport. I requested from the
approach controller a special vector at low altitude along
Waikiki Beach, which he granted with no problem, as traffic was negligible this time late at night. We flew down the
beach at below five hundred feet, zoomed up into a climbing
turn to one thousand, and joined right base for Runway 4R
as we contacted the tower controller for landing clearance.

We came in on a long, low final with Ronnie at the
controls. She pulled off another beautiful touchdown and
rolled off at the first taxiway. She handed over to me and
began the after landing checks, while I took the brakes and
rudder pedals and taxied us to Bradley Pacific Aviation on
the huge general aviation ramp, under the patient guidance
of the ground controller. A ramp guy was waiting for us
with fluorescent wands, to bring us into our parking spot
squeezed between two corporate jets. Our huge wingspan
extended over each outer wing of the jets on our left and
right. The ramp was full of private aircraft, mostly mid-
sized jets of Lear, Hawker and Challenger types, with a

smattering of larger international types and a few medium range Cessna Citations of various models.

Beyer was already in the back completing the mountain of paperwork required by U.S. Border Patrol and Customs for a foreign-registered aircraft. I stretched and yawned mightily, absolutely exhausted by the arduous and lengthy flight, then climbed out of my seat, stiffly crouched through the several compartment hatches towards the aft of the plane, and heaved myself through the blister and over the side to the ground.

I stretched and looked around, something bothering me that I couldn't put my finger on for a moment; then I realized what it was. Except for the ramp agent, who was patiently waiting to lead us inside for the Bradley FBO paperwork, the tarmac was completely deserted, which was not in itself unusual at this time of night. But the fact that we had just arrived from a long overseas flight in a most unusual aircraft should have had Customs and Border Patrol officers, fire trucks and maybe even cops crawling all over us; especially bearing in mind Beyer's latest revelations. We should have had some kind of welcoming committee; but nothing – nobody.

Suddenly I was squatting on my knees, the back of my neck again prickling with the primeval sense of danger that I had become so used to – as both hunter and hunted.

Something was definitely not right! I sensed it before I saw it, and then, just a glimpse of a shadow withdrawing into the darker gloom of the rear corner of the FBO building. Just as quickly as I thought about giving chase, I abandoned the idea. It could easily be a trap to get me back there and away from the relative safety of the lighted area where the aircraft was parked.

Just then, Beyer and Ronnie came down the ladder behind me, and any further notion of chase was gone. I was about to mention the shadowy figure to them, but then thought better of that too; no point in worrying them any more about our enemies lurking in the night.

We trudged wearily into the brightly lighted FBO, and began the tiresome paperwork requests for fuel, ramp fees, rental car, so forth, while Beyer got on the phone.

"What are you doing now?" I asked, curious as to who he might know well enough to wake at this hour of a Honolulu morning.

"Calling the hotel, of course, old horse! You don't actually expect me to spend the night reclining here in the pilot's lounge, I hope."

"Well, not exactly. I assumed that you had a reasonably priced hotel already chosen for us."

"That I have laddie; that I have. I am waiting for the general manager of the Royal Hawaiian to come on the line as we speak...."

"The *general manager of the Royal Hawaiian?*" I echoed, once more dumbfounded by his temerity. "You mean to tell me you are on personal terms with the manager of one of the most famous hotels in the world, as if we could even think about affording to stay there!"

"Why, naturally. And as for the expense, don't worry about that. Ms. Kelly Horan, the GM, has already assured me that our suites will be 'on the house', thanks to a little favor she owes me for a rather large convention and banquet I organized for her a few years ago."

"Naturally," I echoed. I was about to add something petty like "I should have known," when he chipped in again, beginning a not unexpected history lesson on the founding of this famous hotel.

As we climbed into a gray Lincoln rental the ramp guy had brought round front for us, Beyer launched into another of his now familiar dissertations.

10

"The Royal Hawaiian opened its doors to guests on February first, 1927 with a formal gala attended by over twelve hundred guests. The hotel quickly became an icon of Hawaii's glory days. The original resort was built with a price tag of about $4 million and was a six-story, 400-room structure, fashioned in a Moorish style which was popular during the time period and influenced by screen star Rudolph Valentino. The site of The Royal Hawaiian boasts a majestic lineage. The area was used as a playground for King Kamehameha the 1st, after he conquered the island of Oahu. Queen Kaahumanu's Summer Palace was previously located in what is now the resort's Coconut Grove garden. During World War II, The Royal Hawaiian was leased exclusively to the U.S. Navy as a rest and recreation center for the Pacific Fleet, most notably the fleet's submarine crews. The resort reopened to the public in February 1947. Of course, the inspiring and distinctive character of The Royal Hawaiian is known throughout the world as a destination of unparalleled romance and luxury. The 'Pink Palace of the Pacific' emerged from a complete renovation of the historic building on January 20, 2009 as one of the world's elite collection of resorts. The distinctive architecture remains, of course, as well as the elegant details that are reminiscent of the hotel's storied past. The restored resort highlights the indigenous culture and history of the islands, offering authentic and refined service and an elevated ambiance of unrivaled …..."

"Beyer?"

"Yes?"

"Where do you *find* this stuff?"

"Blaine, do what you do best and just drive. I am sure Ronnie is interested in the history of these beautiful islands, even if you are not!"

So I 'just drove', until we swept into the magnificent grounds of The Royal Hawaiian.

He was right, as usual! We had barely gotten the car stopped before we were surrounded by a bevy of bellhops, porters, and other assorted Royal Hawaiian staff, relieving us of our bags and ushering us into the opulently arched, open-air main lobby, which had been welcoming affluent and influential men and women from around the world since the early nineteen hundreds, most of whom arrived in Hawaii by the new mode of luxury transport, the Pan American flying boat Clipper Service.

From out of nowhere, much to the overwhelming joy of our hairy friend Beyer, an elegant woman in her mid-forties, clad in a casual but very business-like light gray suit, came striding up to greet us. She had short, brown hair, perfectly coiffed for her almost angular and not unattractive features. She had bright green eyes, an easy, elegant manner, and as she caught Beyer's eye, she flashed him a brilliant, affable smile. She did not arrest her pace as she approached us and much to my surprise – although by now I should have expected no less – she strode right up to Beyer, reached for his hand as if to shake it, then pulled him close and gave him a huge hug which he joyously reciprocated, making them look like a pair of dancing bears.

"My *dear* Kelly! You look absolutely stunning, as usual. I don't think you have aged a day in these last – how many years has it been now?"

She grinned again and replied, "Almost ten, and you are as big a liar as I remember, and perhaps just a wee bit more slender in the girth – something my executive chef will have no problem rectifying, I am sure."

"Ah, my dear, you flatter an old man. If I am indeed more willowy, it is because my young friend here, Mitchell Blaine, keeps me ever on the go with some nefarious new adventure, many of which keep me from genuine epicurean repast, sometimes for days at a time.

"Speaking of whom, Blaine, be pleased to meet the most famous hotelier in the world, Ms. Kelly Horan. Ms. Horan, it is with dubious honor that I present Mitchell Blaine, the most infamous aviator extant; a legend in his own mind."

We shook hands and grinned at each other, amused at Beyer's unrestrained joviality.

"And now I must introduce you to the most charming young lady – aside from yourself of course – that it has been my joy to meet for many a long year. Kelly Horan, please say hello to Ronnie McCall, an aviatrix whose skill and daring are most certainly equal to that of Captain Blaine himself, and whose personal tragic circumstances have brought us all together at this time and place in history."

Ronnie curtsied slightly, and took Kelly's firm, outstretched hand. It was obvious that they took to each other immediately, something rather rare in the arena of professional women, who are at the very least wary of each other, and more often than not, hostile or antagonistic from the gitgo.

"Welcome," Kelly greeted her warmly. "Come; let us make you all comfortable in my magnificent establishment. I have your suites ready – the finest in the house of course. But first, while my staff takes your belongings up for you, let me buy you all a drink or three in the Mai Tai Bar, on the beach of course. One of the more stunning views of Waikiki you will find, the hour is late, most of my guests have already retired, and it is a perfect night to watch and listen to the surf roll in under the moon and stars. And of course, I can't wait to hear what brings you so far, in what I have already heard is rather an ancient and magnificent flying machine, the likes of which have probably not been seen since the U.S. Navy left here at the end of the war."

So saying, she led us to the famous Mai Tai Bar, spoke quietly into her barman's ear, and ordered up four of those most renowned rum, Curacao and lime drinks! And of course, they were quite magnificent, prepared according to the original Trader Vic's recipe, and as was to be expected, initiating a Beyer-type oration on the origin and history of the famous cocktail.

After Beyer's monologue and the rest of the small talk had died down to a silent appreciation of the night, we gazed up beyond palm fronds gently swaying in the warm breeze, and watched in awe as bright moonlight illuminated an immense build-up of cumulonimbus clouds out over the ocean, towering up to the base of the troposphere, lightning flashing from one to the next, the developing stage of what was about to be one hell of a storm; the forerunner of that line of weather forecast along our previous route of flight, which we had just managed to avoid.

"Of course, you know that the average thunderstorm lasts only about fifty-five minutes, from the developing stage through the dissipating stage," elucidated Beyer. "The developing stage of a thunderstorm is marked by cumulus cloud that is being pushed upward by a rising column of air. The cumulus cloud soon resembles a tower as the updraft continues to develop. There is little or no rain during this stage, and only occasional lightning. The developing stage lasts about 10 minutes.

"The storm then enters the mature stage, when the updraft continues to feed on itself. When the weight of water vapor in the cloud can no longer be held aloft, precipitation begins to fall, and a downdraft begins. When the downdraft and rain-cooled air spreads out across the ground, it forms a gust front sometimes known as horizontal wind shear. The mature stage is the most likely time for hail, heavy rain, frequent lightning such as we are seeing now, strong winds, and tornadoes. Eventually, the updraft is overcome by the downdraft, beginning the dissipating stage. At the ground, the gust front moves out a long distance from the storm and cuts off the warm moist air that was feeding the thunderstorm. Rainfall decreases in intensity, but lightning remains a danger......."

Beyer's voice trailed off as he realized that we were all staring at him in literally thunderstruck awe!

"*What?*" he inquired of the group in general.

Ronnie spoke first. "Beyer, for the rest of my life, whenever I see a thunderstorm, I will remember this moment. And when I am flying through a seemingly endless line of squalls, being tossed around for hours at a time, I will remember your comforting words that a thunderstorm only lasts fifty-five minutes!"

"Couldn't have said it better myself, Ronnie," I added, yawning mightily as the combined effects of the Mai Tais and the incredibly long flight finally began to take their toll. "As for me, Miz Kelly, can you please point me in the direction of my room, and lead me thereto, before I collapse right here in the sand. I would not want your early rising guests to trip over my body littering your immaculate beach."

"Not so fast," that worthy lady replied. "All of you have managed so far to fend off with small talk any question about your adventures. Nobody is being pointed in the direction of their quarters until somebody first satisfies my morbid curiosity!"

"Oh very well, Kelly," Beyer replied, glancing in the direction of the barman to make sure he was out of earshot. "The truth is, in a nutshell, that both Ronnie's husband and brother have mysteriously disappeared while on duty with the air force in Texas, and she has engaged us to find them."

It was too dark to see her expression change, but her response said it all. "So *that's* it," she exclaimed, slapping her knee with a resounding crack. "I should have *guessed* it had something to do with you lot. Thanks a bunch, friend Beyer!"

"What, my dear lady, are you ranting about?" was his sincerely surprised reply.

"Simply that for the last week or more, I have had some very obnoxious and self-important types wandering about my hotel, asking strange questions of me and my staff, and I don't like it!"

It was my turn to be surprised. "What kind of obnoxious types, Kelly? You mean government types, or civilian?

"Government, unless they were sporting fake badges. They were civilian dressed, but showed ID from some federal government department with initials I never even heard of; AF something or other."

"AFOSI?"

"That's it! Who *are* these people, and what do they want with you?"

Beyer answered first, as only he could. I didn't know what to say, and was certainly alarmed, although not surprised, that these guys were here ahead of us. I had expected something like this, of course, but not quite so soon.

He lowered his voice again, and leaned toward Kelly. "Air Force Office of Special Investigation; they are the U.S. Air Force criminal and anti-terrorist investigation and enforcement arm, and they also happen to be the branch that both Ronnie's husband and brother were attached to immediately before their sudden and very mysterious disappearance about six months ago in Texas."

"Oh my....But what has somebody disappearing in Texas got to do with anything here in Hawaii, or Australia, for that matter? And what have government anti-terrorist people got to do with you, and why me and *MY* hotel, for heaven's sake?"

He answered her question with one of his own; a typical Beyer ploy. "Kelly, do you know and trust all your staff at the hotel? Particularly the reservations staff. Who besides yourself would have known we were going to be staying at your hotel?"

"I interview and hire everyone who works here. I have hundreds of staff, and I know them all by name – and their families. In fact, we are one big family here, and I know and trust every one of them," she said proudly.

"What about reservations? Do you have a way of blocking off rooms for your own special guests, as we discussed on the phone?"

"Of course! Your names are not listed anywhere in the reservation system, as you requested, and I told none of these characters anything about you. As far as they're concerned, I never heard of you until today, and I greet all my guests exactly the way I greeted you on your arrival. Well, almost! Nor did I tell any of my staff about you."

"Did any of these people take rooms here?"

"No. As far as I know, after they asked their fool questions, they left and I haven't seen any of them since. Doesn't mean they're not still snooping around though. There are plenty of places to hide around here, especially if you're an expert at it, as these types obviously are."

"So, before tonight, when they may have followed us from the airport, the only way they could have known about us and our activity from before we left Australia, would have been to monitor our phone calls. Kelly, this could get very nasty, and we don't want you or your people to be in any kind of danger. Are you sure you want us as guests in your hotel?"

"I insist! More than ever now. If there is anything I can do to assist this nefarious scheme of yours …"

"As a matter of fact, my dear lady, there is. We can't be too careful. We don't know who these people are, or what they are capable of, but we do know that at least two attempts have been made on our lives since we left Australia, by parties so far unknown. Blaine's band-aided scalp is indicative of one of them! I suggest that for the short time we will be with you, we all stick together, not go anywhere alone, and dine only in your outstanding restaurants, with no names or room numbers assigned to the meal orders."

"You're not suggesting someone might try to poison you, surely?"

"I was thinking more of possible surprise visits to our quarters, but now that you mention it, let's just say we can't be too careful! Furthermore, I think our rooms should be adjacent, as private as possible, and facing the ocean. I suggest the……"

"Already taken care of, Beyer. Your friend Blaine and Ms. McCall will be in the Royal Hawaiian Suite, and you, my reclusive friend, will be in the King Kamehameha Suite, aptly suited to your own celebrated position, and both of them the finest in the house, of course."

"But ….." Ronnie began to object.

"Don't worry, my dear. The Royal Hawaiian Suite is the largest, most elegant two bedroom suite in the hotel.

Both rooms have their own en-suite bathrooms, with a common living and kitchen area. I did not specifically plan it that way, but now that I know a little more about your situation, I think it was very perspicacious of me after all, what?" she ended, imitating Beyer.

"I could not have said it better myself, old girl," Beyer replied, grinning hugely.

"Very well, then, it's all settled. I will personally escort you up momentarily, but first," she leaned forward conspiratorially, "please do tell me more about this fantastic adventure of yours."

Beyer proceeded to tell her as much as he could safely impart, in as short a time as possible, which for him was about another hour – I think. By the time he was half way through, his voice was just an annoying buzz in my ears, and I was having difficulty holding my cocktail tumbler and staying upright in my chair.

It seemed like it was not very long, though, before we all arose and more or less staggered back through that magnificent, though at the moment deserted lobby, found the elevators, and in short order, our respective suites.

Beyer bid us goodnight, pausing a moment to whisper some quiet words to Kelly before closing his door.

As promised, our bags had already been delivered, and placed outside the doors of our rooms in the suite. The short walk had given me enough renewed alertness and sobriety to raise an uneasy wariness of my new surroundings. Even in my present semi-inebriated condition, I felt the dawning of some new and perhaps unfounded dread.

I turned towards the door where our bags were set, unlocked and opened it, hefted the bags and ushered Ronnie inside, but almost before I closed the door, I was spun around and kissed most definitely and assuredly – a heretofore unknown act of random kindness by the lady in distress! Naturally, I felt obligated to return the favor, but she pulled away in predictable reluctance and in a husky voice said, "Mitch, I .....don't want us to ...."

"Shusssh," the ever-valiant knight errant replied, as I took said lady gently by the hand and guided her towards my room. She resisted for only a moment, and then let herself be so led.

The living room balcony doors were wide open, exposing the wide, black velvet night. A big, bright moon slid in and out of those lofty CBs we had been recently admiring from the bar below. A slight breeze riffled the diaphanous drapes, hinting at the onslaught of wind and rain to come.

I changed course midstream, and steered her out on to the balcony, more to gain time to gather my own wits, than to show her the view of magnificent Waikiki Beach, Diamond Head, and the interminable dark sea and sky beyond. Except for a couple of very large and opulent cruisers anchored in the bay off Waikiki, their brass and stainless bright-work glinting in the moonlight, the sea was empty. Distant thunder rumbled ever nearer. Lighting darted from one huge towering cloud to the next. A distinctive odor of ozone and sulphur tainted the air, drifting in on the now stiffening breeze.

We gazed out to sea for a moment in awe and wonder at nature's magnificent light and sound show. She turned towards me, stepped into my arms, put hers around my waist, and drew herself to me.

The rain began suddenly and came down so hard, we were almost soaked before we could take the few steps back into the shelter of the living room.

A huge clap of thunder boomed right outside the open door. She shrieked and leapt into my arms. She was obviously ready to surrender and I was very, very tempted to carry her to my bed, but something stopped me. Perhaps my own not-so-gallant white knight sense of fair play and chivalry had something to do with it; or maybe I just couldn't live with the idea of stealing the wife of the man whose life I was supposed to be trying to save!

In any case, the moment had passed and there was nothing to say or do, except to carry the rain-soaked lady to her own room, lay her gently on the bed, and kiss her lightly on the forehead. She smiled demurely up at me, thankful that we had not made a mistake that neither of us could live with.

The unanticipated and astonishing turn of events had left me empty and lonely. As often as I had thought about it, I had not really expected to be offered as a gift, the woman with whom I was rapidly falling in love – all over again!

I returned to the living room with mixed feelings of smugness and remorse at my doubtful altruistic honor. Leaning against the balcony door frame, I stood watching and listening to the pouring rain and the pounding surf, driven by the relentless continuance of the gradually abating storm.

11

I awoke early, despite my fatigue, that faint sense of unease in the back of my consciousness returning to spoil thoughts of the night before. It was almost dawn and I could just make out the gray horizon of sea and sky beyond the windows. The uneasiness continued. I could not go back to sleep. I dropped my legs to the floor, creaked slowly upright, grabbed my duffel and hefted it on to the bed.

Pulling on a pair of khaki shorts and an old gray t-shirt, I stepped out on to the balcony into the pink awakening light of a bright, new day. The air was chilly; the storm had gone, the sky was clear, the sea was blue and tranquil. There was nobody on the beach, and distant Diamond Head beckoned as it had done for thousands of years. The only vessel in sight was one of the white cruisers still riding at anchor, dipping up and down in a slight swell.

I took a deep breath of crisp, clean ocean air, stepped back inside to the kitchen and put on a pot of coffee. The uneasiness I had felt earlier seemed to have been baseless, as dawn brightened into full, clear light of morning. I pottered around waiting for the coffee to brew, then poured myself a cup and stepped back out on to the balcony just as a golden sun was rising behind the hotel, its molten rays striking the beach and advancing to the solitary cruiser in the bay.

As in the moonlight last night, the rays made her bright-work and brass gleam. The undulating ocean swells sparkled with a million glittering points of dazzling light, and I squinted into a blinding glare.

I sensed the presence of my lady behind me, and turned to welcome her to the magnificent new day. She was about six feet back and to my right, yawning, stretching and smiling mightily at me. As I spun to greet her, I was horrified to see a tiny red spot appear, dead center between her breasts, on the front of the sleeveless yellow shirt she was wearing.

The enamel coffee mug fell from my hand and smashed on the floor.

Former restlessness erupted into a fury of volatile action as a colossal rush of adrenalin lunged me towards her, knowing I was already too late. There was no sound of a shot. They were using a big gun, with a very effective silencer! Even if there had been a sound, it would have come long after she had been cooling meat on the red tiles.

As I knocked her to the floor, I felt the shockwave of the passing slug and heard the sound of impact as it passed right through the back wall of the suite; a big caliber, plenty of foot pounds, a product of mass and velocity. That much slug, in shoulder, hip, thigh or upper arm, she wouldn't have a chance. The massive hydrostatic shock would have killed her, even if they hadn't got her dead center.

She was screaming! I lay on top of her, waiting for the next round; the one that would take me out of the world of sunshine and girls and beaches and booze forever. Nothing stirred. There was no second round. The only sound was the heavy, distant growl of a big engine firing up and revving to maximum r.p.m.

I took a chance and raised my head above the level of the floor. As I peered out under the lower balcony rail, I saw that big white cruiser curving in a fast clip away from the beach and down towards Diamond Head, churning up a huge bow wave as it departed the scene of almost sudden death.

There was no fuss, no commotion. Nobody had heard or seen a thing. The beach was still practically empty, and the few hardy souls that were up for their early morning stroll or swim had not noticed anything unusual. Had it not been for an absurd piece of timing and luck – and the fact that they had used a modern technology laser sight instead of a good old-fashioned sniper scope – with a good old-fashioned sniper behind it – they might have gotten away with it!

And they were *not going* to get away with it! They had had it all their way since this fiasco began. They had creased my own valuable skull, they had somehow managed to bring us within seconds of ditching in the Pacific, and they had almost killed my new-found love before I had gotten to explore all the wonderful, warm, scented ebony sweetness of her. And they were *not* going to get another crack at it! Not if I had anything to say about it, they weren't!

I jacked myself up from off of her, reached down and pulled her still trembling body into my arms, instinctively ducking below the line of fire as I drew her back into the bedroom.

"Wha…what was that?" she whimpered with rasping voice, unable to comprehend what had almost happened to her.

In response, I picked her up, placed her gently back on the bed, and then reached for the house phone and dialed zero.

"Yes sir? How may I connect your call?"

"King Kamehameha Suite, please."

"Yes sir, right away."

Beyer came on after several rings. "Good morning, old fruit. What time is it? Seems like a beautiful morning out…."

"Who do you know in the Coast Guard, Beyer?"

"What? I don't understand ……"

"Do you know anybody in high officialdom in the U.S. Coast Guard?"

"Yes, of course. But what …."

"Call him right away. I want them to find and shadow a boat for us. We're out of here! Right now! Is the bird fueled and ready to fly?"

"Yes, of course," he said again, "but I don't under…."

I briefly explained to him what had just happened, ending in another question. "What kind of security did you find for the plane last night? Has she been under observation all night?"

"Absolutely, old boy. Under physical and video surveillance all night, as requested, by a trusted private security firm. No government involved – at least, not by us anyway."

"Great. Get packed. We need to be airborne ASAP. We're going to find that boat, blast the sucker out of the water, then keep right on going as planned!"

"But ...."

"See you downstairs in fifteen minutes. Have our car ready, and explain to Kelly that we can't stay. Don't give her any details." I hung up on him.

Ronnie was sitting on the edge of the bed, staring wide-eyed at me. "Are you out of your mind? We can't just ..."

"Now don't *you* start with me, mate! Whoever they are, they just tried to kill you – again – and I've had about enough of their one-sided little games of hide and shoot. It's our turn!"

With that, I locked myself in the bathroom for a very quick and invigorating cold shower, stepped out and instructed Ronnie to do the same, climbed into an old green light-weight air force flight suit I dug out of my bag, and threw the rest of my stuff back into same.

While I was waiting for Ronnie to get herself hastily dressed into a pair of raggedy blue denim shorts, loose fitting sleeveless white blouse and a pair of old gray sneakers, I pulled a Ruger Redhawk 'Alaskan' 44 magnum out of its oiled wrapped sheath, checked the load, spun the cylinder and jammed it back into a well-worn brown leather shoulder holster. I was ready to sally forth into the fray!

I tossed the rig back into the bag, zipped it up, and said brusquely, "Let's go, before those mongrels get too far away. With any luck, we'll catch them in the open where I can sink 'em in deep water!"

Her eyes widened, her mouth opened, then closed again as she saw the expression on my face and thought better of what she was about to say.

Two minutes later, we were downstairs in that splendid lobby once more. Beyer was already there, making our apologies and saying his personal goodbyes to his old friend Kelly. I added my own sincere gratitude for her help and hospitality, and said I hoped we would see her again soon under more pleasant circumstances.

The car was already pulled up in the driveway. We threw our stuff in the trunk, I jumped into the driver's seat, stepped on the gas, and we went roaring off into the madness of early morning rush hour in downtown Honolulu. I ducked and weaved in and out of the traffic, its lunatic drivers honking, blaring and glaring at me all the way to the airport.

En-route, I asked Beyer critical questions about the status of the bird. He assured me she was serviced, fueled to the gunnels, and that we had already been cleared for a hasty departure. I didn't know how he had managed to arrange all this, and right now it was the last thing on my mind. All I wanted was to get in the air and after the people – government or otherwise – who had the unmitigated temerity to keep trying to kill my girl!

Twenty minutes later, we were pulling up beside the 'Wayward Wind'. I screeched to a halt and flung the door open in one movement, leapt out and yelled, "Ronnie, you get up front and run the pre-flight. I'll check around the outside. I don't trust anybody right now. I'm going to make sure nobody left us any nasty surprises that might go off before or after we get airborne."

So saying, I began a careful inspection of the entire aircraft, from bow cleat to aft keel. I checked the underside, the landing gear and brake lines. Then I crawled top-side and checked the fuel and oil tanks for quantity, quality and cap security. I checked for any leaks or fresh stains that I had not been aware of before; any signs of recent tampering. Nothing seemed unusual or amiss.

While I was doing all this inspecting, Beyer was heaving our bags aboard and coordinating with the line guy to take the car back to the FBO. When I spotted him struggling up the ladder into the blister, I yelled over to him.

"Check that equipment in the tunnel. Make sure it's ready!"

"Aye, skipper. Don't worry. It will indeed be ready, by the time we get airborne!"

I jumped to the ground and made one last circuit around the ship, my trained airman's eye looking for anything I didn't like. I found nothing. As I came around the starboard wing, I motioned to Ronnie, who was craning her head out the right pilot's sliding window. I gave her the traditional circular motion of my forefinger, signaling her to start engines. She grinned down at me and cranked the big Pratt. It began its sluggish whining and clattering, the prop turned slowly, then with a colossal belch of oily blue smoke, bellowed with the now familiar and nostalgic roar of a huge radial piston engine coming to life. She did the same with the port engine as I strode around the nose to the left side blister, scrambled awkwardly up the ladder, removed it from its brackets, threw it inside and closed the blister.

I stooped and crawled through the hatches and up into the cockpit, settled myself comfortably into my seat, put on my headset, and began the pre-takeoff checks with my co-pilot – and now, for the second time in my life, my would-be new love as well – a strange mixture of pleasure and dread churning in the pit of my stomach.

"O.K., me old china, let's get this show on the road! Get us a taxi clearance from Bradley Pacific to 26R. The wind's out of the west, fortunately, so it will be the shortest taxi to the longest runway. We're gonna need every inch of it too. Tell 'em we want a VFR local flight."

Not waiting for a reply, I switched the service interphone to the rear compartment. "Beyer! Are you on?"

"Right here, old horse. What's up?"

"What did you find out from your mate at the Coast Guard?"

"They're heading southeast at high speed towards either Molokai or Lanai. There's a cutter on the way to intercept them."

"*WHAT?* Why?"

"Couldn't help it old trout. When they ran a check and discovered they were sporting a phony registration, official curiosity kicked in, and they want to find out who they are and what they are doing in these waters."

"Damn! Ronnie, if the tower asks, tell 'em we will be northeast bound."

"But Beyer just said…."

"Never mind what Beyer said. Just do it, O.K."

As she got on the radio to talk to the tower, I grabbed the twin overhead throttles, shoved them forward with an uncharacteristic disregard for the health of those ancient engines, and began the short taxi to the east end of runway

26R for takeoff. We got take off clearance immediately. I rolled on to the runway, applied full power as smoothly as possible under the frantic circumstances, and we were airborne despite our enormous fuel load in half the length of the runway, wheeling around in a right climbing turn over the airport at four hundred feet off the deck.

I got back on the intercom and yelled to Beyer again.

"Beyer, we'll only be able to fool them for about ten minutes. They'll be listening out on ATC VHF as well as the maritime frequencies. They will be watching and waiting for us, and I suspect they have more armament than the sniper rifle they tried to get Ronnie with. Get that gun ready to shoot, and you're going to have to make it count the first time. If they have SAMs or RPGs, we won't stand a chance when we expose our belly to 'em at less than a hundred knots and fifty feet above! One round in these fuel tanks and we're goners! So don't give 'em a chance. Get 'em with your first salvo!"

"Righto, old boy. You can count on me."

"I'll let you know when we are getting close. Stand by."

"Roger that."

I glanced at Ronnie, and she was giving me that look again.

"What do you want me to do, Mitch?" she asked, apprehension rising in her voice.

In response, I winked at her and said "Go back and give him a hand. I'll take care of things up here. I'll call you back when I need you."

I did not tell her that the real reason I wanted her out of the cockpit was in case we took their first salvo head on, right in the face!

She shrugged her slender brown shoulders, released her harness, climbed out of her seat, brushed her lips affectionately on my right cheek as she squeezed by, and started back to the tail of the aircraft. I shouted after her, "Put a headset on when you get there. I can't wait to hear Beyer's running enlightenment on *this* one."

"O.K. I can't either," she laughed as she retreated aft through the hatchway.

As soon as she was in the rear tunnel, Beyer handed her a headset, she plugged it in, and called back to me. "Alright, I'm on. What do you want me to do now?"

"Let Beyer tell you, but keep the hot mike open."

So saying, our huge hairy friend launched into another of his now familiar monologues. "Now, my child, what we have here is an M134D-H Hybrid Gatling Gun.

"It is the latest design from Dillon Aero, which combines the M134D-T titanium model with the housing of the M134D steel gun. The hybrid version is only two pounds heavier than the titanium gun, yet it has over three times the service life.

"This Gatling Gun is the finest small caliber defense weapon available. It is a six barreled, electrically driven machine gun chambered in 7.62 mm and fires at a rate of 3,000 rounds per minute. It is capable of long periods of sustained fire without damage to the weapon, making it an excellent choice for our sometimes, shall we say, difficult, situations. It has a life expectancy in excess of one million rounds and an average time between stoppages of 30,000 rounds. In the unlikely event of a jam, the weapon can be made operational again in under a minute. The multi-barrel design means that each barrel only experiences a 500 round per minute rate of fire. This allows for repeated long bursts of fire and a barrel group life of over two hundred thousand rounds; an astounding record!"

I heard her try to interrupt him several times, to no avail. I could imagine her black eyes rolling in impatient frustration.

Finally, she spat out, "Beyer!"

"Yes, my child?"

"I don't give a *damn* about the sales pitch. Just show me how to *shoot* the bloody thing!"

"Why, yes of *course*, my dear girl. Now, the tunnel of the aircraft, which was originally designed to house a single thirty caliber machine gun, has been modified with this special mount which can be lowered by an electric motor down into the firing position. It has an upper limit so that the gun cannot be fired accidentally into our own tail, and yet has a virtually unlimited field of fire below in all directions. The weapon is very simple to use, with this four thousand round box magazine, extra ammo box, double handgrip, and a guarded firing button instead of the standard trigger. It can be....."

"Beyer?" she interrupted again.

"Yes?"

"I *get* it! Just show me what to point the damn thing at."

I was heading us southeast now, descending to almost zero feet above the gentle swells of the ocean and bearing straight for the white dot I could now just scarcely make out in the distance. As we drew closer, I could see she was making straight for Lanai at high speed. The bow wash and wake made her easy to spot.

I inched the Cat even closer to the waves, hoping the cruiser's radar would not pick us up until it was too late for them to get a bead on us. I shoved the throttles all the way forward to emergency power and closed the range at our top speed of a hundred and sixty miles an hour – almost four times the speed of the target ahead.

About ten miles off her port bow, I could see another vessel closing on her; the Coast Guard cutter, and she was going to beat me to the punch if I didn't do something right now.

I estimated the cruiser's range at about five miles. We would be on her in just over two minutes.

12

I grabbed the marine channel microphone and transmitted, hoping they would believe the bluff.

"Unidentified cruiser two zero miles southeast of Oahu, bound for Lanai; heave to. This is U.S. Coast Guard cutter off your port bow. I repeat, heave to and stand by to receive a boarding party. If you fail to comply immediately, you will be fired upon."

There were several seconds of silence; enough time to take their attention off their stern and get me close.

The cutter's skipper didn't like it a bit!

"Aircraft transmitting on marine channel fourteen identify yourself immediately. I say again, identify yourself immediately. You are impersonating a United States Coast Guard vessel, which is a federal crime. Identify yourself, I say!"

Another brief respite, as they absorbed what the Coast Guard commander had said. Then the silence was suddenly broken by a jabber of voices on the radio, from both the cutter and the cruiser, immediately followed by a trail of white smoke as a SAM was launched from the cruiser's aft deck. I yelled over the intercom for Beyer and Ronnie to brace for impact and get ready to bail out. Of course, at zero altitude and a hundred and sixty miles an hour, they had little chance of survival even if they did make it over the side, but I didn't have time to think about that.

I yanked hard to the left and dragged the nose of my lumbering aircraft to port, directly head on to the incoming missile. It was tracking true, at twice the speed of sound; only micro-seconds to impact. Strictly no go! I held the Cat steady, squinted my eyes almost closed, gritted my teeth, and did something I rarely did; I prayed!

At precisely the moment of impact, the missile veered away to port, its exhaust plume curling harmlessly behind. I silently thanked God and Northrop Grumman, designers of the new Guardian anti-missile defense device mounted to the mid under-belly of the Cat. There was not time for further thought or prayer. I knew they had no chance for a second shot; we were on top of them!

Now it was *MY* turn!

I heaved the yoke back into my gut, and the old girl violently shuddered as she struggled for altitude. I felt the jarring impact as our left outboard wing ripped the mast-head off the boat; I cranked the yoke hard right, shoving in a big boot-full of right rudder as I did so. She yawed and quivered on the edge of a stall, and then we were climbing away with a clear tail shot.

"Beyer! Take the shot! She's all yours. Ronnie! Stand by to help if that bloody gun jams or runs out of ammo. You'll only get one crack at it."

"Righto, old horse; I've got a bead on the buggers as we speak."

And indeed, as he spoke, I heard the familiar whirring thunder, and felt the deck under my feet shuddering as the Gatling gun opened fire. Moments later, I heard a tremendous explosion as thousands of rounds of 7.62 mil tore into every inch of that damned boat, including the fuel tanks and weapons stores. The fireball overtook the aircraft, and we rocked and rolled almost uncontrollably as we fled from the scene of annihilation.

A grim satisfaction settled in my belly as I turned much more gently back to where a few moments before had been a fifty feet cruiser. Nothing remained except a plume of gray smoke, a few pieces of burning wreckage and a black, spreading stain of oil.

For a few moments I was unconscious of the chatter in my headset. First I heard Beyer hollering with unfamiliar vehemence, 'Got `em! Got the blighters!' Then I became aware of a renewed chatter on the marine radio as I heard the commander of the Coast Guard cutter yelling at us again to 'identify yourselves, land immediately and surrender'.

Good luck, chum!

I eased off the pressure on the yoke and rudder, and kept the 'Wayward Wind' coming around in a much gentler turn to the right, putting as much distance as I could between us and the cutter, in case he too decided to try his luck with me. They were supposed to be the good guys, and I could not justify firing on them, even in self-defense.

I put the PBY in a gentle cruise climb and switched off the marine band radio to cut out the ranting of the Coast Guard skipper. Flipping the transmit button back to the Honolulu departure frequency, I keyed the mike and spoke.

"Honolulu Departure, this is Catalina flying boat Victor Hotel Papa Bravo Yankee. We have a VFR flight plan on file, twenty miles southeast of Oahu, setting heading for the mainland, destination Los Angeles. Cruise altitude niner thousand five hundred, and we will remain in radio contact with Center on HF for flight following."

"Papa Bravo Yankee, this is Honolulu Departure. Radar contact. We have your flight plan. Confirm time to destination and fuel and souls on board."

"Time to LAX, twenty hours, seventeen minutes; souls on board, three."

"Say again time en-route, Papa Bravo Yankee," he came back incredulously, thinking he had misheard me.

"I say again, twenty hours, seventeen minutes."

Switching him off, I re-set 'transmit' to the intercom.

"O.K., you guys. You can stow that cannon and come forward. We're mainland bound!"

A few minutes later, they both came forward through the aircraft and deposited themselves in their respective seats, grinning at each other and chattering all the while about their great victory, neither one of them apparently aware of their own near demise.

"Did you *see* that, Mitch?" Ronnie asked incredulously, grinning from ear to ear. "I've never seen anything like it in my *life*. One minute that boat was there, and the next it was gone. That was *some* shooting, Beyer!"

"Much as I appreciate your compliment and enthusiasm my dear, one does not exactly have to be a proficient marksman to destroy a target with *that* weapon. It is literally like shooting fish in the proverbial barrel with a twenty gauge shotgun."

"When you two are through slapping each other on the back," I interjected, "you should both be aware that they got off a shot at us before you took them out. The only thing that saved us was the new anti-missile device strapped to our belly – another little safety measure Beyer insisted on to preserve his precious and generous hide."

"You mean it actually worked?" that worthy replied, and then added rather superfluously, "Well, of course it worked or we wouldn't be here, would we, Blaine old rope?"

I simply turned and stared at him over my sunglasses, then responded lightheartedly: "I have contacted departure control, and let them know we are heading for Los Angeles – nonstop, of course, as there is no place *to* stop between here and there. I also let them know that ....."

"Ah, that is not strictly accurate, my boy," Beyer interrupted.

"I also let them know......" I repeated, and then stopped myself. "What do you mean? Which part is not strictly accurate?"

"We are not actually going to Los Angeles – or Texas, for that matter."

"We're not........?"

"You see, I have done some further calculations, and have estimated that with the fuel we have on board, we *should* be able to make our authentic destination of Page, Arizona, in about twenty-three and a half hours – if the present winds aloft hold true, of course."

"Of course! If the present winds ....Page, *Arizona?*" my voice trailed off again in stunned astonishment. "*WHAT* are you raving about now, Beyer? Did they get you with a stray shot after all?"

"Simply this, old horse; the distance from Honolulu to Page, Arizona, is two thousand five hundred and eighty four nautical miles. So, at an average ground speed of ….."

"Beyer!"

"Well …. ," he began somewhat hesitantly, "what I was trying to tell you both, before we were so rudely interrupted with these latest revolting developments, is that Page, Arizona, is the nearest airport where we can get fuel and the other necessities we may need for an extended period of isolation and survival in the Utah desert."

I had to restrain myself from reaching back and grasping his shirtfront to strike him. Instead, with great apprehension, I said, "I *know* I am going to regret this, but nearest airport to what?"

"Why, the entrance to our destination in the Escalante River Canyon, of course!"

"*WHAT??*" Ronnie and I shouted simultaneously.

"Beyer," I said, trying to remain as calm as possible. "Would you *please* enlighten us both as to whether you are in need of serious psychiatric assistance right now, before we get too far from these islands, or whether you are in fact considering taking this ship to the absolute limit of her endurance, putting us down in the middle of the Navajo Nation, then guiding us into one of the most hostile, inaccessible regions of the United States, on a quest to confront an enemy of unknown strength and origin?"

"Precisely, my boy!"

"I give up. I am not even going to ask. It seems, as you so succinctly announced, that we have about twenty four hours to kill. I can't *wait* for this one. Fire away!"

"Very well. It all came to me rather unexpectedly."

"Naturally!"

"I had been brooding on something Ronnie said about the Navajo who died mysteriously in the tunnel at the Super Collider. Ronnie, you said that he had 'a strange, wriggly shaped tattoo on his upper left arm'. This bothered me, because it did not seem that this should have been something significant that would have been revealed to you. Also, had it in fact *been* significant, why disclose it at all?

"So I had a friend – again someone who has access to such files – but happily, *not* Nathan Price, fax me a picture of the tattoo on the body. I then uploaded it into my computer, and began a scan of all similar patterns on bodies, clothing, tattoos, writings – anything I could think of, related to the Navajo that might produce a similar design. Nothing came up; no match in the data base. At least, not until it dawned on me that, bearing in mind our previous discussion about dimensional portals; it could be a *place*, and not a *thing!*"

"Whoa. Hold up, old friend," I interjected again. "Why would a so-called 'guardian' of a sacred place be wearing a picture of the damn thing on his arm?"

"I wondered the very same thing, Blaine. Great minds do *occasionally* think alike. The answer is often quoted as 'Occam's Razor', which in a nutshell is – incorrectly, I hasten to add – summarized as 'all things being equal, the simplest explanation is more likely than a complex one'. But actually, that is not strictly correct. The original principle states that among competing hypotheses, the one which makes the fewest assumptions should be chosen."

"Oh, well I am *so* glad you clarified that," I chipped in. "I would have been *VERY* confused had you not done so. Beyer, I say again; *what the HELL are you raving about?*"

"Well, as I mentioned before, these so-called portals, if my suspicions are correct, are inter-linked. Should one be familiar with the schematic detailing how they connect, one in theory may be able to enter at one location and exit at another of one's choosing, presumably without any physical harm, as our friend in the tunnel in Texas had probably used the portal located there to enter the SSC.

"But to answer your question, Blaine, I believe – to quote yourself – he was wearing the damn thing on his arm as a means not only to enter the SSC, but to exit at the gateway of his choosing. I think it was some kind of key or identifying code, to allow unhindered access. Furthermore, I believe he had been placed there, possibly by someone who has authority over such paranormal activities, for the very purpose of protecting – or guarding – access to the entrance.

"The problem is, someone – or something – unauthorized came through that gate and the guardian detected it, but was killed before he could sound the alarm."

"Beyer, I've heard you spin some beauties, but that is the most preposterous thing I ever heard," I responded unconvincingly, the familiar chill creeping up my spine.

I was about to make another cynical comment, when Ronnie added a tangential thought of her own. "Beyer, are you by any chance trying to suggest that my husband and brother, either of their own volition or under duress, slipped through this so-called portal in Texas, then somehow ended up in an as yet undisclosed location in the middle of - *Utah?*"

"Well, not exactly. I believe their Navajo friend may have had something to do with it before he so inconveniently died. I think either he or whatever came through immediately before that, may have somehow inadvertently left the gate open long enough for your brother to get through, and I assume the same fate happened at an earlier time to your husband."

"But....but if any of that's true, it means that somebody *else*, who also knows about this, and who *wanted* me to know that Jeff is still alive, *expected* me to try to ....."

".....do exactly what we are doing, and lead them to the other end of the rainbow," I finished her sentence for her, "which explains why we have had virtually no opposition to our proceeding this far, unnoticed or unopposed by any U.S. government authorities – except for our erstwhile unfriendlies a while back."

Beyer opened his mouth to speak again, but I continued with my own train of thought. "However, if what Ronnie supposes is true, then why would they be trying to kill her?"

This time, Beyer did interject before I could answer my own question.

"Because, old fruit, there are at least *two* factions at work here. As you just surmised, there is one group connected with Masters and McCall, led by the nefarious Nathan Price, which it seems, is attempting to get us to do their dirty work for them by leading them to the portal. And apparently there is perhaps one other, authorized by any means necessary to *prevent* us from discovering the entrance by making *all of us* disappear, in order to protect their own agenda, which is obviously to cover up the existence of the portals.

"At first, I had no clue. But now I believe, bearing in mind the nature of our quest, that it may be something even more sinister; something that has been around for eons, and has in fact become part of Navajo legend about their own creation.

"Unfortunately, I believe that we have stumbled onto something intangibly, incalculably evil, and possibly supernatural. And of course, when we enter into *their* territory, we are totally alone and quite expendable."

"But WHAT, *dammit?*"

"I am afraid we won't know the answer to that until we get there."

"Get *where*, exactly?"

"Ronnie mentioned an 'as yet undisclosed location in the middle of Utah'. Well, it is no longer undisclosed. I found a match for that tattoo."

"You *did?*" Ronnie exclaimed.

"It is the outline of a canyon far up the Escalante River. It is unmarked on any map. However, the Navajo call it ….well, I can't pronounce it in their language, but in English it is close enough to 'Canyon of Those Who Came Before'."

"Before *what?*" I persevered hopelessly.

"Before everything; you see, the Navajo – and Hopi for that matter, who have similar creation legends – believe they, or more specifically their ancestors, commonly referred to as the Anasazi, entered this world through holes in the ground from worlds that had existed before. This creation myth suggests that they emerged from underground chambers which have a single entrance at the top.

"Navajo origin stories begin with a First World of darkness. From this Dark World, the Dine – their word for 'the People' – began a journey of emergence into the world of the present. The First World was small in size, a floating island in mist or water. The creatures of the First World are thought of as the Mist People. This world, being small in size, became crowded, and the people quarreled and fought among themselves, and in all ways made living very unhappy.

"So, because of the strife in the First World, First Man, and First Woman, followed by all the others, climbed up from the World of Darkness and Dampness to the Second or Blue World. However, foreign gods in human form were rapidly destroying the people by corrupting them. These monsters made the Second World unpleasant for those who had come from the First World. There was fighting and killing, so they decided to move again. They found an opening in the World of Blue Haze and they climbed through this and led the people up into the Third or Yellow world.

"The beings were happy in the Yellow World. But this world was infested with great giants, offspring of the foreign gods. They escaped to another world. This was the Fourth, White World. This is the place where all beings live today.

"Hopi legend also tells that the current earth is the Fourth World to be inhabited. The story is essentially the same, and states that in each previous world, the people, though originally happy, became disobedient and lived contrary to the creator's plan; they engaged in sexual promiscuity, fought one another and would not live in harmony. Thus, the most obedient were led to the next higher world, with physical changes occurring both in the people in the course of their journey, and in the environment of the next world. In some stories, these former worlds were then destroyed along with their wicked inhabitants, whereas in others the good people were simply led away from the chaos. As I said before, it all sounds rather familiar, doesn't it?"

I dared not reply, fearing that my limited recollection of the Book of Genesis would be too inadequate for a rational response.

"Which brings us to our present dilemma," he continued. "If there is even a grain of truth whatsoever to these legends, and the method of actually passing from one world to the next was by way of some kind of dimensional portals, and if we actually enter the one that I seem to have re-discovered, we stand a good chance of either being stranded in another world infested by creatures of unknown origin, or being killed by them before we can locate Masters and McCall – assuming they have not fallen victim to the same fate – before we can make our escape."

I had listened to this foolishness until the hairs on the back of my neck were stiff with apprehension of the unknown – the greatest fear of all! Several hours seemed to have gone by, and I desperately needed to get out of my seat, stretch, walk around and visit the head.

"Beyer, either you are stark, raving mad, or you have gotten us into the direst situation we have encountered since we first began our crazy adventures together. I'm not so sure I don't want to turn us around, head back to the beaches and booze of Hawaii, and leave all this nonsense behind us before it's too late. But it is already too late, isn't it, 'old trout'", I mimicked as I struggled out of my seat, forcing him to back out of his so that I could squeeze past him and exit the cockpit.

I did not realize how much time had elapsed since we left the safety of Hawaii and ventured forth into the North Pacific, west coast U.S.A. bound. It was early morning when we had caught up with and destroyed the mystery cruiser and its crew. However, from what Beyer so vociferously described, they were rank amateurs compared to what lay ahead!

Twilight was rapidly enveloping the 'Wayward Wind' as we plodded doggedly north-eastward over another two thousand miles of empty ocean. There was nothing to see on the horizon except the darkening sky, a trillion stars now beginning to blaze in the frosty, uncharted heavens.

I lingered for a moment in the companionway in the space behind my bear-like friend, who had re-seated himself on the totally inadequate jump seat to continue his discourse with Ronnie. I felt the familiar, gentle sway of the aircraft on the autopilot, and was comforted by the muffled roar of the Pratts. This was *my* world; tangible and real. I yawned and stretched mightily, contorted myself into the tiny head, then retreated back to the galley where I found that Beyer had left a pot of coffee on the warmer. Pouring a mug, I stepped over the coaming into the main cabin, slid into the dinette, and sat staring out the Perspex porthole at barely visible whitecaps on a black, inhospitable ocean thousands of feet below.

Reflecting again on Beyer's latest revelations, I could not help but shudder at the thought of what lay ahead. Having spent more than half my life aloft, strapped into the cockpits of hundreds of different aircraft, dozens of different makes and models from fighters to commercial jet transports to float planes and flying boats, I had over twenty thousand hours in my log books. I had witnessed every inexplicable and fantastic wonder of nature that a pilot could see in a lifetime of airborne adventure. But I had never seen a so-called UFO – although many pilots claim they have – nor had I ever encountered anything that could be remotely suggestive of supernatural. I was frankly and morbidly curious about what was before us. Yet at the same time I felt a deep and abiding sense of dread. There was something menacing out there; some awful enigma that, when revealed, could change our lives forever. I was too simple a man with too simple an outlook on the joys of being alive to get involved with something ungodly or supernatural. I did not want to even think about what awaited us around the final bend of that canyon in Utah!

It suddenly occurred to me that our almost fatal descent into the maw of the south Pacific shortly after Beyer's apparent discovery of a 'new' cluster of stars a few days ago might have something to do with his present conjecture, and that thought made me squirm in my seat, glance furtively out the window again, and listen for the slightest change in pitch of the old, reliable Pratt and Whitney engines.

Nothing was amiss, however; no abnormal rumble, vibration or noise that was not a perfectly comfortable and familiar element of this seventy year old flying boat's personality. Comforted by the muted, steady roar of the engines, we drifted north-east with the night, nudged along by favorable tailwinds. I shook myself awake after discovering my head resting on one arm on the dinette table, my fingers still hooked into the empty coffee mug.

13

I glanced at my watch and was shocked to discover that almost eighteen hours had gone by since we took off from Honolulu; over three hours since I had left the cockpit! Ronnie was up there by herself, with no reprieve from either Beyer's banal banter or the constant strain of flying and navigating by herself. Struggling out of the dinette, I crawled forward to find Beyer's head resting on his ample chest with his hairy arms folded as he dozed sitting up. I slapped him on the shoulder, startled him into semi-consciousness, and motioned with my thumb for him to vacate his seat.

Shaking himself fully awake, he bellowed "Oho, so his lordship finally condescends to joining the ranks of the working class, what?"

Ignoring his causticity, I inquired as to the routine of the flight, and was promptly assured that everything was 'absolutely peachy, old boy!'

Ronnie, however, glanced back at me with a pained expression that told me she either had to use the bathroom, or relieve herself from Beyer's inimitable profundity, or both. I again raised my thumb rearwards in signal for her to bail out and take a break, to which she responded eagerly. She scrambled out of her seat, planted a quick, sly kiss on my cheek as she eased by me, and disappeared into the back of the plane.

I climbed into the left seat, fiddled with the GPS for a moment, adjusted our course a couple of degrees to allow for some extra drift we had picked up, then scanned the instruments with suspicious eye, the habit of a lifetime of so doing. Beyer returned to his jump seat, which although woefully inadequate, was still easier for him to mount than to attempt to gather his bulk into the co-pilot's seat.

"Going to be a beautiful sunrise," he commented with an unaccustomed appreciation of nature.

"Sunrise?" I repeated, squinting out the forward windshield.

"How can it be sunrise?" I added, realizing the inanity of the question as I remembered the short day and night that had passed since we set heading from Hawaii, flying towards the sun as we were.

"Yes, I guess you're right, Beyer. We must be getting pretty close to the coast."

As if in answer to my spoken thoughts, the H.F. radio crackled and a tinny voice from L.A. air traffic control center came faintly through the headset. "Flying boat Victor Hotel Papa Bravo Yankee, this is L.A. center. Do you read?"

I picked up the mike and responded immediately, almost shouting as if he could hear me better. "This is Papa Bravo Yankee. We are ...." I hesitated for a moment as I again checked out position on the GPS. "We are one hundred eighty miles northwest of L.A., on the two niner five bearing, niner thousand five hundred, estimating over Cayucos Beach, at zero six three five local, destination Kilo Papa Golf Alpha at one one one seven local."

"Copy, Papa Bravo Yankee. Verify you are not landing at LAX?"

"That's affirmative. Change of flight plan. We are now direct Page, Arizona. I say again, direct Page, Arizona. Request flight following until arrival," I added superfluously, knowing full damn well that we were being watched on radar every mile of the way until touchdown, at which time I expected an armed reception committee! In fact, I almost expected summary execution immediately upon our arrival!

"Very well, Papa Bravo Yankee. Understand requesting flight following to Page, Arizona. Advise cancellation of flight plan in the pattern or on the ground."

"Papa Bravo Yankee, roger."

"Well, that was easy. Too easy," I mused aloud.

"Not to worry, old fruit," Beyer chipped in, reading my thoughts as usual. "I took the liberty while you were in dreamland of sending a message on the Sat-phone that we were changing our plans and proceeding directly to Page. They are expecting us."

"Oh, I'll just bet they are," I responded cynically. "I'll just bet they are."

"Not quite what I meant, Mitch old boy. I mean, as well as flight service, I personally contacted the FBO there and they are waiting for us with a gas truck; a *big* gas truck! Also, they have a rental car and hotel lined up as well. I dare say we will all need another good night's rest before we venture into the unknown."

"If we're not arrested, summarily executed and buried somewhere in the outback, that is," I added morbidly.

"Don't be so melodramatic Blaine! These people *want* us to do their dirty work for them, remember? You said so yourself!"

"Yeah, and I also remember your mentioning the minor detail that there was another faction at work trying to *prevent* us from reaching our destination, no matter what the cost."

At that moment, Ronnie re-emerged from the dim passageway behind Beyer's bulk, squeezed past him and back into her seat.

"So, what did I miss? Anything important?"

I opened my mouth to reply, but Beyer beat me to it.

"Nothing at all my dear, nothing at all; except that we have altered course slightly, and are now on the direct track to Page, Arizona."

"Oh. Well, that's good," she said, stifling a yawn. "What's our remaining flight time," she inquired, checking the GPS to answer her own question.

"About another four hours, if we don't run out of gas somewhere over the Sierras," I responded dryly, tapping the fuel gauges which were all bouncing around just above the quarter mark.

Fifteen minutes later, we roared over the magnificent California coast halfway between the beach cities of Cayucos and Morro Bay. The brilliant blue Pacific gave way to aqua, white-capped surf pounding creamy colored sand, then almost as quickly was replaced by verdant rolling hills, the trademark of coastal southwest California.

Our mood changed from the dreary hum-drum silence of long, over water flight to that of excited chatter as we pointed out various landmarks and features of the constantly changing terrain. The GPS now really did earn its keep as it marked off cities and towns passing sedately below. We skirted the southern foothills of the Sierra Nevada range. Sequoia National Forest, Mount Whitney, Olancha Peak and the infamous Death Valley drifted under our port wing.

Then we were over the state line and into Nevada. Charleston Peak and the ever expanding garish urban sprawl of Las Vegas floated past our starboard beam. The earlier chill morning air was now replaced by stifling desert heat as we began a gradual descent to two thousand feet above the steadily rising terrain of the Colorado Plateau. Past Lake Meade we flew, as we crossed the state line into Arizona.

The breathtaking, awesome splendor of the Grand Canyon came into view on our right side, and we eased over to get a better view, remaining outside the special use VFR airspace so we didn't draw any more attention to ourselves than was already suspected.

South of the canyon, off in the far distance we could clearly make out the snow-capped tops of the San Francisco Peaks, dominated by the highest mountain in Arizona, Humphrey's Peak at 12,633 feet. We departed the North Rim then turned northeast towards Page, dropping down to follow the Colorado River a thousand feet above the rim. We crossed over the twin bridges of Marble Canyon, then on up the river over Horseshoe Bend, and cut across directly to Page.

None of us had spoken a word for the last hour, sitting in silent awe as the brilliant colors of this red, barren, broken land kept us captivated with its stunning beauty.

I grabbed the microphone and transmitted on the airport CTAF frequency, advising our location.

"Page traffic, this is flying boat Papa Bravo Yankee, inbound from Horseshoe Bend at fifteen hundred, joining a ten mile final for runway thirty three. Any traffic please advise."

14

As we descended to the airfield, I felt pangs of nostalgia as I recalled my former visits to this isolated area of the United States. House-boating on Lake Powell and hiking and riding the back country had been one of my favorite things to do in my early years, before the NPS and BLM, with their ever-expanding rules, regulations and oversight, made it virtually impossible to go anywhere without permits, guides and ceaseless and insistent supervision.

Edward Abbey's 'Desert Solitaire' is one of my favorite books. His irreverent and anarchistic portrayal of this country before government autocracy totally ruined it often made me wish I had lived here long before the days of their infernal interference in the wilderness!

Now, as we began our final descent into that fantastic realm of the Navajo Nation, with its infinite and multilayered panorama of spires, towers and buttes, I again admired the extraordinarily striking contours and colors of the canyons, cliffs and mesas glowing vermillion and purple in the mid-morning light. I was overcome with feelings of familiar serenity, despite the hazardous circumstances of our mission.

In the foreground, magnificent Lake Powell itself grew larger as the beginning of its almost two thousand miles of coastline drew near. The pink and beige sandstone cliffs dropped down to talus slopes and sandy beaches for as far as the eye could see. In the distance were the red hills of Utah, spectacular realms of Canyonlands and Arches National Parks, peaks of the Sierra La Sals still clad in snow, and about to receive a new dumping as the weather grew colder in this unbelievably glorious desert landscape; this land of the Anasazi, their cliff dwellings long abandoned, many now forever inaccessible under hundreds of feet of water behind Glen Canyon Dam. And into the maze of this back country we would shortly be venturing. When we rested, refueled and restocked at Page, we would take off for the Escalante River Canyons and the heart of our adventure, and hopefully discover an answer to the riddle behind the mysterious disappearance of Ronnie McCall's husband and brother.

"Beyer, see if you can raise American Aviation on one twenty two point eight and ask 'em if Bob Hogan is around. He's the chief pilot; or he was, the last time I was out here flying for them several years ago."

"Roger, old boy, wilco," he responded effusively. "American Aviation, this is Papa Bravo Yankee on a five mile final for runway three three. Is Bob Hogan available, by any chance?"

"Papa Bravo Yankee, this is American Aviation. Standby please. I'll put him on."

A moment's pause, and then he came on the radio.

"This is Bob Hogan."

I grabbed for my mike.

"G'day Bob. I *know* you won't guess who this is."

"I already know who this is! Word travels fast around here, even as far out in the boonies as we are! How the hell are you, Mitch?"

"We're all fine. Can't wait to down a few cold ones with you. We'll be on the ground in one minute. Where do you want us?"

"Park her right beside the terminal on the southeast apron, next to the Twin Otter. We're waiting for you."

"You got it. See ya in a few."

I stowed the mike and began the landing ritual with Ronnie.

"Gear down, Ronnie. Landing checklist."

"Roger, skipper," she responded with a familiar grin. "Gear down."

We ran the checklist as I straightened the 'Wayward Wind' out on final, crabbing her in to allow for a pretty good left crosswind, and then giving her a hefty bootful of right rudder to straighten us out on the centerline, easing the nose up moments before touchdown. The old girl squeaked gently on to the asphalt of runway thirty three, glad to be done with her natural element for a while. I stood on the brakes and managed to get her slowed enough to get off on the first high speed taxiway to the left.

I brought us in, sneaked between the Twin Otter and the terminal, and shut off the mixtures and the magnetos. The props slowed and stopped as the good old reliable Pratts, which had kept us aloft for almost twenty four hours now, clattered to a whining halt. We sat there for a few minutes, already baking in that famous 'dry' oven heat, still partly stunned, with ears ringing in the sudden and absolute silence after an eternity of deafening racket.

When I could hear the tick of cooling metal, I asked Ronnie for the shutdown checklist.

As we were finishing it up, a golf cart pulled up beside my cockpit window. I slid it open just as my friend Bob Hogan, still nimble at late sixty something, jumped out of the cart and squinted up at me.

"Are you kidding me?" he grinned, shading his eyes from the desert glare. "Come on down out of there and I'll buy you that cold one."

"You're on, me old china," I responded with boyish zeal, "Can't wait! Who are all those people," I added, jerking my head in the direction of a throng of mostly geriatric types milling around behind the low brick wall outside the terminal, excitedly pointing and gesturing at us.

"That's your reception committee. No, seriously, that's our latest busload of French tourists waiting to go out on the next scenic. No doubt they think they're getting a special treat today; probably have the idea they are going up with you in that crate."

"Watch your language!" I pulled my head back inside the cockpit.

"Beyer, get on the phone and …."

"Get us a car and a hotel with a cool, dark bar and a big, bright swimming pool," my friend finished the sentence for me. "Already done, old trout. I imagine your chum down below has the arrangements well in hand."

"Naturally," I responded sheepishly. "I should have guessed."

He didn't hear me. He was already back at the port blister starting to hand luggage down to Bob's ramp guys by the time Ronnie and I struggled out of our seats and hobbled towards the rear of the aircraft, every joint in our exhausted bodies crying out for relief from long hours in the cramped spaces of our ancient flying machine.

I dropped to the burning asphalt, disregarding the boarding ladder, and then handed Ronnie down. We stood there under the scorching sun allowing the blistering heat to soak into our weary bones.

Bob came up and shook hands vigorously, saying "It's good to see you again Mitch, after all this time. I thought you were going to come and fly with us again for another season, but you never showed up; gave up on you when I didn't hear from you for a few years."

"I know. Sorry about that Bob. Got busy with other projects," I added, nodding my head in the direction of the Catalina and Ronnie at the same time.

"I should have guessed. Anyway, got you all squared away at the Courtyard in town. Great place to stay, beautiful view of the desert, a nice big pool and a quiet bar with good prices. Think you'll like it!"

"Sounds too good to be true. Can't wait!"

"You want gas I take it?"

"Like the man said, 'fill `er up! And I do mean squeeze in every last drop! She'll probably take about fourteen hundred gallons. You got that much available?"

"Sure do, pardner. I heard you were coming."

"Yeah. My pal Beyer knows his stuff all right."

"Beyer?" he repeated, scratching his head. "Who's Beyer?"

"My mountain of a friend over there, helping to unload our gear."

Bob glanced in his direction and said, "He is a large one, ain't he?"

I was about to respond when, glancing beyond the crowd and into the terminal, I caught a glimpse of a beautiful young woman clad in traditional Navajo dress. My eyes rested on her only for a moment, but that moment was long enough for me to register that she wore a long, fringed, buckskin dress with tall matching moccasin boots. She wore a plain brown belt around a slender waist, with a similar band around her black, straight, hair, parted in the middle and pulled back into twin braids. I saw no jewelry.

I turned to Bob and, nodding in the direction of the terminal window, asked, "Who is that Navajo girl over there in the terminal, staring out at us?"

He gazed in the direction I was indicating, and replied, "What Navajo girl?"

Turning back to the window, I repeated, "That ……"

My sentence remained unfinished and my jaw dropped when I realized that she was gone.

"You've been out in the sun too long already? You just got here!"

"I know I'm not seeing things, Bob. She was there a minute ago."

"Well, she's not there now, and I have no idea who you're talking about. Besides, seems to me you already have your hands full with one handsome young woman in tow. Getting a bit greedy, aren't ya?"

"Very amusing! Lead the way to that cool bar and cold beer!"

"I'll do better than that. I am going to take you all there myself, as soon as you're ready."

"Give me five minutes to button up the ship, and we'll be with you," I replied.

"Ronnie, Beyer," I yelled over the din of an arriving private jet, "get the control locks and chocks in. Bob here is going to give us a ride to the hotel."

"Roger *that*," they eagerly replied in unison.

Five minutes later, Bob's line guys had transferred our gear from the golf cart into the back of his dusty old Chevy pickup. Ronnie and I were crowded into the so-called 'crew cab' in the back, as Beyer had elected to squeeze himself into the normally ample room of the front seat.

Bob left instructions with his lead hand to top off the 'Wayward Wind' and, as requested by me, to keep two eyes on her at all times, day and night, no exceptions, until we returned.

After an interesting, guided historical ten minute tour through downtown Page, with enough colorful discourse to match one of Beyer's never-ending dissertations, we arrived at the Courtyard which to our pleasant surprise overlooked the entire red rock vista of canyon, dam and blue lake behind it.

Bob introduced us to the gals at reception, with whom he was well acquainted of course, then sauntered off to wait for us in the bar.

We quickly checked into our respective rooms. I changed out of my malodorous, sweat-stained flight suit into an old pair of comfortable tan slacks, blue knit shirt and well-worn boat shoes, and was about to leave the room when on an impulse I could not fathom, I pulled the Ruger out of my bag, removed it from the shoulder rig and shoved it into a belly holster which I slipped under my shirt in my waistband.

I then joined Bob, Ronnie and Beyer in the bar. Lori, one of the very pretty Native American receptionists, came out to drop off a set of keys and a rental contract for me to sign. The vehicle was a new Jeep Wrangler, very appropriate for the kind of terrain we might be exploring before heading off into parts unknown in the 'Wayward Wind'.

As we sat at a table in the deserted, pleasantly quiet and private bar, three more cold, frothy beers were placed before us, joining Bob's, which was already half empty.

I positioned myself opposite Hogan, facing the plate glass windows and door which led out to the pool. Beyer sat on his right and Ronnie on his left, so that we could easily converse. I had an idea that Beyer might wish to regale him with some spurious details of our adventures thus far.

But before any of us got a word out, Bob gulped down another long swig of his beer, wiped his mouth with the back of a dusty hand, and floored us when he quizzically remarked, "So …. I don't suppose your arrival has anything to do with a certain uppity air force general swooping down out of the blue this morning on our isolated, peaceful little community in an AC-130 gunship bristling with thirty millimeter Bushmasters, escorted by a brace of equally bristling F-16s, would it?"

"*Whaat?*" we echoed, as our jaws dropped simultaneously. Beyer was, of course, the first to recover his composure.

"Nathan Price, *damn* him!" he exclaimed, muttering an indistinguishable profanity under his breath. And then he added the obvious question on everyone's lips. "What in heaven's name is *he* doing here?"

"I just asked you the same question. Who, pray tell, is Nathan Price?" Hogan inquired, fixing his bright blue gaze on each of us in turn with raised and wrinkled brow.

Again, Beyer stepped in to the rescue, with rapid and devious response.

"Ah, you apparently just met him. General Nathan Price is an ex-colleague of mine. We worked on the same, shall we say, project a few years ago. He knew we were due to arrive here today. He must have ... been in the neighborhood as it were, and decided to drop in on a surprise visit."

Well, I thought, he wasn't out-and-out lying, which was impossible for Beyer. It was more or less true, even if incomplete.

"So if he's a buddy of yours, why was he snooping around every FBO on the field asking a lot of fool questions about you? And if he was so eager to see you, why did he jump into that big bird of his and fly away as soon as he knew you were about to arrive?"

"That is a *very* good question," Beyer responded, scratching his several days old stubble of whiskers; "a very good question indeed; one which remains to be answered.

But I am sure that in the coming days, we will become privy to General Price's objectives ....like it or not."

I began to squirm uncomfortably in my seat, glanced at Beyer and wondered how he was going to dig himself out of that one. Hogan was a friend of mine, and I surely did not want him getting involved in something that could at the very least be dangerous and more than likely fatal.

Trying to think up a suitable lie myself, I was gazing out through the plate glass windows at the deserted pool area when I was shocked to lock eyes with the same Navajo girl I had seen at the airport, staring in at me from outside the glass. I was definitely not seeing things this time!

"Hogan! Turn around slowly. There she is again!"

He did as requested, but even though he hardly moved his head, by the time he could shift his eyes to the window, she had disappeared. I had no idea how she did it. She was simply there one second and gone the next. This was getting a little weird!

"Are you sure you're not imagining things?" Hogan inquired. "After all, you have apparently been awake for over twenty four hours. You could be hallucinating."

Ronnie and Beyer were now staring at me, wondering what Hogan was talking about.

"Wait right here, all of you!"

"Where are you going?" Beyer inquired, as I pushed my chair back, leapt to my feet with astounding agility considering my present totally exhausted condition, and strode to the glass exit out to the pool.

"I am going to find that girl and ask her very politely what she wants of me, and why she keeps disappearing. I'll be back!"

I made the door in three bounds, and was outside looking around the empty pool area within no more than thirty seconds of first spotting her. But she was nowhere in sight. I searched all around the pool area, went back inside by another entrance, walked up to the reception desk and, before realizing the inanity of the question, asked Lori, the same girl who had brought me the car keys, if she had seen a Navajo girl in the lobby a few minutes ago.

She flashed me a polite, automatic smile and told me that she undeniably sees many Navajo maidens come and go. Translation: since it was their country, they come and go as they please, and who am I to ask.

I thanked her anyway, stepped briskly out through the main entrance, shaded my eyes against the desert glare and squinted up and down the main road. No sign of her!

I suddenly realized that I had unconsciously grabbed the Jeep keys off the table as I stood up, and they were still in my hand. Searching quickly around the parking lot, I found the tan Wrangler – the only one of its kind in the lot – climbed in, started up, skidded out of the driveway, turned left, and roared off down North Lake Powell Boulevard just in time to spot a gray Chevy van a hundred yards ahead, fast approaching the intersection of Highway 89. He hooked right and headed northwest out of town at high speed. I followed with an acute sense of foreboding growing in the pit of my gut. I had no idea where I was going, what the hell I was looking for, or what I would encounter up ahead.

I was soon to wish I had stayed in the cool safety of the hotel bar!

15

The van approached the Glen Canyon Bridge, but did not attempt to slow to the 20 mile per hour speed limit. He was doing fifty when he went across, almost hitting a couple of wayward pedestrians casually strolling over the vehicular bridge, off the dedicated walkway.

I followed at a more sedate pace, not wanting to draw attention to myself at this early point of my stay in Page. Minutes later, we were heading out into the vast red empty expanse of buttes, mesas and canyons, ripping along the practically empty highway at a fast clip.

I had not realized how quickly the morning had passed. The sun was already in the western sky dropping to the horizon, and the fantastic orange and burgundy cliffs were beginning to surrender to subtle hues of rose, and in the expanding shadows, deep lavender. Had I been on a scenic drive, I would have stopped to take in the awesome beauty of this strange, enchanted land. Instead, I was on a quest; of what ilk I did not know. But something sinister lurked ahead. That much I was certain. I felt it in the back of my neck now, as surely as I had a hundred times before!

Then I realized that I had lost sight of the van. Somewhere up ahead in that daunting desert landscape, it had disappeared. I brought the Jeep to a halt, switched off the ignition, stepped out and squinted into the fading glare; no sign of it.

Nothing out there but empty space and pervasive silence – except for the wind; the ever-present whistling of the hot, dusty wind as it moaned around buttes and ridges and stirred the ceaseless, tinkling motion of the shifting, whispering sand.

I stood there in that scorching heat, shading my eyes with my hand, looking around for any sign of life. An abrupt movement in my peripheral vision startled me and I turned to spy a giant hairy desert scorpion, stinger and claws raised high, scuttling away over a dune to the cover of a nearby clump of creosote.

My skin crawled with a primeval chill, despite the heat.

Then, almost as if the scorpion had deliberately drawn my attention in that direction, my eyes locked on a plume of red dust disappearing around a butte far ahead and off to the right of the main paved road. I jumped back in the Jeep, left a couple of layers of black rubber on the pavement, and set out in pursuit.

A few miles past the 'Welcome to Utah' sign on Highway 89, I came to the only trail he could have taken, a faint pall of red dust rapidly dissipating in the hot breeze. I yanked the wheel hard right, skidded on to the dusty track, and gunned the engine as it led down into a sandy wash and up the other side. I came up out of the wash just in time to see the trail of telltale dust leading me into a jumbled maze of washes, arroyos and canyons towering above me on all sides.

I found myself in a deep ravine which narrowed as I drove further in. The dust trail petered out but there was no further sign of the fleeing van. I stopped the engine and listened. Again, a profound, eerie silence; no.....not so much silence, I realized, but a hushed stillness, as if the cliffs around me were watching and waiting for something. I peered around in the gathering gloom, alert and uneasy. There was no sign of the van, yet there was nowhere it could have gone. The chasm ahead looked too narrow for any vehicle, let alone one the size of that van.

Every fiber of my being told me I was being led into a trap.

Why was I here? What had possessed me to leave the beauty and comfort of my sybaritic life on the water in Sydney Harbor and fly half-way 'round the world to this incredibly barren, hostile landscape of rocks, sand, snakes and scorpions?

What would I find here? If I had to admit it to myself, I was afraid; of what? I had visited almost every continent on earth – had been exposed to many different cultures, religions and bizarre rituals in my years of traveling the globe.

Why this sudden fear of the unknown? What was it I was afraid of? Did I sense something out here that was truly beyond my experience and comprehension – something actually outside my ability to control?

I searched my memory back through the years, but could not identify a single incident that had caused me such morbid apprehension. The truth was, I sensed something positively evil – a malevolence that was almost tangible! And yet, everything in range of my normal senses seemed to be as it should; nothing out of the ordinary. But *something* was definitely, palpably wrong!

I decided that discretion was the better part of valor, started the Jeep, and backed up far enough to turn around in the narrow ravine.

It was then that an inexplicable terror came over me. I floored the accelerator, but it was too late. Something moved ahead of me in the dim shadows of the canyon. Then she materialized out of the gloom about twenty feet in front of me. I slammed on the brakes and came to a sliding stop no more than a foot from her. She did not as much as flinch. She made no motion whatsoever to protect herself from the impact of the onrushing Jeep. She just stood there, as if she knew and expected that the vehicle would stop in time.

For a moment I sat there staring at her, gripping the wheel of the Jeep as if it was my only contact with reality – whatever that was! This time I prudently left the engine running, and with my heart pounding, climbed out and took a couple of steps to face her. She was stunning! One of the most beautiful women I had ever seen, she made no move to advance or retreat. She simply stared at me with calm nonchalance, as if almost having the life crushed out of her – assuming she was in fact alive – and not simply an apparition, was an everyday event for her! She wore the same traditional Navajo outfit, but up close she was even more striking than I had surmised. She had a unique, slender figure which was sharply outlined in the glare of the Jeep's headlights. She had sleek, dusky skin, a shade or two lighter than her outfit.

However, the most startling thing about her was her eyes! They were large, obsidian and almond-shaped. At first I thought they were completely devoid of expression, but then I realized that I was staring into two bottomless wells of unplumbed depth and feeling.

I was about to speak when I sensed someone – or something – else; some indefinable presence, lurking in the lengthening shadows around the Jeep. The presence was accompanied by a fetid, animal stench and a soft, dry rasping sound reminiscent of cottonwood leaves rustling in a slight breeze. I slowly reached for the comforting grip of the Ruger in its belly holster under my shirt. But before I could touch the walnut butt of the revolver, she uttered an indescribably dreadful sound that was more like the menacing snarl of a wolf than anything emanating from a human throat.

Then she spoke – with a voice soft and ominous - that froze me in position.

"Do not! Your puny weapon cannot harm them. They will kill you!"

My hand dropped to my side as I spoke, not recognizing my own voice. "Who are *they*, and who are you? What do you want with me? You have been following me since I arrived. What is your name?"

"*They* are my protectors. *My* name does not matter. You would not understand it if I told you. You must leave here. You and your friends are in much danger. "

"I cannot," I replied, trying to sound forceful. "My friends and I seek two men who may be held prisoner in another place near here. We must try to find this place and ......"

"The men you seek are dead. And the place you speak of, you cannot go. If you do, you also will never return to your people. No-one ever leaves – or lives to speak of this place; *no-one!* It is not possible."

"Nothing is 'not possible'! The men I seek are *not* dead, and we *will* find them – and the place you say we cannot go – we *will* go, and we will return, and expose this place to my people."

"You are a fool, white man. Do you not think your people have tried for generations to learn the secret of our worlds? All you succeed in doing is making it more difficult for us to live our lives in peace. We have been hunted for many years by the mighty ones before the white man came. Our lives, our homes – our way of life – have been destroyed. If you continue with your experiments and your interference, you will release them and they will destroy your world too!"

"The 'mighty ones'? Who are they?"

"You will find out soon enough, Mitchel Blaine, if you persist in your quest. Perhaps your friend Beyer will be able to explain them to you. Although even his speculations are nowhere near the truth! Your kind have for years made assumptions, re-written history, and given lectures on the demise of my people. You have all been wrong! You will discover for yourselves *how* wrong if you do not stop now."

"How do you know my name – and how do you know about my friend Beyer? Who *are* you?"

"You are a fool," she said again, "but a brave fool. Go! Discover, if you can, the secrets of my world. It will not be easy, since you have buried it under your big water.

"You are already dead, but you do not know it," she added ominously.

I had not noticed the passage of time in the thickening gloom of that canyon. As I stared at her, she seemed to dissolve into the lengthening shadows, and the awful presence and odor that I had detected faded away with her. I was left with an unshakable sensation that something was still watching and waiting for me to move – to try to run – and that whatever was still lurking there was not going to let me leave that dreadful place!

As I climbed back into the comforting reality of the Jeep, I peered all around into the gathering darkness, but there was no more sign of her. I slammed the auto-shifter into 'Drive' and again floored the accelerator, spewing a huge plume of dust up in my wake, as I spun the wheels and fled!

I could not get out of that canyon fast enough. The headlights picked up the faint hint of vehicle tracks which had led me into this mess as I retraced my previous trail. My imagination began to run away with me as the crags and overhangs of the ravine seemed to close in on me. Then that horrible feeling that I was being watched morphed into reality.

Glancing in the rearview mirror, I was appalled to discover that my senses were not deceiving me. Something *was* following me – and it was gaining on me! I was terrified! I tore out of the ravine and on to the trail leading into open desert, hurtling towards the main road.

I did not want to look into that mirror again, but when I did, there was nothing there. The feeling of relief was short-lived, however, when what I had previously glimpsed in the mirror appeared next to me, *loping alongside the Jeep, which was doing sixty miles an hour!*

My natural survival instinct kicked in and I swerved towards the creature, trying desperately to knock it down. At first I thought it was an animal, but then it became all too obvious that it was a man – or at least, something that resembled a man, apparently covered in an animal skin of some kind.

Then the thing turned to face me and my horror intensified as I spied under that animal hood two red, glowing coals staring out at me. Again, I veered left in another attempt to run it down, but then, just as I thought things could not get worse, the creature began to extend a bony claw towards me. Strictly no go! This thing – whatever it was – was not going to get the better of me. I reached under my shirt, grabbed the Ruger, and fired without aiming.

16

Point blank, the explosion and muzzle flash of that miniature cannon in the fading twilight momentarily blinded me. When I looked again, the thing was gone. I did not know whether I had gotten it, or whether it had simply decided that a .44 magnum at close range was more than a match for it. In any case, the creature seemed to have disappeared. I kept the Jeep at high speed, almost leaping over that first wash I had encountered, days ago it seemed, and back on to the main road.

At seventy miles an hour, I roared over the Utah state line. A hundred yards later, the 'Welcome to Arizona' sign appeared in the headlights. So did the Coconino County Sheriff's cruiser, parked right under the sign, as if just waiting for me to return. It was too late for me to even pretend to slow down, so I kept right on going.

Moments later, his headlights came on, and so did all his other flashers. Then he hit the siren and I knew it would only make matters worse if I didn't stop. At least, I thought, I would have some very official and well-armed company on this lonely road, if my recent nightmare decided to show up again!

I slowed and pulled over to the shoulder of the narrow, two lane highway. While I was waiting for him to stop behind me and check my rental's license tag in his computer,

I dragged my wallet out of my hip pocket and withdrew my Australian driver's license. His lights were shining right into the open Jeep, so with as little movement as possible, using the back of my seat as my only cover, I eased the Ruger out of my belt and shoved it under the seat, then put my hands back on the wheel where he could see them.

Moments later, he sidled carefully up to the driver's side, one hand holding a flashlight, the other on the holstered butt of his service pistol. He shined the light in the Jeep, looking for any obvious weapon. Then, holding the light in my eyes, he spoke with a smooth, laconic western drawl.

"Captain Blaine, I presume."

I was shocked! "Good evening, officer. How is it, may I ask, that everyone in this country knows who I am, when I have only been here five minutes?"

"First of all, it's not officer. My name is William T. Briddle and I am the sheriff of Coconino County. And it is no accident that I am personally out here on this lonely highway when I should be home in Flagstaff having supper with my wife. I have over forty patrol officers and deputies who could be on this road tonight, but *you* apparently warranted my personal attention."

"I don't understand. I was simply out for an evening drive and I happened to be ....."

"Stow it, Blaine! Your friends have already reported you missing, and when I discovered that you came in on that big bird of yours, and that you are more or less responsible for an air force AC-130 gunship gallivanting all over my airspace with no radio communication, almost colliding with one of my patrol aircraft with not so much as an apology or a beg your pardon, I get a might peeved."

"How could I possibly be responsible for something like that?"

He ignored the question. "Are you carrying?" he inquired casually?

"No," I replied honestly.

"How about stepping out and letting me decide for myself."

The casual tone was an order, not a request, so I opened the door and slowly climbed out.

"Turn around, spread 'em, and put your hands on the hood."

I did as instructed, and waited silently while he briskly and professionally checked for a weapon.

"O.K. You can turn around."

I did so, leaning casually back with my rump on the hood and my arms folded.

"Now. Let's start again. Exactly why are you out here in the middle of nowhere, roaring across my state line at seventy miles an hour, as if you had the devil on your tail?"

"I did!"

"You did what?"

"Have the devil on my tail."

I proceeded to inform him of my recent encounter, leaving out, for now, the part about the gun.

He stared at me suspiciously, then said, "Get back in the Jeep and follow me. Don't get lost again. We need to chat!"

I did as requested, and followed him at a more sedate pace back into Page. He drove across the dam, up the hill, and pulled off into Denny's parking lot. He waited until I had parked beside him, then led me inside the restaurant.

"Evening, sheriff," one of the girls said, beaming at him with a genuine smile of welcome. "Your usual booth?"

"Please, Lou."

He strode over to a window booth with a stunning view of the dam, the canyon below it, and the plateau beyond, still painted with the faint afterglow of a glorious desert sunset. He threw his Smoky Bear hat on the table, dropped into the booth, and pulled a pack of cigarettes from a side pocket of his coat. He offered me one, which I declined with a shake of my head, and lit up.

While he was thus engaged, I took stock of his features. He was about mid-fiftyish, heavy-set, just beginning to show the belly bulge of too much sedentary confinement. He had a strong, square head with short, wiry blond hair. He had the wrinkled, leathered look of long years in the open. He had an easy, infectious grin, which could be very misleading. He was obviously not a man to be trifled with. He had creases around his bright blue eyes, now squinted against the smog his cigarette was producing.

After he had succeeded in almost filling the restaurant with a huge exhalation of smoke, he spoke again.

"Now, what's all this talk about a skin walker?"

"A what?" I replied, puzzled by the term.

"Blaine, this is Navajo and Hopi country. These people have strange rituals and beliefs that defy the generally accepted paradigms of the white man. I have been around here long enough to have witnessed some very bizarre goings-on, some of which I have never been able to fully explain in terms of what we believe to be normal.

"So why don't you tell me exactly what you were doing out there in that back country, and more to the point, exactly what you experienced?"

I sighed and began to enlighten him as to everything that had happened since I first saw the girl in the terminal at the airport. I still prudently left out the part involving the gun.

It took a while. By the time I had finished, he had smoked three cigarettes and gulped down several cups of strong, black coffee which the waitress had brought us immediately we had sat down.

"Blaine, I need to know why you are here, and I don't want any run-around. From what you have told me so far, you have already upset some very powerful folks around here. I have over eighteen and a half thousand square miles in my county, including the Grand Canyon, and a population of only a hundred and thirty-some thousand, which equates to about seven people per square mile. It's a lot of territory to cover – wild and desolate – and I don't want my bailiwick to suddenly be the focal point of murder, mayhem and meddling by federal agents who think they know everything, but have no clue when it comes to local ways and rituals."

As I was about to reply, his radio crackled and a muffled, tinny voice came on to his receiver. "Billy, are you there?"

Obviously annoyed, he grabbed the mike off his shoulder. "I'm here," he growled. "What's up, Floyd?"

"Those people want to know if you found their buddy."

"Tell 'em he's sitting across from me right now, and that I will bring him back to them in a half hour or so. I need to talk to them too, and that includes Bob Hogan. Don't let him leave yet. Are they still in the bar at the Courtyard?"

"That's affirmative, boss."

"Good. Keep 'em there!"

The radio crackled again, but he ignored it.

"O.K. Now, where were we? Oh yeah. You were about to tell me all about how it is that you have apparently flown half way around the world, just to come visit my little town in the outback of Arizona. Right?"

I looked at him again, sizing him up. He could be a valuable ally in the forthcoming fray, especially if what I had just experienced was any indication of what we might be up against.

I took a chance. "Are you a good cop, Sheriff?"

His eyes tightened to narrow slits, barely revealing the bright blue flash of indignation in them. At that moment, I realized that I did not want to be on the wrong side of Sheriff William T. Briddle.

"Blaine, I can think of a hundred reasons to have you thrown in the can. Don't make me use one of 'em!"

Then his tone softened. "It is an elected office. I have been in law enforcement in Arizona for over thirty-seven years, starting from the ground up as a deputy. It runs in the family. My granddaddy was an Arizona Ranger when this was still the Wild West. This is my third term as sheriff of Coconino County. I am not in anyone's pocket, nor they in mine. There is no politician, lobbyist, businessman or self-titled preacher who has his hooks in me. They know I can't be bought! The day I decide I need that kind of money is the day I quit for good, and go to admiring the mountains while rockin' on my back porch. Does that answer your question?"

"Indubitably, as my friend Beyer would say. Thank you!"

"So. Let's start again; at the beginning."

"I think, now that I feel I know you better, Sheriff Briddle…"

"Billy. Now that I know you better, Blaine."

"Mitch," I rejoined. "I think it would be better if we took that ride up the hill to the Courtyard. It would be more beneficial all-around if you heard the whole story from Beyer and Ronnie ….."

"Who is Ronnie?"

"The reason we are here in the first place. It's because of her – actually her husband and her brother, who have both apparently disappeared somewhere in this area – that we ended up here. It's a long, long story and I think it would make more sense if you heard it from her and Beyer, who is very knowledgeable about all matters pertaining to the case."

"Case? You're not meddling in official police business by any chance, are you?"

"I *call* it a case, but actually we're just doing a favor for a friend; a very good and old friend, who needs our help."

"Are you in the habit of doing favors for friends, which just happen to resemble official inquiries? Because that could be broadly interpreted as private investigation without a license – which of course is a misdemeanor in most states, including this one."

I thought about that for a minute. "Like I said Billy, we are simply doing a favor – at great personal expense, I might add – for a friend, who just happens to be very close to me."

"Yeah, *right!'* he replied, not impressed. "But let's get out of here."

He grabbed his hat, left a five dollar bill to cover the coffee and a tip, slipped out of the booth, and waving a general salute to all in the restaurant, stepped outside.

"Follow me up the hill," he barked as he opened the door of his cruiser.

"Sheriff?"

"What?" he said, looking over at me, expectantly.

"I forgot to mention one minor detail. I think I should tell you that I do have a piece."

He grinned. "I know. I was wondering when you'd get around to it."

He dropped heavily into his seat and roared away up the hill, leaving me standing there in the hot desert evening, looking like the idiot that I was.

"Well, I'll be damned," I muttered to myself as I followed him.

He was waiting for me as I pulled into the Courtyard parking lot moments later.

"How did you know?"

"My business to know, Blaine. I'd be a long time dead already if I didn't know stuff like that. Don't you think I've seen that move a hundred times before?"

"What move?"

"That bit about you squirming around in your seat to hide the piece under it, while pretending to dig for your wallet. Don't you think that's the first thing I look for from way back before I even pull in behind a suspect? It's even easier these days, with the camera rolling. If I think I've missed something, I just replay the tape and zoom in."

"Yeah, I'd forgotten big brother is watching us from afar at all times now. Then why did you frisk me?"

"Never know when a suspect has a second, or even a third one hidden on him. There's been many a good cop killed by carelessness like that. Is it licensed?"

"What?"

"You heard me. Is it licensed?"

"Oh. No. Not here anyway. It is where I come from."

"Well, keep it stashed and don't get careless with it – not in my territory anyway. You may need it where you're going, so I'm not going to take it away from you. But I want to see that license – for my own edification."

"What do you mean, 'where I'm going'? How do you know where I am going?"

"I don't. Yet. But I suspect that if what you have already told me is true, your destination lies across the border somewhere in the canyon lands of Utah. That's wild country up there – unknown, uncharted and dangerous. There are stories ……"

"What kind of stories?"

"Let's get inside. I'm officially off duty now that I have found you, and I need a drink!"

"Sounds good to me. I was right in the middle of one when I got sidetracked and almost killed. I know I need one too."

So saying, we stepped into the Courtyard bar, where my friends were still sitting. Despite their fatigue after our long flight, they were anxiously awaiting my return. Hogan had notified his crew back at the airport that he would not be back tonight, and he too was still in the bar.

As it was well on into the evening now, there were several other guests sitting at the bar itself, and at the tables in the bar area and adjoining restaurant.

Ronnie, Beyer and Hogan all got up in unison when they spotted us, and waited for us to join them before they sat down again.

The sheriff and Bob Hogan greeted each other warmly and shook hands like the old friends they obviously were.

Beyer, of course, was the next to speak. "Blaine! Where the hell have you been? You stormed out of here almost five hours ago with a burr under your tail about some imaginary Navajo girl. We had no idea what had happened to you, so when you did not come back, we ....."

"Called out the cavalry," I ended the sentence for him. "And for once, old friend, I am very pleased that you did!"

"You are? I thought you would be abusing me and ranting about my not minding my own business, so forth....."

"Not this time Beyer. I am very glad that Sheriff Briddle took it upon himself to personally ascertain my whereabouts. Or I may not be here to tell the tale."

Briddle scowled at me as we sat down. Then, not to be sidetracked, he said sharply, "Now, will somebody *please* order me a tall, cold beer and then tell me the *hell* what you people are doing here, and why you have managed to single-handedly demolish the peace and quiet of my county within just a few hours of your very dramatic arrival – not to mention provoking the wrath of the locals – to the point of apparently invoking their particular form of very potent witchcraft to try to scare you off!"

They all stared accusingly at me. Beyer looked from me to the sheriff and back again.

"Blaine?"

Before I could defend myself, Sheriff Briddle answered for me.

"He seems to have had an encounter with a Navajo skin walker," he replied casually.

It was apparent from their shocked reaction that everybody except me knew what the term meant.

"Skin walker? Oh my..... *Skin walker?*" Beyer repeated, unable to believe what he was hearing. "Do you have any idea, Blaine, what you have done?"

He could tell by my vacant expression that I had no clue.

"No, apparently not!"

Before I could reply, Beyer spoke to the sheriff. "Do you mind if I ask Blaine a couple of questions? It might have a very important bearing on the situation."

The sheriff huffed and sighed, and said, "Oh all right. Go ahead! It's not as if I have anything else to do tonight. Actually, it might help me – to see if he can tell his story exactly the same way twice!"

"Well Blaine, what in heaven's name have you gotten us into now?" Beyer inquired with acerbity.

So I told him, as briefly as possible, but without leaving out any important details, what I had encountered in the desert. This time, I did not omit the part about shooting at the creature.

They all waited in stunned silence and utter astonishment until I had finished.

Beyer scratched his massive, bewhiskered jaw and, ignoring the sheriff's attempt at interjection, launched into one of his inimitable discourses.

"Hmmm. A skin walker is a *very* powerful medicine man. Now let me see," he mused. "In the religious and cultural lore of Southwestern tribes, there are entities who can alter their shapes at will to assume the characteristics of certain animals. Most of the world's cultures have their own shape shifter legends.

"The Navajo, Hopi, Utes, and other tribes each have their own version of the skin walker story. Basically they boil down to the same thing – a malevolent witch capable of transforming itself into a wolf, coyote, bear, bird, or any other animal. The witch might wear the hide or skin of the animal identity it wants to assume, and when the transformation is complete, the human witch inherits the speed, strength, or cunning of the animal whose shape it has taken.

"Skin walkers are very strong. They can run faster than a car and can jump high cliffs without any effort at all. These creatures are purely evil in intent. I am no expert on it, but the general view is that skin walkers do all sorts of terrible things; they make people sick, they commit murders. They are horrific and evil beings who must kill a sibling or other relative to be initiated as a skin walker. They supposedly can turn themselves into were-animals and travel in supernatural ways.

"At night, their eyes glow red like hot coals. It is said that if you see the face of a skin walker, he has to kill you. However, if you see one and recognize who it is, *he* will die. Although they are generally believed to prey only on Native Americans, there are reports from Anglos claiming they have encountered skin walkers while driving on or near tribal lands."

Beyer interrupted his own monologue and looked questioningly at Briddle.

"I believe that one Arizona Highway Patrol officer is reported to have said that while patrolling a stretch of highway south of Kayenta, he had two separate encounters with a ghastly creature that seemingly attached itself to the door of his vehicle. But then to his horror, he realized that the ghoulish thing wasn't attached to his door after all. Instead, he said, it was running alongside his vehicle as he cruised down the highway at a high rate of speed...."

"That is *exactly* what happened to me," I interjected, overcome with a renewed feeling of apprehension as I recalled my recent terrifying experience.

"I also know I was led into a trap. Whoever was driving that van knew I would follow, and that I would be forced into that dead-end ravine. What happened to the van, I have no idea."

"But why, Blaine? Why you? And what about the girl? Are you saying that she is in fact the skin walker herself, or that the creature was in some way protecting her?"

"No. There were other *things* there that she said were her 'protectors'. I didn't see them, but I did hear and smell them. She came across as being apprehensive, despite her so-called protectors – whatever they were. As for her *being* the creature, I don't know about that. All I know is that about the same time she vanished, the thing appeared in my rear-view mirror, and the next thing I knew, it was running along beside me at sixty plus miles an hour!

"But the girl seemed very, very afraid that we would discover where she came from and that we would somehow destroy her world. In fact, she implied that we had *already* destroyed it with what she called the big water. I have no idea what she was talking about."

17

"Big Water?" he repeated.

He thought for a moment, then exclaimed, "Of course! The lake! Whatever she was talking about has been inundated by hundreds of feet of water backed up behind the dam, not to mention dozens of feet of silt and muck on the bottom. The environmentalists and archeologists have been complaining since the dam was completed in nineteen sixty three about all the cultural history of the Anasazi in Glen Canyon that was lost by the backing up of Lake Powell."

"Anasazi? You mean to tell me you think ….? But they've been gone for hundreds of years. How could she be …?"

"I don't *know* Blaine! And as a matter of fact, *Anasazi* is not their real name. Modern Pueblo people dislike the term, which they consider an ethnic slur. It is actually a Navajo word which means ancient enemy, foreigner, or outsider – although it has been in common use for about seventy years.

"But what I *do* know is that we have to get out there post haste. Pronto. Immediately! I suspect we are on the verge of discovering something bigger than any of us could have possibly imagined."

Now the sheriff spoke again – this time with authority and official demeanor.

"Nobody is going the hell *anywhere* until *somebody* explains to me why you are here in the first place!"

"I am so sorry, Sheriff Briddle," Beyer cajoled in his most placatory style. "In the excitement of the evening's revelations, I forgot you were patiently awaiting an explanation of our arrival in your territory. Please forgive us, and allow me to explain."

So saying, he launched into a classic Beyer soliloquy, with necessary diversions, as to exactly what had brought us into Sheriff Billy Briddle's life at this particular moment in time.

Ronnie, Hogan, Briddle and I remained silent during this monologue.

It took a while. The bartender was calling for last rounds by the time he had finished.

Hogan was the first to speak when Beyer finally wound down.

"I wouldn't be in *too* much of a hurry to get out there, if I was you," he allowed. "Stranger things than what happened to you, Mitch, have been reported up in that Utah canyon country. I can't speak for the sheriff here, but my pilots occasionally come back from scenic flights up that way with stories of weird phenomena. Personally, I have never seen anything, but....."

"What kind of phenomena, Bob? After what just happened to me, I wouldn't be much surprised by anything. But I do have to admit to you all that I was scared back there; scared straight! I encountered something out of my control – something totally foreign to my experience – and I didn't like it at all!"

Hogan looked askance at the sheriff and shrugged his shoulders.

Then Sheriff Briddle chipped in. "Like I started to tell you before, Blaine. There are stories about that country up around the San Juan and Escalante River canyons. You have seen the Wahweap and Antelope marinas from the air. So you know that there are thousands of boats out there. At any given moment, there are dozens of 'em scattered over an area of hundreds of square miles of lake.

"Most of them are rentals, operated by amateurs. Some of them – the high dollar ones – are owned and operated by wealthy, flamboyant out-of-towners, who don't know a thing about boats. But it doesn't seem to matter what kind of boat, or who is running it. Every now and then, one disappears with all hands. And it doesn't have to be a houseboat either. Sometimes, it's just a ski-boat or even a jet-ski.

"But even with all the search and rescue manpower I have available in my department and that of my counterparts in Utah – not to mention the BLM and the NPS – we still can't find any trace of boats reported missing in some of those canyons. No wreckage, no bodies, no radio calls or sightings – nothing! I mean, no trace! We have searched by air and water. We have sent down divers at the last reported locations. Again, nothing! It's as if those vessels just disappeared off the face of the earth!"

Recalling Beyer's dissertation about the Navajo and Hopi stories of other worlds, I was again overwhelmed by that feeling of morose uneasiness that was becoming very familiar lately. What the hell was I afraid of? I had *never* felt this way. Why now? What *was* it out there – apart from my recent encounter with an entity the like of which I had never even heard of – that was striking such abject terror into my very bones?

"There's something else," Briddle added, looking at Hogan. "I have never mentioned this to you before, Bob, because as you know, my aircraft are based in Flagstaff and not here at Page. But a couple of my pilots have reported similar incidents as you describe, while on those very search and rescue missions up there in the same area. In clear conditions, no weather, they reported strange sensations of spatial disorientation, loss of situational awareness, feelings of anxiety.

"They said the country suddenly looked strange – whatever that means – and that they almost got lost when they were flying low over the water on their search patterns because sometimes the canyons seemed to close in on them, as if they had unwittingly flown into a dead end. Even when they reversed course and climbed higher, the walls of the canyon behind them appeared to have changed their contour so that it seemed there was no way out! Then, all of a sudden, they were above the rim again."

I looked at Beyer. He shook his head slightly, as if reading my thoughts. He had not mentioned, in his lengthy summary of our mission, his little discourse on the story of the Navajo and Hopi creation.

"What?" Briddle asked, looking from Beyer to me and back again. He did not miss a thing. I was beginning to like this man.

"I take it sheriff," Beyer said, "that since you have lived in this area your whole life, you have heard the Navajo and Hopi creation myths? Those referring to emergence from 'other worlds'?"

"Of course! Who hasn't? What of it?"

"What if there is something to it? What if the experiences of your pilots bear out such stories? And what about the disappearances you speak of? People and vessels just don't vanish into thin air. Is it possible that there is some kind of portal or gateway up there – perhaps even more than one – into another world of which we have no knowledge? After all, this whole adventure began with the vanishing of Ronnie's husband and brother through an apparently similar doorway."

"But what has something that happened fifteen hundred miles away in Texas got to do with what's going on out here?" Briddle asked thoughtfully.

"We were wondering the same thing ourselves – until I discovered that the strange mark on the dead guard in that tunnel in Texas had only one computer match; that of an apparently unmapped side canyon up in the Escalante River!"

The sheriff remained silent and thoughtful for a moment, then said, "That's wild and for the most part, still unexplored country up there. Oh, there have been plenty of tourists in the more easily accessible canyons and surrounding area. There's a plethora of photographs posted on line to prove it! But there are still many places they can't get to by boat or vehicle, and that even the Navajo and Hopi shy clear of, because of ancient fears and myths about them! There's a literal maze of mesas, canyons, washes, ravines that you couldn't get to in a lifetime of exploration. In fact, up in Canyonlands, there is an area actually called The Maze, and it is still relatively unexplored, even today.

"I know the sheriff of Kane County, in which most of the area you speak of is located. He's a good man, but he is limited in what he can do. His county is not as big as mine, area-wise, but it might as well be. It's almost four thousand square miles, with an estimated population of only about five thousand. He has a smaller department, and he is based hundreds of miles away in Kanab on the west side of the county. And I know that he would not like anyone meddling in what could be considered official police business any more than I would.

"However, because of the circumstances – and the fact that you lot seem to be more or less professionals – and you have the means and the capability to get out there, I am not going to inform him of your mission – yet! I am going to give you two days. If I don't hear from you by then, I'm coming looking for you – with manpower from every local and state department I can muster! I'll leave the feds out. Like I said, I have no time for meddling bureaucrats!"

"Sheriff, you are a true professional yourself. We appreciate your understanding and your acquiescence," Beyer replied, in his most conciliatory tone.

"Don't suck up to me Beyer! Like I told Blaine here, I can't be bought and I can't be fooled. I am only doing this because it happens to be in somebody else's bailiwick – not mine! Two days! Forty-eight hours. Then I inform Sheriff Smith that I suspect there are some strange goings-on in his territory, and I will be happy to co-operate with him in any way I can to get to the bottom of it. Now. I don't know about you lot, but I have to get to bed. I do have other duties to attend to besides playing nursemaid to a bunch of aviation adventurers out to get themselves killed."

"You're not driving all the way back to Flagstaff tonight, are you Billy?" Hogan inquired. "You are welcome to stay with me and Alice, you know."

"Thanks for the thought, Bob. But I am bunking in with one of my deputies tonight. I'll head back south in the morning. Don't want to run into one of Blaine's zombies in the middle of nowhere," he added, winking at me.

"Don't even joke about that Billy," I responded. "I'm rattled enough about what happened to me, and I usually don't scare that easily."

"I can tell. I will be looking into that too. I am going to ask a few questions around town. I know a lot of the locals and their customs. I've never been invited to any of their special ceremonies, because I am a 'bilaganna' and I *am* the law, but I've given them no reason not to trust me. I don't make a habit of arresting or bothering people just because they are Navajo or Hopi. After all, it *is* their land – not ours! And I have instructed my officers likewise. I hear of anyone in my department who goes around intimidating or bullying *anybody* just because they are 'Dine', they are out of a job – with no references. Pronto!"

With that, Sheriff Billy Briddle got up, retrieved and donned his hat, shook hands all round, and bid us good evening.

As he ambled out into the night, Beyer commented, "He's a good man. And a good man to have on our side. I feel a whole lot better about what we are getting into, knowing he is aware of our plans."

"Yeah. Me too. Well, I have definitely had enough excitement for one night. I suspect we have another long day tomorrow, so I suggest we all hit the sack."

I turned to Hogan and said, "Thanks for your help, Bob. I am sure that the sheriff's knowing you as he does, and trusting you, helped allay his fears about us and our intentions. We're grateful to you!"

"No problem Mitch. I'll be getting along. But you take care, hear. I wasn't kidding about that country up yonder. I don't want to have to send up a search party for you, and maybe lose one or two of my pilots as well. Your bird will be ready to go in the morning. Give me a call when you're up, and I'll come get you. You can buy me breakfast!"

"It's a deal. I'll give you a buzz as soon as I wake. Despite the fact that I am exhausted, I doubt I will be able to sleep well tonight."

With that, we all arose, said goodnight, and headed to our rooms as Hogan departed. We had adjoining rooms on the ground floor, just down the hall from the bar. Beyer, for once short on words, bid us a hasty "See you two in the morning. Sleep tight. I suspect we may have a long day. But I must tell you, Mitch, I have a bad feeling about this."

"Don't worry old friend," I reassured him. "We have always come out of these scrapes relatively unscathed – so far."

"This is different. There is something about this venture that doesn't smell right. I can't put my finger on it, but …. Oh well, goodnight all."

With that, he turned and locked himself in his room.

"Well Ronnie, what about you? What about…..us?"

She gave me that tender look I had become so fond of and, stretching up, brushed my lips with hers and whispered in my ear, "Not tonight, darling. I agree with Beyer. I am afraid. Very afraid that something unnatural is going on here. I'm not sure if I will be able to sleep, but I want to be alone for a little bit – to think. Do you understand, Mitch?"

"Not really. But my adjoining door will be unlocked. If you get scared in the night, I'm only a few feet away."

"Thanks Mitch. I.…I don't know how to feel right now. Things are so different from what I expected. And as we get closer to the end, I become more afraid. I don't understand myself."

I took her in my arms and held her tight, the natural, musky scent of her arousing me despite my fatigue.

"It's O.K., baby. Tomorrow we'll find out what's waiting for us around the bend. I'll see you in the morning," I said, afraid to share with her what was really on my mind.

18

Alone in my king size bed, in a clammy nightmare of fear, torment and monstrous beings in hot pursuit, I awoke with a start, to stare into the red, glowing eyes of that hideous creature hovering over me. Terrified out of my wits, I grabbed for the Ruger under my pillow, turned and was about to fire when I realized that I was still coming up out of the dream.

I forced myself awake, aware that I was drenched in sweat, and that the area of sheet where I had been lying was similarly soaked! I sat there for a moment, shaking off that awful vision, and peering around the dark room, fearful that the creature was still lurking there.

Glancing at the bedside clock, I noted that it was just after five in the morning. Ruger still in hand, I stumbled out of bed, padded silently over to the connecting door to Ronnie's room, quietly opened it and checked on her. I could just barely make out her shapely silhouette framed in a faint glow from the outside pool lights, filtering through a crack between the heavy drapes

She was snoring softly, and seemed to be suffering from no such hallucinations as I had just experienced. But as I gently closed the adjoining door, I carried an uneasy after-image of something – some shadowy substance – flickering swiftly away from the space between the drapes.

What the *hell* was wrong with me? I could not remember a time in my life up until this moment when I had been so afraid. But afraid of what? I had faced the fear of aerial battle, the fear of being ensnared in strange and bizarre rituals in foreign lands from Africa to the Caribbean, the fear of flying in weather so bad it could rip an aircraft apart, and – up until this moment – my greatest fear of all; that of personal combat with a knife. *Nothing* scared the hell out of me as much as facing a proficient combatant handy with a blade! So what *was* it about this particular mission that was causing such angst to penetrate to the very core of my being?

Like Beyer had said, *something* really stank about this affair. But what? On the face of it, apart from a couple of odd occurrences, it seemed to be a routine job to find two missing airmen, who just happened to be related to the girl in the next room, except for the minor detail, of course, that we seemed to be involved in something of a supernatural nature; from the so-called portals, to the skin walker, to the Navajo girl who claimed to be from 'another place'.

Well, the hell with it! I needed some fresh air in my lungs, and I needed to think.

I stepped back into my room, pulled on a pair of shorts, running shoes and an old tee shirt. Still reluctant to let go of the comfort of the Ruger, I stuck it in its belly holster, jammed it inside my shorts and headed out the door. Striding through the empty lobby, I went out through the front door and began running along the same route I had previously taken in the Jeep, hoping I would not again see the gray van or the creature of my nightmares.

I ran a good couple of miles around the block. Thankful for the fact that it seemed I was the only one up and about this early, I stopped, chest heaving, lungs and legs aching from the uncommon exercise, to watch the sun come up over bleak, barren ridges and climb over Tower Butte, turning the stark desert landscape from deep purple to vermillion fire, and raising the temperature twenty degrees in a matter of minutes. This awesome spectacle took my mind of my recent nightmare and reminded me of the beauty in the world that I was so fond of admiring every day. I prayed I would live to relish a few more of these wonderful days of life, before my luck finally ran out!

Walking briskly back to the hotel, I returned to my room, showered and changed into my grimy old flight suit, and went into the dining room. I entered just in time to join Beyer, Ronnie and Hogan, who had already arrived to take us to the airport, sitting down to breakfast.

With his customary effusive greeting Beyer bellowed, "Oho, the sleeping beauty was not sleeping at all! How long have you been up, old chap?"

"I don't know. All night it seems. I had a terrible nightmare."

"Oh? What kind of nightmare?" Beyer inquired, chomping on a piece of toast.

I slumped into a chair next to Ronnie and poured myself a large mug of coffee.

"My friend from yesterday was back. I was tossing and turning and then I remember waking sometime after five, soaked in sweat, and looking up into those terrible, glowing red coals hovering a couple of feet above my face. I didn't see anything else – except those awful red eyes. I grabbed my gun and was about to shoot, when I realized that it was just a horrible dream."

Glancing at Ronnie, I noticed she had a strange expression on her face. She had just picked up her cup to pour herself some coffee. She dropped the cup, stared at me, and said, "Oh my ….!

She stopped speaking and sat there swallowing, with her mouth opening and closing like a beached fish.

"What's the matter, mate?" I asked, staring at her.

"I ….. I had … the same dream!" she stammered. "I woke up terrified. I tried to scream, but no sound came out. It seemed like I was somehow frozen."

"*What?*" we all cried in unison.

A chill ran all the way down and up my spine, when I recalled the momentary, darting, flickering shadow I had glimpsed as I opened Ronnie's door.

It had *not* been a dream. The thing had actually *been* in there, and I had *left* it with her!

"Are you sure?" I asked her, as that primal fear rose in me again.

"Yes," she replied, unable to say more.

The others simply sat and stared bug-eyed at both of us. "That does it! Let's eat up and get out of here. Whatever that thing is, it's either trying to scare the hell out of both of us, or it's trying to kill us – or both. Either way, it's not going to get the better of me! If it shows up anywhere near where we're headed, I am going to put it out of its misery, once and for all!

"Oh Mitch. I….. I'm having second thoughts about all this. Do you think we should go on? I have a dreadful feeling that something really, really bad is going to happen ….."

"Rubbish, my child," Beyer interjected consolingly, patting her gently on the shoulder. 'Tis a lovely morning, as anyone can see, and a beautiful day for flying up the river and into the unknown. We shall break our fast and be on our way, what?"

"I suppose so," she replied reluctantly.

Hogan spoke up and, obviously attempting to dispel the gloom that had settled on us, said "Your bird is fueled and ready to go, Mitch. I had a good look over her myself. Everything seems to be shipshape, and my chief line guy stayed with her personally all night as requested."

"Thanks Bob. I appreciate it. That's one load off my mind. Any sign of our mysterious AC-130 lately?"

"No. He seems to have disappeared off the radar, so to speak. Not that we have any radar around here, for hundreds of miles."

"Good. Let's finish up here. Even though we have plenty of food on board," I said, looking questioningly at Beyer, "we may not get a chance to eat again for a while."

He answered my question with a nod, so we tried to allay the foreboding we all no doubt felt, and got on with a more or less silent breakfast.

Thirty minutes later we were in Hogan's truck again, heading back out to the airport. Unlike yesterday, however, the mood was much more somber, and Hogan had hardly a word to say in the seven or eight minute drive. He drove us right up to the '*Wayward Wind*', where we piled out and began our pre-flight duties.

"Ronnie, you hop up inside and start the cockpit check."

She acknowledged with a grin and a cursory salute. Now that she was back in her element, she was rapidly cheering up.

"I'll walk around her and make sure everything is O.K. Beyer, you …."

"I know, I know. Start the mundane chore of loading all our appurtenances, and checking our supplies. One of these days, Blaine, I am going to insist on your engaging the services of an actual, professional loadmaster for these missions!"

"Whine, whine, whine," I retorted as I began my external pre-flight. "Then you would be complaining that you had nothing to do."

Hogan went inside the FBO to catch up with his pilots, most of whom had been hovering wistfully around the PBY, and organize their daily routine as we prepared the bird for flight. About twenty minutes later, we were all buttoned up and ready to go. When Bob came back out to the aircraft, I thanked him for his help and we said our goodbyes.

"You be careful up there, Mitch. Keep in touch. I doubt if you will have a cell phone signal out there in the boonies, and you will probably be out of VHF range, but I'll be listening on the CTAF frequency if you need any help. I will brief my pilots to do the same when they are up. I'll call Briddle pronto if you need back-up."

"You *do* that. He's a good man, and a good cop. I could use him. Thanks again Bob. See you in a day or two – I hope!"

So saying, I swung up into the bird, closed and locked the blister, and made my way forward to the sweltering cockpit. Beyer was already up front, securing the galley and making sure we had everything we needed for an extended stay.....wherever we ended up.

I slid with practiced ease into the left seat, strapped myself in, reached sideways, gave Ronnie a quick, surreptitious kiss on her left cheek, and said, "O.K., baby. Let's get this show on the road. We have a dragon or three to slay."

She flashed me that brilliant white smile, returned the kiss, and said, "All right, Mitch. Whatever lies ahead, I trust you implicitly."

We ran our pre-start checks, cleared the area with Bob, who was waiting below, and cranked the old Pratts grudgingly back into life.

As we trundled out on to Runway 33, Ronnie made the radio call on the common traffic advisory frequency and Beyer squeezed himself on to the jump seat between us and said, "Where is that infernal GPS?"

"What?" I retorted. "After almost ten thousand miles of Pacific crossing, *now* you want the GPS?"

"Only way to find our elusive location, old boy. As I mentioned before, the place in question has only one computer match, whose co-ordinates I have carefully studied. If I am correct, it is only about forty miles from here, as the crow flies. But as the '*Wayward Wind*' flies, that is, up-lake to the Escalante River arm, it will be a trifle longer – about fifty-five miles."

"And why, pray tell, do we have to fly up-lake, instead of directly?" I inquired.

"For one thing, old rope, to throw of anyone who might be shadowing us," he said, pointing skyward, "and for another, there are so many canyons, ravines and grottos up there, and so many of them look alike, that we will have to fly up river at about a thousand feet above the rim, to get an accurate look at the lay of the land. We need to check out places near our destination where we can put this bird in the water. There appears to be no place long enough or smooth enough – apart from a couple of rough looking mesa tops – to try to put her down on the ground. And we surely don't want to take a chance on breaking anything. We will be another one of Briddle's riddles if we get stuck up there!"

"Very funny," I replied. "However, as Ronnie just stated, I will trust your judgment implicitly, Beyer. Let's go!"

So saying, I eased the throttles up to take-off power, the engines bellowed in response, and we were rolling. The bulbous snout of the '*Wayward Wind*' sniffed the hot breeze, eager to be back in her element. She was heavily laden with fuel, but she gained speed quickly and four thousand feet of runway later, we were airborne.

I banked her sharply northeast over Antelope Island and set heading up the lake at a thousand feet, as Beyer had requested. The ground elevation above sea level in this area was roughly four thousand feet, and we were flying at five, which gave us ample view of the lake and its contours as it wound its serpentine way up towards the junction of the Colorado and Green Rivers, about a hundred and twenty miles further north.

The scenery was spectacular, of course, and it momentarily took our minds off the importance and danger of our mission; red rock, deep blue lake, boundless cerulean sky punctuated here and there with puffy cotton wool cumulus drifting east on a light breeze. I gazed down in awe at the unbounded expanse of the Kaiparowits Plateau, again reminded of my previous visits to this strange, enchanted land. Nowhere on earth did I feel more at home – except for the great Outback of my own country – so similar to that over which I was flying right now.

A thousand feet below, dozens of houseboats plied up and down the main waterway. It was late October, and most of the tourists had gone home for the fall and winter. Still, there were enough boats, jet skis and other assorted water toys to create wakes which reflected a thousand points of lights off the sparkling blue water, blinding us in their glare. Other houseboats were moored in the many bays or nudged up on the countless pink, sandy beaches formed by the waters of the Colorado River as it backed up behind Glen Canyon Dam.

I pulled the power all the way back to cruise at a minimal ninety-five knots, so as to get a better view and a clearer picture of the scenery below. I had an aviation VFR sectional chart on my lap. I wanted to be very sure about my position at every moment along this short journey. Beyer had pre-programmed the GPS so that it counted down the distance, latitude and longitude to our destination.

Rainbow Bridge and Navajo Mountain, most sacred of sights to the Dine`, drifted past us on the right. Then, also on the right, came the San Juan River arm of the lake.

A few miles further on and we came to the junction of the Colorado and the Escalante. Somewhere up ahead in that wild and broken country, an unknown evil lurked; the Escalante Enigma.

As we turned northwest to follow the winding upper reaches of the river, Beyer became more and more excited, hopping around on his seat and pointing at every rock outcrop, ravine, mesa and arch that could possibly lead us to our elusive destination.

"Not far to go now," he shouted in my ear over the din of the engines. "On the left – there! Fifty Mile Canyon. That should lead us into the spot we're looking for. It's an unmarked side canyon up in there somewhere. You'll have to go down, Mitch! Drop to five hundred above the rim, turn left up the main arm and we should be on top of it. We can orbit around until the GPS says we're right overhead, then we can spiral down into it."

"If it's wide enough and long enough," I added helpfully.

"Precisely."

I did as he requested, easing the 'Wayward Wind' down to five hundred feet over the plateau. I spiraled us around, inching lower and lower, checking out the walls of the canyon. As I did so, I took note of the surrounding terrain above the rim. We seemed to be dropping into a deep depression, reminiscent of a meteor crater. It was about a half mile across, and in the middle of the crater there was a low mesa, bare on top except for what looked like some odd rows in the earth, parallel to the length of the mesa.

I had no time for further observation. Suddenly, the GPS started bleeping madly, accompanied by Beyer's clamorous yelling, "There, there, down there!"

I squinted into the glare where he was pointing, and spied a narrow side canyon, almost indiscernible from the air. My professional aviator's eye immediately began measuring width, length and height of the rock walls, judging distance for landing in and getting out of the slot. It seemed like there was plenty of room for my wing span, but I could not be sure about the distance for landing and takeoff. Like many of the others, this one was no different in that it turned almost ninety degrees on itself in places.

Pulling the power back almost to idle, I let her down below the rim, lining up on the longest stretch I could find in that narrowing defile. As I did so, I had the strange sensation that the walls of the thing were closing in on me. I uneasily remembered experiencing that very same feeling as I had been lured into that box canyon in the Jeep! But it was too late now. We were committed.

The chasm up ahead was indeed becoming more confined, and there was no room for a go around. If I tried to climb out from this point, as heavy as we were, we would be unable to turn, and we would plow straight into the sheer cliff ahead, where the river curved back on itself.

The perpendicular walls now towered above me.

"Ronnie," I shouted, "Floats down. Props and mixtures full forward! Be on the lookout for rocks, debris or sandbars in the water. We'll only get one shot at this!"

"Roger, Mitch. I'm on it!" she replied, hitting the float switch.

I eased the nose up a hair and pulled the throttles all the way off. Moments later, we were gliding on to the calm, blue water of the lake. The hull kissed the surface with a familiar, satisfying hiss. I pulled the yoke all the way back into my belly, the nose came up, and she settled into the water. For a moment, we sat there gently rolling in our own wake. Then I cracked the throttles a half inch or so, and we were drifting forward into the constricted gorge.

I wiped the sweat off my brow. Ronnie sat there gazing around at the red rock cliffs surrounding us. Beyer jumped excitedly off his perch, opened the overhead hatch and squeezed his bulk up through it to sit on the canopy roof with his legs dangling down in my face.

Except for the now muted clatter of the engines at idle power, there was no sound. A hushed, ominous stillness seemed to pervade the very essence of the place. As we taxied slowly up-river into the increasingly restrictive gorge, the heat became almost intolerable. Yet, the air itself was clearer, sharper, than it was before we had descended into the canyon. I shaded my eyes and stared up past the vertical red walls. The sky appeared to be darker than the bright azure I was accustomed to, and the sun, now almost directly overhead, seemed to be whiter, hotter, than I ever remembered.

Beyer began kicking my right shoulder with his huge, bare, dangling feet. Irritated, I looked up at him through the overhead canopy. He was gesticulating wildly at the rock wall only a few feet off our left wing. My eyes followed his jabbing, pointing finger. For a few moments, I could not see what he was so excited about. Then I spotted it. Far above, in an alcove below an overhang jutting out from the rim, were the unmistakable remains of a cliff dwelling – a big one! The stone walls were crumbling, the years of abandoned neglect and decay plainly evident, but still, it was an impressive sight.

I pointed it out to Ronnie, whose gaze followed mine. She became very excited. "Can I get up on top with Beyer?" she pleaded.

"Sure. Go ahead. Let me know if you spot any more of them."

"I already did. Look!" she exclaimed.

I now squinted up to where she was pointing, and sure enough, there were more ruins below the rim, just before the bend in the river up ahead.

How did they do it, I wondered. How did an ancient people, working with only primitive tools, manage to quarry and carve those bricks, and somehow hoist them up almost vertical cliffs? And how did they then form them into veritable miniature cities on slender ledges barely long enough or wide enough to support such incredible architecture?

My thoughts were rudely interrupted by Beyer's frantic yelling.

"Blaine! We're there. Round that next bend up ahead, and we should be there."

I acknowledge with a raised thumb and pulled the throttles all the way off, preparing to shut the engines down and drift silently in to wherever we were going.

Beyer dropped back down into the cockpit and stooped over my shoulder, glancing from the GPS in his hand to the view through the windshield.

Then, while he was staring at the magic box, he muttered, "That's odd."

"What's odd?" I inquired, still concentrating my gaze on the towering cliffs above.

"The GPS. It seems to have lost its signal. A moment ago, it was pointing us directly to the bend in the river ahead, and now it is dead. No bearings at all."

"Probably no satellites overhead this canyon right now," I opined.

"You're right," he replied calmly. But his next comment chilled me, despite the oppressive heat. "No satellites. None at all. This unit is telling me there are no satellites to detect!"

"What? That's impossible. There are – how many? Thirty-two of the damn things? There are *always* at least a couple overhead any given position on the earth at any given time, aren't there?"

"Absolutely correct, old rope. But that is not what this device is saying. It is indicating that there *are no satellites in the sky - period!*"

"What?" I repeated, stupefied by the implication.

"There is something else," he added.

"Don't tell me."

"This unit, unless it is completely on the blink, is indicating no history – no record of there ever being anything to track, and our present and previous positions are not even in its memory!"

"Oh great! Don't tell me we have just drifted into the Twilight Zone."

"I am afraid," he replied reluctantly, "that for all intents and purposes, old boy, that is *exactly* what has happened."

Not wanting to believe him, I sat silently, squinting ahead at the rapidly approaching bend in the river, trying to guesstimate whether the width of the canyon walls was sufficient to allow my wingspan around the curve. Ronnie, unaware of Beyer's latest revelation, sat happily on the canopy above, searching for more ruins.

Then it was too late. There was no room to turn around, and the bend was upon us. I tugged again at the throttles, vainly trying to reduce the taxi speed even further. But unless I actually shut down the engines, I could go no slower.

I eased in left rudder, along with some right aileron, forcing the right float on to the water to prevent the left one from going under and pivoting the nose of the plane around into the left cliff face. I could not see the wing tips from my seat in the cockpit, so I yelled up to Ronnie, "How's it look? Are the tips going to clear?"

"I think so. Just barely. If the floats were up, I don't think we'd make it."

"Terrific!" I muttered to myself.

Then we were around the bend, coasting into a wide bay about two miles long, with a sheer rock wall on the right, and a broad, pink sandy beach on the left. The beach was a couple of hundred feet long and about half as wide, sloping back until it ended abruptly at the foot of the left cliff face.

As we coasted into the beach I stared with awe, mouth agape, comprehending at last part of the answer to the enigma.

Ronnie was shouting from the canopy above. "Mitch? Beyer? Do you see them?"

"We see 'em," I called back, stunned by the spectacle before me.

19

High and dry along the beach were the rotting, rusting hulks of at least a dozen houseboats, plus a score or more of other assorted small craft. I could tell at first glance that, judging by the style and state of disrepair, some of the boats were very old – fifty or more years – and others were – or had been – almost new when they were 'lost'.

I looked up at Beyer, who was similarly dumbfounded by the sight.

"Well," he said, sighing deeply, "at least now we know where all the missing vessels ended up."

"But how?"

"I suspect we are about to find out, old horse. Let's beach the *'Wayward Wind'*, get her secured, and go exploring. I believe the answer not only to the riddle of our missing airmen, but also to that of all these boats that were thought to have disappeared into thin air, is about to present itself."

"Ronnie," I shouted, "come on down from there. We're going to beach and secure the plane. I'll need you on the rudders while Beyer and I swing her round."

"O.K., I'm coming down."

So saying, she leapt down into her seat. "What do you want me to do, Mitch?" she asked, scowling as she stared at the sight on the beach.

"Just stand by on the rudders. I'm going to turn her parallel to the beach as we get close in. We're going to jump out, swing her tail around, and secure her with her nose pointing out into the bay – just in case."

"In case what?"

"In case we have to get out of here in a hurry!"

"That's what I thought," she replied. "Well, we're here now. Let's get on with it," she added matter-of-factly.

"That's my girl!"

As we coasted into shallow water, I pulled the mixtures, snapped off the magnetos, and using the last of her momentum, swung the plane to the right.

"Full right rudder, now!"

She complied immediately. As she did so, I squirmed out of my seat and doubled back through the fuselage to join Beyer, who was standing by in the left blister with lines and anchors. He had already heaved two of the anchors out the right blister, and they were wedged in the sand.

I doffed my old boat shoes, we jumped over the side, and I dived around behind the pivoting tail to secure the right anchors more firmly at the forty-five and thirty degree angles, while Beyer did the same with the left. We tugged simultaneously as the longitudinal axis of the aircraft came at right angles to the shore, and then she was fast, her tail firmly wedged on the beach.

I wiped my sweating brow with a sand-covered forearm.

"Good work, old friend," I said to Beyer, unable to avert my eyes from the derelicts on the beach behind him.

"Well, let's get Ronnie out of there and go take a look," he said, reading my thoughts. "Obviously, part of the mystery lies down there with those boats."

"Before we go anywhere, let me go back aboard and get a little protection."

"Oh don't be so theatrical, Blaine. It is broad daylight, high noon, and those vessels have plainly been abandoned for a very long time. And there's not a boogeyman in sight," he added sarcastically.

"Humor me," I replied, wading out the few feet to the left blister again.

I climbed aboard as Ronnie was coming back through the plane. I grasped her waist, pulled her into me, hugged her tightly, and gave her a long, tender kiss.

"What was that for?" she asked when I let her breath again.

"Let's just say we might not get another chance, and I want you to know how I feel – always!"

"I already know, Mitch. And I feel the same way. But ….let's go find those dragons, shall we?"

"Yes, ma'am. But let me go get something to slay them with," I responded, ducking through the cockpit and into the forward locker compartment. I shoved aside some anchor chain, pulled on a ring, and yanked up an almost invisible hatch cover.

The double hull behind the nose gear well was dry, and the long metal ammo box was still secured safely in place on the port bulkhead. A thick rubber gasket around the upper rim kept it free from moisture. I opened the lid, reached in, and pulled out the forty-four magnum Winchester carbine and the Browning Maxus twelve gauge power action shotgun. The Ruger Red Hawk was now in its holster under my left armpit.

I did not bother to take extra shells. If Blaine's Last Stand took more than what was already loaded, it couldn't be done.

Crawling out of the locker, I hurried back through the aircraft and joined Ronnie and Beyer on the beach. I tossed the shotgun to Beyer remarking flippantly, "I know how you hate these things Beyer, and I also know what a lousy shot you are, so you'd better take the shotgun, as usual."

He reached and caught it mid-air, with a feigned lack of dexterity. I knew from previous experience that he knew how to use it if he had to, however damned reluctantly!

"Ronnie, do you know how to use a rifle or a hand-gun?"

"Yes, but ….."

"Take the rifle. I'll keep the Ruger – for now!"

"Mitch, you're scaring me. What are you expecting to find down there?"

"I don't know. But somehow I have a feeling it's not going to be pretty."

We put our shoes back on and began trudging down the beach toward the wrecks. I didn't know how Beyer and Ronnie felt, but my sixth sense told me that something really, really evil was afoot.

As we drew closer to the first derelict, I could tell that it was a fifty-something feet houseboat, probably a Gibson by the layout, not more than a couple of years old, but already weathered and forlorn, making it appear a lot older than it was. The stainless steel was no longer stainless, the fiberglass hull was badly battered and holed in places, the glass ports and windows filmy and opaque.

There was a steel ladder hanging from the stern at the aft lounge deck. I took the lead and with mounting trepidation, climbed aboard. As I set foot on the deck, I was horrified at the mess. It was as if somebody had come aboard with a wrecking ball and simply demolished the whole damn boat. Absolute chaos!

There were personal things scattered everywhere. Clothing, ripped and tossed about; food remnants, glassware, silverware, all the trappings of a modern houseboat littered and cast aside, as if those monstrous predators in my nightmare had deliberately set out to destroy the boat. And there were signs of fire on the deck. I waited for Beyer and Ronnie to join me, then warily stepped into the main saloon. It was worse inside, and a nauseating odor of burnt meat permeated the entire cabin and below decks area.

Then, as my eyes adjusted to the interior light, I saw the bones scattered about.

Beyer was right behind me, and turned to keep Ronnie from entering the cabin. "Stay outside, my dear, and keep watch. We don't know who – or what – may be observing us from up there," he said, jerking his head in the direction of the cliff tops far above.

He turned back to the cabin, and with clinical curiosity, stooped to examine the bones. "These are human bones, of course. This is a femur, and all the others are obviously those of several people; all murdered violently and mercilessly, I suspect."

"Is there any other way?" I observed.

"It would appear that when the people who lived on these boats discovered that they had been somehow trapped in a place from which there was no escape, they stayed with the boats for shelter and comfort. They probably tried to explore, as we will have to do, to find another way out, but in the end remained close to the comforting confines of their vessels until they were attacked."

"Attacked?" I echoed.

He was idly running his fingers along the length of that femur when he remarked, "These bones appear to be marked. Let's go topside. I want to examine them in more detail. Do you think Ronnie is up to seeing them?"

"She's got a thick hide. In any case, she is going to have to toughen up pretty quickly, by the look of things around here."

So saying, we went back on deck. Ronnie did not flinch as Beyer brought the femur, a shattered skull and a couple of other smaller bones out into the bright, white glare of the late-morning sun.

"As I thought," Beyer continued, "these bones have been hacked and broken with a very primitive blade – either stone or steel. Archeologists have long suspected that the Anasazi were engaged in cannibalism. The breaking of long bones to get at marrow, cut marks made by knives, the burning of bones, splinters resulting from placing a bone on a rock and pounding it with another rock, all signs of extreme violence and cannibalism."

"But I thought the Anasazi were supposed to be a peaceful, agricultural people," I argued, looking around with renewed apprehension.

"I believe they were. I think the archeologists – in their infinite ignorance – have gotten it wrong. I suspect they, like these more recent visitors, were the victims of much more aggressive predators. It probably explains why the Anasazi began building their homes high in the cliff faces over years of constant aggression and attack. Unfortunately for these poor sods, however, they had no such opportunity."

"But the Anasazi vanished hundreds of years ago. These people have only been disappearing for the last fifty years or so. Are you saying that whoever killed off the ancient people are still around?"

"I don't know. We will need to explore further to find out. Let's examine some of the other boats."

So saying, we inspected the next couple of vessels on the beach. In every case, the scene was the same; chaos and carnage!

As we left the scene of devastation, walking briskly back up the beach, I stubbed the toe of my shoe on a rock half buried in the sand. I stooped down and brushed away the sand to discover a very old fire pit strewn with more fragments of bone. We hurried back to the comforting reality of the 'Wayward Wind' swinging gently on her hooks. It was then that I remembered something Beyer had said.

"Beyer, what did you mean back there when you said, and I quote, 'they probably tried to explore, as we will have to do, to find another way out?'"

He looked at me, then nodded his head out towards the other side of the bay, where we had come around the bend in the river. I followed his eyes, and was astonished to see that the bend was no longer there. Unless some trick of light and depth perception was deceiving me, there was nothing on the other side of the bay but a continuous cliff face, hundreds of feet high, curving around from there to the upper end of the beach where we were standing!

"That's impossible," I said, thunderstruck by the implication.

"Well, impossible or not, I think we have the answer as to why those boats never left this bay. Something of which we have no knowledge is occurring around us, and I think we should start immediately looking for that other way out."

"What makes you think there *is* another way out?"

"Whoever – or whatever – slaughtered all those people are not here, are they?"

I looked around again with mounting dread in my heart, unable to suppress the lump in my throat. There *seemed* to be no way out, but over there where that rock wall met the beach, there appeared to be a slim crevasse winding between the towering cliffs.

"O.K.," I said, recovering some of my composure, "let's go find it."

I checked the anchors on the plane again, to make sure they were all fast, then we began striding rapidly towards the slot. As we approached, I could tell that it was indeed a very narrow cleft in the cliff face. We stopped at the entrance, all of us acutely aware that this could be a very neat trap, just like the one I was enticed into yesterday.

It was no more than three feet wide, tighter in places, with jagged edges of rock protruding out from the sides at uneven levels. I pulled the Ruger from its holster, checked the load, and replaced it. Then I led the way into the slot. There was only room in there for single file, so I put Ronnie behind me and Beyer brought up in the rear. It was tough going, but I found that by getting down on all fours in the tight spots, it was easier to negotiate the twists and turns in the crevasse.

At one point, I looked up to see how deep this thing was. It must have been several hundred feet to the top. I could barely make out a slender band of dark blue sky overhead, so if it turned out that there was no end – or worse yet – a dead end ahead, perhaps there was a chance that we could climb out, using all the jagged projections as steps. I did not have to think about that for too long.

A few moments later, scrabbling along on all fours, I came to a wider place in the slot, and then it opened out into a chasm perhaps ten feet wide. We plodded steadily and warily along, until suddenly the chasm opened out into a broad, deep basin. It was like a hidden valley, perhaps a mile across, with rock walls all around, cottonwood trees standing beside a tiny stream than seemed to spring from somewhere on the far side of the basin and disappear in the rocks to our left.

I stood there for a moment, sensing a vague familiarity about the place. In the middle stood a low mesa, the top of which was obscured by sloping sides which were about fifty feet high.

Then I remembered! This was the crater I had seen from the air, just before the GPS went on the blink!

"Beyer?"

"Yes, I know. But look behind you."

I followed his gaze to the rock wall from which we had just emerged. About midway between the floor of the basin and the top of the cliff overhang was another ruin, smaller than what we had previously seen, and apparently incomplete. It appeared that whoever had started building it had either been interrupted, or had decided for whatever reason not to finish it.

"Let's take a look," I said, setting out towards the rock face.

"Are you sure, Mitch?" Ronnie said, speaking for the first time since we had left the beach.

"Sure. It's just a ruin. Probably nothing but rattlers to worry about. Besides, we may not even be able to get up to it, since we forgot in our haste to bring along any rope or other climbing essentials."

"Typical of Blaine, of course," Beyer said. "He remembers to bring the weapons, which will probably be useless, but forgets the important life-saving items – like rope, food and water, so forth."

"Hey. Who needs water? We've got a whole stream full of cool, clear water right here in front of us."

"You didn't *know* that when we left the plane, Blaine," he said, not meaning to wax poetic.

"You're right! But never mind. Let's see how these ancients used to live," I said excitedly, as I reached the base of the cliff.

It turned out that we did not need climbing equipment or ropes. There were footholds carved into the rock face all the way up to the lower level of the edifice. At intervals of ten feet or so, there were larger alcoves or shallow caves, where material was probably stored until it could be hoisted further up the cliff to the construction site.

I climbed the stone footholds to the first of these staging points, where I waited for Ronnie and Beyer to join me.

"Throw up your guns," I said. "I'll catch 'em. We need to keep them with us – just in case!"

I caught the weapons as they were tossed up to me. Beyer and Ronnie followed, scrambling up the rock face, and we proceeded on to the ruin quickly and with relative ease. I was the first to the top, and as I stepped over a low stone wall, I could tell that this was indeed an unfinished project.

An overhang from the cliff above sheltered the entire structure so well that it looked as though it had been abandoned only within the past few decades – not hundreds of years ago.

Behind the wall stood an almost complete building, its roof formed by the overhang. Another structure, possibly used as a granary or storage shelter, adjoined the first. Along a narrow ledge, behind the wall, we came upon two more dwellings and another larger granary. Looking over the edge of the wall, we could see beneath us a magnificent, panoramic view of the basin below. Directly beneath us, the cliff plunged straight down, then gradually tapered off to a slope that dropped another few hundred feet to the valley floor.

We decided to inspect this latest and more complete example of the work of the ancients. Beyer led us inside the doorway of this dwelling, carefully checking around for any of the less friendly reptiles which usually inhabited such places.

There were a few shards of their famous pottery, the odd piece of broken sandal, a few bits of straw basket, but nothing significant in the way of artifacts.

I looked around and noted that Ronnie was watching Beyer as he stretched up and gently wiped with his fingertips at something on the rear wall of the room. I walked over and stood by Ronnie for a few moments, curiosity getting the better of me.

"What are you doing, old rope?" I asked, imitating his customary salutation. "Found an interesting petroglyph, have we?"

"You could say that," he responded, turning slowly to face us. "Except that it is not a petroglyph. At least, not in the traditional sense."

"What other sense is there?" I inquired ruefully, suspecting that we were about to be assaulted with another of Beyer's infamous monologues.

"I simply mean, *old chap*," he replied, that it is not a form of writing customarily attributed to the early people of *this* continent."

"Well, what is it then?"

"In a word, my friends, it is ancient *Hebrew!*"

"*What?*" we both responded, stunned by this latest revelation.

"Are you sure?"

"Positive!"

"And I *know* you know what it says," I cynically replied.

"Naturally."

"Well, don't keep us in suspense, Beyer! What the hell does it say?"

20

"It says, roughly speaking, of course, and I paraphrase for your benefit, 'The Neph'ilim were on the earth in those days and afterward. During that time the sons of the true God continued to have relations with the daughters of men, and these bore sons to them. They were the *mighty ones* of old, the men of fame.'

"I emphasize 'mighty ones' for your benefit."

"Where have I heard that before? It sounds familiar."

"It should, if you know your Bible. It is a direct quotation from Genesis, Chapter Six, and Verse Four."

"Oh no. You are *not* going to lay that on me, Beyer! Please do *not* tell me that what we have here were ancient people who were not only familiar with the Hebrew Scriptures, but also used that knowledge to describe the origin and ancestry of their enemies?"

"Precisely, my boy!"

"Now I've heard everything."

"Not quite!"

"Mitch, what in blazes is he talking about?

"He is trying to tell us, Ronnie, in his own sweet way, that this land is inhabited by giants – man-eating giants apparently – who have lived around here for a few thousand years – give or take – and that the other 'normal' people who lived here started building up in the cliffs to survive their constant attacks."

"Oh my ….." she began.

"Exactly, my child. But there is something else."

"Oh?" I was afraid to ask.

"It was not the 'normal' people, to use Blaine's inadequate description, who wrote this. I believe it is much older than that, and that it was written by the Anasazi's ancestors."

"You mean, those from the 'other worlds' you mentioned?"

"Now you are catching on."

"Who just *happened* to discover the existence of the gateways, and found their way here from the Land of Goshen," I quipped.

"More or less."

"There is one major flaw in your theory, Beyer," I countered.

"Such as?"

"If I remember the rest of the story, the materialized 'bad' angels and their offspring, the giants – along with everyone else in the world except for Noah and his family – were all destroyed in the great flood."

"True, but remember even after that, and ostensibly confirmed by the discovery of enormous human bones and footprints in many parts of the world, there were other giants recorded in Biblical history. Take, for example the story of Goliath. He was allegedly nine and a half feet tall, the weight of his armor alone was a hundred and twenty six pounds, and just the iron blade of his spear – not counting the shaft, which was reported to have been the length and girth of a small tree – was about fifteen pounds.

"He was from a race of titans who were part of the Rephaim nation. At the time that he confronted David, he ..... Blaine! What the blazes are you looking at?"

I had lost interest in what he was saying. I was standing on the ledge behind the stone wall, gazing along the cliff at something that had caught my eye. Higher in the rock and about a hundred feet along to my right was the almost invisible outer wall of another cliff dwelling. However, this one appeared complete, and was so perfectly camouflaged that it blended into the surrounding rock face. I would not have spotted it, had it not been for a flash of sunlight bouncing off something bright embedded the wall.

"Beyer, take a look at this," I responded, excitement growing within me.

"What is it?"

"You tell me," I said, as I pointed up at the wall in the cliff.

"Good grief! That appears to be a perfectly *intact* cliff house. That's not possible, unless .....no. It can't be!"

"Can't be what?"

"Never mind. But we have to find a way up there. Now!"

"Are you crazy?"

"Maybe. But let's go."

"Exactly how do you expect us to get up there? The climb up here was a breeze compared to that. That's straight up a vertical cliff, hundreds of feet high."

"Precisely. That's why there has to be a way up there from here."

"What? Are you nuts?"

"Perhaps, but let's take a look, shall we?"

Without waiting for us, he set forth along the narrow rocky trail behind the low stone wall.

We were right behind him, of course, and soon found that the trail ended at a sheer drop to the valley below. It appeared that Beyer had been wrong for once. Frustrated, I inspected the cliff face adjacent to where they stood looking over the edge of the precipice. I stepped back a few paces from the end of the trail, and it was then that I spotted a small crevice in the rock, just prior to where the stone wall ended. It was neatly hidden by the face of the rock itself, and would never be spotted on a cursory glance.

While Beyer and Ronnie were still gazing over the brink, I examined it more closely. The opening was barely more than a foot and half wide, and closed at the top at a level of about five feet. But it was obviously possible, if one stooped or crawled, to get into the space. I got down on all fours and eased myself into the aperture. It was painstaking, and painful, as sharp edges protruded from the rock, perhaps designed to discourage further investigation.

I reached into my tattered flight suit, pulled out a lighter I kept handy, and crawled on my hands and knees for what must have been twenty feet or so, cautiously feeling my way ahead of the dim flame for any obvious signs of booby trap or biting type creature.

The space seemed to be narrowing even further, but just when I thought I was going to have to back out the way I came in, a gust of warm air blew out the lighter's tiny flame. I rounded a sharp curve in the crawl space and there ahead of me was daylight shining into the mouth of a small cave. I had reached the end of the tunnel, to no avail.

Peering over the edge of the grotto, I had almost the same view as from end of the trail behind me.

Then, glancing to the right, I spotted a slender ledge no more than a foot wide just outside the mouth of the cave, winding up along the rock face towards the dwelling, now visible diagonally above me. I stretched forward as far as I could without throwing myself off the brink, and peered to the left. There, standing at the end of the trail, I could see Beyer and Ronnie about twenty feet away.

"Hey! Beyer. Ronnie," I called out.

They looked around for a moment, wondering where my voice was coming from.

"Blaine! What the hell are you doing over there? We thought you had fallen off the cliff!"

"Look around behind you," I replied. "There's a small passageway in the rock. It might barely be wide enough for you to get through, Beyer. But be careful. There are a lot of sharp rocks sticking out the sides in there. Don't get stuck, whatever you do!"

"Very amusing. All right. Hang on. We'll be with you in a jiffy."

Ronnie came through first, as her tiny frame allowed her to get around the projections with relative ease.

It took longer than a jiffy for Beyer, with tremendous effort, to squeeze his bulk along that constricted crawl space, but after about ten minutes, he finally emerged, battered, scraped and bloody.

"Blaine, I swear on the grave of my sainted grandmother....."

"I know. Forget it! I found your way up to the cliff house. Look!" I said, pointing to the narrow ledge.

His eyes followed my finger, and when he spotted it he exclaimed, "No! Absolutely no way. I can't do it. I *won't* do it! Ronnie might be able to make it, but you and I are too big. One slip and we'd be at the bottom of that cliff, a pile of broken bones for those vultures up there to pick at.

"No!" he said again. "I won't do it! You're asking too much of me Blaine."

"We will have to leave the guns behind," I said, ignoring his whining. "We'll need our hands to hang on. I think I see some hand holds in the cliff face. Let's go!"

So saying, I turned to face the wall, eased myself off the edge of the cave and stepped carefully on to the ledge, testing its strength before placing my full weight on it. It seemed solid enough, so with heart pounding and legs trembling, I started up the narrow incline, feeling for handholds as I went. There did seem to be very small niches carved into the rock face at arm's length intervals, obviously to assist with balance.

I inched up the slope, one hesitant side step at a time, with my head to the left and my eyes on the prize, not daring to look down. At one point, I carefully turned my head to the right, to make sure Ronnie and Beyer were still behind me.

It seemed like an eternity, but several minutes later, I was stepping off the ledge and on to another trail behind a stone wall, similar to what we had left below. I waited for Ronnie and Beyer to join me, panting and trembling with fear and effort. Beyer opened his mouth, no doubt to utter another profanity, but I put my finger to my lips to shush him.

I had that eerie feeling in the back of my neck again. I whispered to them, "Keep it quiet. I don't think we're alone up here."

We stepped silently along the path under another huge overhang from the rim above, and moments later, we were behind the external wall of the dwelling, in a huge stone room which was completely intact.

Around the walls, suspended in iron holders, were primitive torches. On low stone benches or tables, there lay some of the most exquisite examples of completely whole, unbroken Puebloan pottery and cookware I had ever seen! Archeologists would kill for such fine examples of genuine, ancient earthenware. In the rear of the room, formed by the back wall of a huge cavern, fire places had been carved into the rock.

Iron cooking utensils lay about on hearths and benches in front of the fireplaces, which still contained coals and ash. Gazing around the room in utter astonishment, we saw that there were other signs of habitation. Sandals, straw baskets, and woven blankets lay about, neatly arranged on the stone benches, and hung on the walls of the room.

"This in fantastic! Unbelievable!" Beyer exclaimed, unable to contain himself any longer.

"There are people still *living* here!"

"But how can that *be?*" Ronnie challenged. "You said yourself that these people had been gone for hundreds of years."

"I did, didn't I? Blaine, tell me again what that girl said to you yesterday about her ancestry."

"She said, if I remember rightly, 'We have been hunted for many years by the mighty ones before the white man came. Our lives, our homes – our way of life – have been destroyed.'"

"There must be some of them left!" he replied. "But if that's true, it would be the most fantastic discovery in modern times. They could tell us so much about their history. They could fill in all the blanks – including those of their other worlds – everything!"

He turned to examine the pottery at close hand, gently picking up one of the pieces.

"These are some of the finest specimens of ancient stoneware I have ever seen.

"Ancestral Puebloans are well known for their pottery. In general, it was used for cooking or storage. As you can see, it is painted gray or black, smooth or textured. These are examples of the most common decorated pottery, black painted designs on white or light gray backgrounds. Decoration is implemented by the fine hatching, and contrasting colors are produced by the use of mineral-based paint on a chalky background.

"The tall cylinders are probably ceremonial vessels, and the narrow-necked jars may be used for liquids. The decorated bowls and plates are obviously what they use for eating. This is an absolutely unbelievable find. These people must have been ....."

"Quiet!" I said sharply.

I had suddenly become aware of something familiar. For a moment, I could not place it. An odor came to my nostrils, faint but definitely not my over-active imagination. Then I heard a low growling coming from somewhere in the back of the cave, and recalled the fetid, animal stench and the rustling sound I had experienced in the ravine yesterday. Was it only yesterday? It seemed like an age ago!

I turned again to the rear of the cave and it was then I noticed dimly outlined doorways, apparently leading to other rooms, carved into the rock. Too late, I reached for my Ruger.

21

I froze as I heard the same words of caution I had received yesterday.

"Do not!" she threatened, as she emerged from the shadows. "They *will* kill you. You should not have come here. I warned you!"

As she came into the light, several creatures appeared with her. They were hideous animals, something like wolves, but with features akin to those of both the coyote and hyena. The rustling sound seemed to emanate from the backs of their throats, as if they had difficulty breathing. But this noise was suppressed when they began that low, ominous growling.

"And I told you we *would* come, and why we *must* come."

"Yes. I did not think you would be so strong. Few people discover the way into this valley, or are able to climb up here from the ruins below. You and your friends are welcome to my home. I am Chosovi. These are my people," she said, sweeping her left arm behind her as several others came out of the shadows of the back rooms.

They had similar features, of varying ages. But some of them looked distinctly European, with fairer skin and lighter hair. A few were dressed in loosely fitting buckskins, and some had normal western clothing.

But then the real shock came. Behind this first small band came another group of varying ages, from very old to very young, dressed in threadbare rags of clothing in various stages of disrepair. The first of these to appear was an old man, I guessed in his eighties, small, wiry, grizzled, weathered.

As he strode up to us, he grinned broadly and held out his hand.

"Ethan Masters," he greeted, plainly overjoyed to see some new and friendly faces.

As Beyer took his hand he said, "Don't I know you? The name sounds familiar."

The man frowned and replied, "You don't know me, but you might know my son."

Ronnie was staring at the man, and when she heard the name, she cried, "Richard's father!"

Then Beyer exclaimed, "Of course!"

The old man jerked his thumb in the direction of the lake and said, "I got trapped in that canyon fifty years ago. Some friends and I had one of the first houseboats on the lake when it was opened to the public in `sixty-three. There were five of us, out for a pleasure cruise in my brand new boat on this brand new lake; me, two other buddies, and a married couple – friends of ours.

"When we got stranded, we began to live off the land. We tried to find a way out. Eventually, we discovered that slot from the beach to this valley. Chosovi's grandparents found us and rescued us before those big ones got to us – fortunately. After a time, I married one of Chosovi's people. We had a son. One day when he was about ten, he wandered away from the community. We never saw him again. We thought he had been taken by *them*, until he showed up again about six months ago – a grown man, and an air force officer!

"My wife and friends had long since died, so you can't believe how glad I was to see my son again.

"I am the only one of the original party left. These other folks, and their offspring," he went on, nodding to the rest of the group, "are the only survivors, from all those boats that got trapped like we did.

"A few of them found the way out. Others chose to stay with the boats and – well, I guess you saw what happened to them. Some of these folks have only been here a few months, some of them – like me – for years. We owe our lives to Chosovi's parents and grandparents, who are all dead now – either taken or died of sickness or old age."

"But what about Richard?" Ronnie implored.

Ethan Masters, looking broken and forlorn, replied, "I think your brother Jeff is in a better position to tell you. He was with him when he disappeared – again."

"*Jeff?*" she cried. "You mean, Jeff is ...."

Before she could finish the sentence, a man of about forty gently shouldered his way through the crowd. His skin was several shades darker than Ronnie's, but the family resemblance was unmistakable. His wiry black hair was long and matted with dirt. He wore the tattered remains of what was once a U.S. Air Force officer's uniform.

Ronnie screamed, shouted his name again, and rushed to greet him.

"Hi sis," her brother grinned, as he limped up to her and hugged her tightly.

This was all too much for Beyer and me. I was stunned and speechless. Beyer was naturally the first to recover.

"But ... this is absolutely fantastic!" he burst out. "Not only have we stumbled across a remnant of a civilization thought to be extinct for centuries, but we have discovered the mystery of the missing boats and their crews *and* found Ronnie's brother. This is unbelievable! Mitchell, we must remain here and learn every detail of their fantastic adventures!"

Remembering his manners, he introduced himself to Jeff McCall.

"My *dear* fellow, I am Doctor Beyer – please just call me Beyer – and this is my friend Mitch Blaine, and of course you know your sister," he added, before realizing the absurdity of his last remark.

He grinned again, and shook Beyer's hand, then mine. "I knew that sooner or later, my sister would cotton on to the fact that I was not dead, and come looking for me."

A few of the crowd had taken seats on the floor around the room, and some of them had begun preparing meals for all. From out of nowhere, they seemed to have gotten fruit, corn, sweet potatoes and some kind of smoked meat – I was not game to ask of what variety – and began serving Ronnie, Beyer and me first.

"Oh Jeff," Ronnie said. "I don't know where to start."

Then she asked with mounting apprehension, "Jeff, where is Richard?"

Jeff, who obviously had a bad leg, flopped down, and staring at the dirt floor, he muttered, "He's dead. I'm sorry sis."

Ronnie put her head in her hands and burst into tears. "I ... I knew it. I had a terrible feeling that....something had happened to him. What happened, Jeff?"

"I don't really know. It's a long story. We both somehow ended up here ....well, not here exactly; down there, on the other side of that mesa. There's some kind of opening there. A rift or something. I don't understand it all, but it seems it's got something to do with what they were experimenting with at the Collider. Chosovi's people have known about it for centuries, apparently. Anyway, one minute I was in Texas, and the next I was down there, and when I got there I discovered that the same thing had happened to Richard. It was almost as if he knew I was coming, and was waiting for me. He brought me here, although it seemed, almost reluctantly. He had been acting very strange before we got here, and afterwards, as time went on, he seemed to become increasingly angry and well ....weird!"

"What do you mean, weird?" she asked.

"I don't know how to describe it exactly. Agitated, I guess. Aggressive and kind of spooky. I really can't explain it. He spent a lot of time by himself, down there. We were all worried about him being taken by those giant warriors or whatever they are, but it seems he had some way of knowing their whereabouts and evading them.

"Anyway, one day we were over on the other side of the mesa, in that same area, hunting for food, when they came upon us. We managed to dodge 'em, though I don't know how. We didn't want to lead them back here, although I think they know about this place. They just can't get up here. Their one disadvantage is that they are big and ungainly. But they can still move incredibly fast for their size.

"I was out in front, Richard was behind me. I looked back and he was gone. The last I saw of him, he was tangling not with one of *them*, but with some kind of creature that had apparently been stalking us."

"Oh my ….no!" she cried. "Not that," she said, looking at me.

The blood had drained from her face, and I felt that huge lump sliding up and down in my throat again. The hairs on the back of my neck were standing straight up.

"The skin walker!" I said.

At that, Chosovi, who had been standing quietly during this entire exchange, looked up sharply. "What do you know of skin walkers?" she asked, anxiously glancing around the room.

"There was one in the canyon yesterday," I replied. "We thought you might be it."

She laughed nervously. "No. It was not me. I felt its presence, but my friends," she nodded her head at those wolf-like creatures, now lying placidly at her feet, kept him away. I think these are the only things – animal or human – he is afraid of."

"He followed me out of the canyon. And he visited me in the hotel room last night. At first, I thought I was having a nightmare, when I woke and found myself staring into those awful red eyes," I replied. "Ronnie saw it too."

"Yes," she said quietly. "It was horrible!"

Her brother was shocked! "What do you mean, Ronnie? When?"

"Last night in my room. I woke up staring into that thing's eyes, just like Mitch described. I tried to scream, but it was like my vocal cords were paralyzed."

That really alarmed both Jeff and Chosovi!

Chosovi scowled and said, "They do not normally bother other people – only the Dine`. Something is very wrong."

Then she frowned at Ronnie and said matter-of-factly, "You really saw him too?"

"Yes."

"Something is very bad. I do not understand, but I think we are not safe here anymore. He knows of this place, and can come here. He goes anywhere he wants to."

She went over to Jeff and sat down close beside him, taking his hand in hers. Second shock in two minutes!

"Chosovi is my wife," he said bluntly, looking at each of us in turn. "After she and her people saved us from those *beings*, we became very close. We fell in love. We married according to her tribal customs three months ago."

"*Whaat?*" Ronnie exclaimed, as taken aback as Beyer and I, at this latest disclosure.

"Yes. I didn't think there was any way I was ever getting out of here again, and frankly I like it here. I like the people, their peaceful way of life. I am going to stay here with them, and the hell with the rest of the crazy world!"

"Well, this *is* an astounding turn of events," said Beyer. "But there are so many things I don't understand. Chosovi, do you know who made the writings on the wall in the ruin below?"

"It has been there since long before my ancestors arrived from the previous world. Many thousands of years. We think those who knew of the doorways came a very long way. Perhaps the guardians know, but they say nothing."

"The guardians?" I chipped in. "You mean, those who guard the portals? Like he who died where Jeff and Richard came from?"

Ethan Masters, who had been silent through this exchange, said "They are a tribe of the Anasazi's ancestors, chosen for their unique skills. Their entire purpose in life – that of protecting the gateways – is ingrained into them from the day they are born. They are afraid of nothing – except perhaps, the skin walkers, who are supposed to be supernatural."

"Well," I replied, "perhaps that explains the terror on the face of the one who died in the tunnel in Texas. But what was the skin….."

I froze as a horrible thought came to my mind.

"Chosovi, would the skinwalker know how to access the entrances without the knowledge of the guardians?"

"Possibly. He seems to know all – to come and go wherever he wishes, and to be whatever he wishes."

I glanced around the room, that creepy feeling raising the hairs on the nape of my neck again. I had a faint notion that I knew how that guardian in the Collider tunnel died, and my suspicions about something else were growing; something I didn't like to think about at all.

I thought for a moment, and spoke to her again. "I *know* these people – especially the older ones – do not go up and down that narrow ledge to get to and from your fields be-low. You must have another way down."

"Yes," she said guardedly.

"You must show us. We have to get down there to that entrance."

"No. It is not possible. The mighty ones are all around that place. And even if we get there, the guardians them-selves will prevent you from getting close."

"We must try. We have to get out of here."

"I can show you the way down, so you can get back to your craft. That is all I can do."

"That won't help much, since our craft is trapped like the others."

"Perhaps not," she replied mysteriously.

"Eat! Then I take you down and show you the way back. We must be very careful. The mighty ones wait for us. They are many, and they are very powerful. You can-not fight them. They are huge, and have much armor and weapons."

"What kind of weapons?"

"Some from their own making, some handed down from their ancestors – great swords and spears – and some taken from the white men they have killed."

"How many are there?"

"We do not know. Many hundreds, perhaps. Our cre-ation story tells of them following our ancestors from the previous world into this one."

"Through the gateways?"

"Yes."

"Well," I sighed, "we have to make a run for it one way or another. Jeff, are you sure you and Chosovi won't come with us?"

"No!" he replied firmly. "My place is here with Chosovi and her people. I can help them; perhaps show them how to make weapons. Or," he grinned, "show them how and where to steal them from the white man, if their guardians will trust me with their portals."

"Do not joke, Jeff," Chosovi chastised him. "You know that is not possible."

He sighed. "I know. But one day, if your people are to survive, you will *have* to trust me."

"Perhaps," she replied, shrugging and drawing closer to him.

Ronnie, who had been silent during this exchange, now spoke up for the first time. "Jeff, did *you* sent me your class ring, to let me know you were still alive?"

"Yes. I had Chosovi take it to the other side, where she could mail it."

"I *knew* it!" Ronnie said.

"You go to and from the other side at will?" I asked Chosovi. "You go through the portals?"

"No! The guardians will not permit it. There are other places – only open sometimes – not guarded."

"You drove the van yesterday?"

"No. One of my people who understands your ways."

"Jeff, you *must* come with us – you and Chosovi!" Ronnie said. "I can't bear the thought of finding you, only to lose you again so quickly."

"You're not losing me, sis. You know exactly where to find me. Just think of it as my living in another state, where you can visit me any time."

"I can fly or drive to other states where there aren't any giants to contend with."

"Yeah, there is that. Well, we're not going, anyway. But as you can see, I am alive, well and happy. And we will help you, Mitch and Beyer to escape. We know the lay of the land, and I'm not as useless as my bad leg makes me appear. I can get around all right. I've managed to avoid them so far, haven't I?"

So saying, he struggled to his feet, and pulled Chosovi up as well. "Come on, girl, let's show these people the way out of here!"

Without another word, he led off, Chosovi behind him.

Ethan Masters, apparently the leader of the survivors, probably in deference to his age and length of time here, asked "How many can you take with you on that bird of yours?"

I looked at the small group and did some quick math in my head.

"Probably as many as would like to come, provided I can get the plane up and out of that blind canyon."

Ethan nodded and said, "We'll take the chance."

He then asked his band of followers who would like to join us.

About a dozen of the younger, more able bodied types agreed and followed us, bringing with them a smattering of simple weapons – mostly bows, knives and axes. A few had small arms, no doubt purloined from the abandoned boats.

Most of the older ones elected to stay behind, feeling it was too late to begin a new life somewhere else in a world that had advanced without them.

Chosovi led us to the back of the large room, through one of the dim doorways, and down a flight of hand-hewn stone steps which wound around the perimeter wall of what appeared to be a large circular well, about ten feet across and of unknown depth.

"Kiva," Beyer offered. "They played an important ceremonial part in the sacred rituals of the ancient people. It is thought that…."

"Beyer!"

"What?"

"Not now!"

"Yes, of course, old boy."

The rough stone wall of the well, or kiva, was dimly lit with torches similar to those above. I glanced back to see the others, the boat survivors, carefully following us down the steep and winding stairway.

Several minutes later, we were standing in the bottom of the kiva, with apparently no way out, until Chosovi pointed to a small aperture in the rock, similar to that which I had discovered on the ledge of the ruin above.

She dived into it like a rabbit on the run, followed by Jeff and Ronnie.

Beyer looked askance, and said, "Oh no. Not again. How many times do I have to do this Blaine?"

"I hope this will be the last time, Beyer. Let's go!"

I got down on my knees and followed the others into the crack. It was not as difficult as the one up top, and after a few minutes of groping on all fours, I found myself back out at the base of the cliff, which towered hundreds of feet above.

I turned around to see Beyer exiting a hole in the wall so perfectly camouflaged as to be almost invisible to the naked eye. His bulk barely squeezed through the gap, and it was obvious that even if they knew about it, the so-called mighty ones would never be able to get through. And I suspected that Chosovi and her people probably had a few surprises stationed at both ends of the hole, including her 'protectors', to discourage any closer inspection.

As soon as the entire party was outside, with Chosovi and Jeff in the lead, we crossed the small stream and headed back towards the base of the cliff from whence we had come, heading towards the opening that led to the beach.

We had not gone a hundred yards when I heard a buzzing sound like that of a swarm of thousands of angry bees. A moment later, an enormous spear the size of a small tree, with a blade wider and longer than my forearm, thudded into the ground a few feet in front of us. I turned to see a horrifying sight! Fifty yards behind us, a dozen or more giant warriors, fully clad in leather armor and helmets, were charging at us with those tree-like spears on high.

Chosovi and Jeff turned and struck out towards the mesa. Its flat top above was obscured by a rough shale and talus slope rising to the surface at a steep angle.

I caught up with them, panting with the effort, and imagining how Beyer and the others, who were not anywhere near the shape I was in, must be feeling.

"Where are we going?" I gasped.

"Up," she said, heading straight at the talus slope.

We clambered up the rough, rocky incline towards the top of the mesa. With our feet slipping and sliding and our hands scraped, cut and bloody from the rough, loose surface, we made tough going of it, but a few minutes later, with the warriors still closing on us, we made it to the rim.

As we scrabbled over the edge of the mesa, we came to a sliding stop, stunned at what awaited us.

22

Not twenty feet ahead, surrounded by two dozen well-armed Air Force Special Ops troops, squatted the enormous bulk of an AC-130 gunship, its left side facing us, bristling with Bushmaster cannon and Equalizer Gatling guns!

At the rear of the extended loading ramp of the aircraft sat an armored Hum-Vee. Beside the airman manning the fifty caliber M2 Browning machine gun, standing nonchalantly with a cigar in his teeth, his forearms crossed on the top of the windshield was a tall, heavy-set man in his mid-fifties, wearing the fatigues and insignia of an air force brigadier general.

I was so shocked by this latest revelation, I just stood there, mouth agape, wondering what else could possibly go wrong.

"Come ahead, all of you," shouted the general. "Quickly, now."

Since we had no choice, with the warriors rapidly climbing the slope behind us, we all hurried towards the waiting aircraft.

As we pulled up short of the Hum-Vee, the general grinned around his cigar and said, "Mornin' Beyer. You sure have led me on a merry chase."

"Nathan?" Beyer responded, as shocked as I was at this astounding development.

"In person. I have been tailing you lot since you arrived in the country. Thought you'd eluded me when I lost you on radar a while back. Some strange phenomenon made all my electronics go on the blink, then I picked you up visually as you were touching down in that lake over yonder. I circled overhead, spotted this mesa and figured I probably had just enough room to get in and out. And here I am, waiting for you. I knew it was just a matter of time."

"But why? Why have you been shadowing us? Why have you been trying to kill us?"

"Kill you?" he roared.

He was silent for a moment, a puzzled look on his bullish features. Then he burst out laughing.

"Kill you? Why, I have been *protecting* your incompetent, sorry hides from *being* killed, ever since you began meddling in national security affairs that don't concern you!"

"But, I don't understand," Beyer replied, as puzzled as I was by this turn of events. "*Somebody* has been trying to kill us ever since before we left Australia on this epic adventure."

Suddenly his troops cocked their automatic weapons with menacing metallic clacks, aiming them right at us.

As I braced for the inevitable, I realized that the weapons were not pointed at *us* — but over our heads. I half turned and was horrified to see that the entire rim of the mesa behind us was lined with hundreds of the giant warriors, just standing there – watching and waiting. For what, I wondered?

General Price raised his arm and pointed directly behind us. "Maybe *he* can answer your question, Beyer."

We turned slowly all the way around and received yet
another jolt to our already stricken senses!

Appearing out of nowhere, and standing not fifteen
feet behind us, cloaked entirely in some kind of animal
skin, his own head crowned by that of a wolf with gaping
jaws, stood......

The skin walker!

His face was obscured in shadow by the mantle's hood.

General Price was not slow in sizing up the situation.
"Kowalski!" he shouted to a staff sergeant standing nearby.
"Get these people on board! All of you, get over here and
into the aircraft – now!"

Except for me, Beyer and Ethan Masters, our group did
as ordered, and hurried up the loading ramp into the plane.

The man-creature pointed a familiar bony claw at us
and hissed, "Yes! It was I. You people have no idea of my
power! Unfortunately, I sent fools on a simple errand to
prevent you from coming here. Being merely human, they
failed! I will not. *None* of you will leave here alive!"

The general glanced over his right shoulder towards
the nose of the plane and shouted, "Olsen! Get those engines fired up. Now!"

I expected the huge Allison turbo-props to start whining into life immediately, but nothing happened!

The aircraft commander craned his head out the left
cockpit window and shouted back. "General, I .... I can't. I
don't seem to have any electrical power. The whole airplane
is dead!"

The skin walker screeched with an evil cackle, "As you *all* will be soon. My power over even your machines is indomitable! I tried to prevent you from coming here; from finding this land. But you would not stop. Now you all must die. The secrets of this place must *never* be revealed!"

"*What* are you talking about?" Beyer uncharacteristically bellowed. "Who are you, and what do you want with us?"

"I want nothing from you, except your deaths. I command the power of your military, and the power of my people. The combination makes me indestructible. Since I discovered the secret of the portals, I can go anywhere, do anything, *my* ancestors did. These warriors," he said, sweeping his cloaked arm in their direction, "are mine to control. They are from the third world, and are the most powerful beings on Earth. And soon, I will lead them to conquer *your* world, as we have conquered so many others, including the people of this land," he shrieked.

Ethan Masters began shuffling towards the creature.

"Don't!" I yelled.

He ignored me. He got right up to within a foot of the thing, leaned into that shadowy visage, and mumbled something to him. The creature shrieked again with an awful howl, reached out, grabbed Ethan by the throat with one bony claw, and lifted him two feet off the ground. The old man began gagging and writhing as his life was choked out of him.

And suddenly it all made sense to me.

As the skin walker dropped the old man's lifeless body like a piece of refuse, he turned to the waiting horde and raised his scrawny arm.

"You forget one thing," I shouted.

He turned to me and said, "What, white man? What can you *possibly* do to me?"

"Who me? Oh, nothing at all. You forgot your own witch rules, that's all."

"*What?*" he hissed.

"Oh, just that it is *you* who will die – if you are seen and recognized – Richard *Masters!*" I yelled.

The thing let out the most blood-curdling scream I had ever heard in my life, and leapt at me. Even though it was fifteen or more feet away, it seemed to cross the distance in one leap, its glowing red eyes mesmerizing me with fear. At the same time, the warriors behind it charged, launching a salvo of those massive spears and arrows into the Special Forces as they did so.

Way too late, I shook off the horrible spell of those evil, ruby eyes, dropped to the ground dragging Beyer with me, pulled my Ruger and fired all six rounds in rapid succession, with no apparent or significant result!

Simultaneously, General Price, standing cool as a cucumber under that incoming hail of projectiles, raised his hand, paused for a moment and calmly said, "Fire!"

The troops, accompanied by the gun crews in the aircraft, lay down a withering stream of shells at the warriors.

The creature, still in mid-air, screamed again as I rolled to one side trying to evade its impact with me. As I did so, its extended claw managed to momentarily grab my throat. Then I saw, in the awful saffron glare of noon, the thing continue its flight for another few yards before it came to rest upright, its body suspended and impaled on a ten foot spear shaft.

Crawling over to it under the continuing barrage of automatic weapons fire, I saw that the animal skin cloaking the thing had fallen off, to reveal the tattered, threadbare remnants of an air force major's uniform. Underneath were the emaciated remains of something I almost did not recognize; something that had once been human. Held on the immense spear shaft which had taken out most of his midriff, he was still barely alive. His head turned slowly towards me, the fiery coals glowed brightly in one last act of defiance, then slowly dimmed. As the fires went out, the eyes reverted those of a human, then closed forever.

Beyer was still lying on the ground beside me, covering his head with his hands, as if they could protect him from spear, sword and projectile. The giant army had retreated back to the rim momentarily to regroup, leaving behind them a pile of dead.

Before I knew what was happening, rough hands were grabbing Beyer and me, picking us up bodily, as if we were sacks of grain, and tossing us on to the loading ramp. The Hum-Vee roared up the ramp as the plane's engines, now apparently freed from the creature's control, began to wind up. The loadmaster and his crew, with clockwork precision, secured the heavy vehicle to the deck in a matter of seconds.

As the Special Forces filed back into the aircraft, I looked out on the scene of devastation and saw that the army of warriors was again charging at us, with no apparent attempt to evade the ship's gunfire. Spears, arrows and some small arms fire begin striking the plane, and a number of the tail end troops went down. With no thought of self-preservation, some of those already safely aboard the now taxiing aircraft jumped to the ground to get the injured and dead back on deck. I did the same thing, hearing above the roar of the engines, a most horrific howling coming from the advancing hoard.

The plane began turning to point down the length of the mesa. I glanced in the direction it was aiming and was appalled at how close to the cliff face at the end of the mesa we were. All the troops, dead and alive, were now on board. The aircraft gathered speed as I leapt for the loading ramp. I reached for an extended hand. The general himself pulled me back to safety.

"I have to get back to the beach," I shouted over the din of the engines. "I can't leave my plane behind. We may never find this place again!"

"I know," General Price yelled back. "I'll fly a low pass over the lake with the ramp down. You and your friends are going to have to take a swim! I'll keep all the others here on my bird."

Beyer, who had been standing nearby waiting for my safe return to the aircraft, shouted "Are you crazy? No! I won't DO it! How many times do I have to *tell* you! I'm too *old* for this, Blaine!"

"No choice, Beyer. It's that, or leave the 'Wayward Wind' behind, and you know that's not an option."

".....insane," was all I heard him yell in reply.

"Ronnie, Jeff, Chosovi," I shouted. "Get back here at the end of the ramp and hold on tight! We'll be flying low and slow over the water. We're going to have to go 'jump in the lake', if you'll excuse the pun!"

Moments later, the AC-130 was airborne, heading straight for the looming cliff face. "Hang on," yelled the general, as the ship banked sharply to the right. We stood at the rear of the ramp, hanging on for dear life to some heavy webbing used to secure cargo.

As the aircraft heeled around in that tight right turn, I peered out over the rear end of the ramp. All I could see was red rock only feet from the huge tail. The plane's huge props must have cleared the cliff face by only inches! Then we were in a steep climb over the top of the cliff. Seconds later we were in negative 'G', as the pilot pushed her over the top and down the other side to the lake below. He leveled out, dropped full flaps, pulled the power all the way back, and we seemed to come to a stop in mid-air.

"Get ready!" Price shouted.

We were only a few feet above the water, doing maybe a hundred and twenty knots. I could not see out the side of the aircraft to tell where we were, but the general was on an intercom with the pilot, measuring distance from the beach and the PBY.

"GO!" he yelled.

Beyer was standing at the end of the ramp clinging desperately to a strap and looking down at the water. He didn't move. I leapt at him from behind, grabbing him around the shoulders as I did so, and out we went together. He didn't have time to think or resist.

Moments later, we hit the water feet first with one almighty splash. The impact and the cold water hit us like a physical blow, and we went several feet under. I struggled up and looked around, frantically hoping that Beyer was

O.K. For a moment I panicked when I did not see him, but then his big, ugly head broke the surface like a breaching humpback whale. Seconds later, Ronnie, Jeff and Chosovi surfaced a few yards away. We all seemed to be in one piece.

Dog-paddling in the deep, cold water, I looked around and saw that we were only about fifty feet out from the 'Wayward Wind'. We struck out for the beach, and a minute or two later, we were all floundering on to the sand, breathless, but apart from a few bruises, undamaged.

The gunship roared overhead and disappeared beyond the canyon rim.

As the others sat puffing and panting on the beach next to the PBY, I came to my senses first. I looked around anxiously, and happened to glance up. There, not a hundred yards away, rappelling down the cliff face from the rim of the plateau above, were dozens of the giant warriors. So *that's* how they got to the beach, I mused.

"Let's MOVE!" I shouted at the top of my voice, pointing at the cliff. "Ronnie! Up front and get the engines cranked up! Chosovi, go with her. Beyer, Jeff, help me with the picks. Cut the ropes if you have to! Let's get out of here!"

As the warriors hit the beach and began running towards us, they launched their terrible spears. Dozens of them landed just short of the aircraft. If even one hit the bird below the waterline, we were literally sunk!

We cut the ropes and bounded up the ladder into the left blister as Ronnie coaxed the engines into clattering life. She shoved the throttles forward, and they backfired with objection at the sudden harsh treatment. Oily gray smoke plumed from the exhausts, and the tail broke free of the beach.

I dropped into my seat, Chosovi in Beyer's usual spot between Ronnie and me. Beyer and Jeff strapped themselves into seats at the former radio operator's desk behind the cockpit.

Glancing at Ronnie, I realized that she had not spoken since before being loaded on to the gunship. She sat stony-faced, determinedly doing her duties.

"Are you O.K., mate?" I asked tenderly.

"That wasn't *really* Richard, was it? It *couldn't* have been. I…I don't understand any of this! They said he was dead."

"He was – in a way. And he is now – forever! I will explain it all to you later, Ronnie. Right now, we have to get out of here!"

She turned to me and brushed away a single, silver tear from her lovely caramel cheek. "O.K., Mitch. I understand."

Chosovi shouted and pointed, "Down that way. Past the boats. You must turn around and go back the way you came!"

"But that's impossible," I yelled back. "There is not enough room."

"Trust me," she said modestly.

I had no choice. I took the throttles from Ronnie as she began the pre-takeoff checks. The old engines were cold-soaked, and the oil temperatures would never be in the green by the time we turned around and lined up. At almost gross weight, I risked blowing pistons and cylinders right off the engines when I gave her full power, as I must, with the impossibly short take-off run available.

"Arm the rockets," I told Ronnie, remembering that I had replaced the JATO's we had used on our previous near death-dive.

"Roger."

I kicked in left rudder and spun her round at the very end of the narrowing lake. As we lined up with the longest run possible towards the other end of the blind canyon, I shoved the throttles all the way up. I hauled the yoke as far back into my belly as I could. The engines bellowed!

"Floats up, Ronnie!"

She snapped the switch and the floats retracted into their wingtip positions.

The warriors were now lining the entire beach in front of the derelict houseboats, launching their weapons at us. Above the din of the engines, I heard and felt several of those massive spears strike the fuselage, accompanied by the thud of small caliber bullets. I would not be able to assess the damage until we were out of harm's way.

The 'Wayward Wind' rose sluggishly on to the planning step. There was not enough lake. We were going to plow straight into the canyon wall at the other end, where we had originally entered the bay.

"Rockets, Ronnie – NOW!"

She hit the switch and we leapt out of the water, climbing away. The cliff face loomed ahead. We could not climb fast enough, and there was no room to turn around.

Chosovi yelled in my ear. "Turn right, when I say; exactly when I say!"

"O.K.," I replied, wondering if these were my last moments on earth.

We were doing over a hundred knots, heading straight at the towering wall of the box canyon.

"TURN!" she yelled.

I jammed in full right rudder and aileron and yanked the PBY around in a hard bank, standing her on her right wing. I clenched my teeth and closed my eyes as the nose of the aircraft was about to slam into the onrushing cliff! Strictly no go! We were dead!

23

Then we went straight through that rock wall, and still in the right bank, were swinging around the bend we had previously encountered as we had taxied in on the water.

I leveled her wings, and we were climbing away, up through the widening gorge. We topped the rim out into the normal glare of bright yellow sunlight, red rock and blue water. We were back!

Beyer, who had apparently been peering over Chosovi's shoulder – speechless for the first time in his life – said, "What the hell was that? What just happened? I don't understand. We should have hit that cliff at a hundred knots and disintegrated! What happened?" he repeated superfluously.

"I don't know, but I suspect it was a mirage – or something," I replied, as puzzled as he was.

"No mirage," Chosovi replied. "A sometime place; one of the entrances to our world. More like – I do not know how to say it – one way …?"

"Glass? A one-way mirror. Of course!" Beyer exclaimed.

"I don't get it," I replied.

"Of course you don't, Blaine. Very simple, really. Chosovi said it is a 'sometime' place. Most of the time, you can go up and down that stretch of the river, never knowing of the existence of that other place. Then, occasionally, and apparently uncontrollably, the portal opens up and allows only one way travel; except that it's not really one way. It just *appears* so because the portal is like a one-way mirror. Once inside, it seems as if the entrance has closed behind you."

"You meant to tell me that all those people could have gotten out, if only..."

"Not necessarily. It depends on the physics of the phenomenon."

"What do you mean?"

"I mean that we don't know enough about it. When the portal closes, is it solid, or does it just *appear* to be solid? Or, does it *begin* to solidify after it closes, then dematerialize as it begins to open. We would have to know when it happens, to try it to find out."

"Didn't we just do that? It wasn't solid a few seconds ago!"

"Yes, but how long has it been like that? An hour, a day? We don't know. It could have just been in the process of changing back. We might have barely made it through before it became solid rock again."

I shuddered as I thought of hitting that rock wall, and broke out in cold sweat.

I looked accusingly at Chosovi. "You knew?"

"I did not know whether it was – solid. No."

"Not at that moment," she continued. "A long time ago, one of my people went through from our side in a canoe. We thought he had gone forever, because he went through that rock. Most of my people are frightened to go near that place because they sometimes disappear and never come back. But then, he did come back – the next day! He spoke of many boats, like the ones on the beach. We did not know where they came from until then."

"But what about your guardians?" Beyer asked.

"They only guard the all-time places – and only on the land. There are not many. They keep the mighty ones away. They sacrifice themselves to lead them away from those places."

"Well, *somebody* got through – and killed your guardian in Texas. And I guess we know who – now!"

"I do not know Texas. I know we lose many guardians. It is their duty … to protect the gateways with their lives!"

"And they all wear symbols of the gateways on their skin?" I asked, thinking of the guard in the Collider tunnel.

"Yes. They must be able to recognize each other, and which gate they guard, or they would be killed by their own kind. They allow no one near the entrances. Not even their own people. They are assigned one gateway – for life. And they expect to die protecting it!"

"Well, that more or less explains that," I said thoughtfully.

Nobody spoke for the next twenty minutes, as we flew southeast, directly back to Page.

As we taxied in, I saw that the AC-130 had arrived and was parked in a remote area at the northeast corner of the field. Several ambulances stood nearby, no doubt off-loading their wounded and dead. Obviously General Price did not want any news media getting hold of the story. The small band of survivors had been taken to the terminal and were being cared for by Hogan's people in a back room.

Nathan Price came striding over to us as we exited the 'Wayward Wind'.

"Everybody all right?" he asked with genuine concern.

"Fine," I replied. "Thanks to you! We need to chat. Do you have time?"

"I'm afraid not."

"What are you going to report?" I asked, concerned about the people in the canyon, and especially about Jeff McCall and Chosovi.

He looked wryly at me, one eyebrow cocked as he read my mind.

"I don't know. But I do know I can't report the truth. For one thing, nobody would believe me. For another, I can't reveal the secret of that canyon. Those people – all of them – need to be left alone. They've been living that way for hundreds of years. We can't change anything! As for McCall, let me go talk to him."

He stepped over to where Jeff and Chosovi, were standing by the ladder of the PBY. He spoke to them quietly for a couple of minutes, put his hands on both their shoulders, and then came back to us.

"He's already served his country well. If he wants to stay and help Chosovi's people, as far as I'm concerned, he's still serving it!"

"I was hoping you'd see it that way. But what about the others?"

"Like I said, Blaine, we can't change anything. We can't interfere. They have been living like that for centuries; hunter and hunted. It's the way of the world. I'm not going to expose their way of life, or their home to our frenetic society, who would do them more harm in one week than those warriors have done in centuries. Leave them alone, I say! What about you? You're a civilian. I can't *order* you not to say anything..."

"Don't worry, general. I never *saw* that canyon. We never found Masters or McCall, and we're headed home after some R and R."

"They were both *my* officers," he mused aloud. "It is I who will have to come up with a plausible explanation for their disappearance."

"General, they've already been missing for six months or more. You just never were able to find 'em – or Eric Laudaman, for that matter. Something to do with the experiments in the collider. An enigma."

"Pretty thin, Blaine," the general replied.

"It'll have to do, won't it? You people always manage to come up with *some* tall story for people who have disappeared or been abducted. And it's *never* aliens – or people from other worlds. No such thing, you say. It's always just mass hysteria! Right?"

"Very amusing, Blaine. Well, good luck to you."

He turned to Beyer, who had been listening to this exchange, curiously silent.

"Beyer? You look bewildered, for once in your life."

"I am. I don't understand any of what happened back there. I am merely a physicist, not some kind of Indiana Jones. I am at a total loss, and I need time to absorb it all. I need to sit down with Jeff, Chosovi and the others and talk with them for about a week."

"Well, keep it under your hat. Like I told Blaine, I am not going to expose them. You lot need to do the same. You need to get those two back to their people ASAP. As for the other survivors, well… we will have to go with what Blaine accuses the air force of. They're all crazy! They somehow got lost up in that canyon country, and all went off their rockers."

"Like you said, general. Pretty thin!"

"You two take care. And stay out of trouble! I can't keep gallivanting around the world at taxpayers' expense making like the U.S. Cavalry every time you get into a scrap, you know."

He glanced over to where Ronnie was sitting alone in one of Hogan's golf carts, head in her hands, her face covered.

"Is she going to be O.K.?"

"I don't know. Why don't you go ask her? After all, she *is* the wife of one of your officers."

"*Ex*-officer. That's something about this affair I never will understand. What happened to him?"

Beyer came to life again. "The oldest story in the world, Nathan. Combine lust for omnipotence with opportunity presented by birthright and circumstance – in this case, his mother being, or being related to someone who practiced the Navajo 'witchery way' – and you have a formula for corruption. As they say, absolute power corrupts absolutely!"

"I guess so. Well, good luck to you both," he said, as he stepped over to where Ronnie sat and joined her in the cart.

He spoke to her for several minutes, then got out and strode over to his Hum-Vee waiting at the terminal exit.

He turned, saluted, jammed a cigar in his teeth and drove off.

Sheriff Briddle spent most of the evening, again at the Marriott, grilling us as to what had transpired during our almost twelve hours of 'disappearance'.

He was not a happy man. He was not at all happy that the mysterious air force gunship had again arrived in his territory, this time with a strange cargo of people, both civilian and military, some of whom had to be transported to the local hospital and morgue!

Finally, with the assistance of the general, who agreed to join us in the Courtyard bar later that evening, after he had tended to his troops, the sheriff was more or less satisfied – at least satisfied that he was never going to know what *really* happened up there.

We told him part of the truth. We told him we had found the missing boats and some of the survivors. He was not happy that they had apparently developed some form of mass amnesia, and could remember nothing of where they had been for weeks, months or years! We did not elaborate on what had happened to the others. He promised to go up there with the sheriff of Kane County, Utah and find out for himself.

We wished him luck!

24

The 'Wayward Wind' swayed gently on her mooring in Wahweap Marina. A light easterly breeze was blowing down the bay.

It was about ten p.m. the following evening. A wide, clear, desert night embraced us. The marina dock lights, and those of a hundred houseboats, reflected a million points of light off the water.

We five were gazing up at a black, diamond-studded sky as we sipped our drinks in the aft compartment.

Ronnie and I sat close together, as did Jeff and Chosovi. Beyer leaned on the open coaming of the left blister.

"When are you two going home?" I asked Jeff McCall.

"Soon," he said, looking at his beautiful bride. "Very soon."

"Do you know the way?" I grinned.

"Chosovi does," he replied confidently.

"Don't forget you owe me two good guns. We left them in the ruin."

"I know."

"Bush telegraph?"

"Desert telegraph."

Ronnie, who had been sitting quietly, nursing her drink, and unaware of our small talk, shook her head and asked for the tenth time, "Why did he marry me? Why? Was he just using me ...for what? I don't *understand!*"

Beyer came over and placed a giant, hairy paw reassuringly on her shoulder. "I'm sure he loved you, my dear. I'm sure he did not even know what was happening to him at first. It must have started when he was very young.

"Remember, his father Ethan said he wandered off when he was only about ten. His mother probably belonged to a cult of those who practiced the 'witchery' or 'frenzy' way; a very powerful form of magic. Any Navajo practicing the witchery way is evil. The intent of such a practice is purely to harm, usually others of their own tribe, but sometimes people outside of it. They are feared and shunned by the rest of the tribe.

"Probably because of this, he left the reservation. He must have acquired an affinity for the white man's world as well, educated himself in our ways, and ultimately found himself in the air force, where he discovered that the power of the department to which he had been attached would be an asset to his particular indigenous talents. He met Jeff and you, and the rest, as they say, is history."

"I don't know what to *do*," she replied. "I feel so lost. So empty!"

"Why don't you come cruising with us?" the ever-hopeful and gallant white knight inquired.

She smiled at me with tear-filled eyes and said, "Didn't I?"

I leaned over and kissed her gently on her lips. The sweet, musky scent of her made me know that I had to keep this girl; to somehow make it up to her for all that she lost.

CPSIA information can be obtained at www.ICGtesting.com
Printed in the USA
LVOW07s2350311014

411499LV00001B/2/P